"So…you were…you were dreaming. About *me*?"

A remark like that from the old Maleah might indicate that she felt flattered. But the new Maleah had changed a lot, and Ian couldn't get a read on what she meant now.

"I guess you could say that."

A tiny smile lifted the corner of her mouth. "Don't know if I've ever been the star of a guy's dream before."

She'd stood center stage in hundreds of dreams during his years at Lincoln. What would she say if he admitted that now?

Only one way to find out…

"It probably won't surprise you to hear that I thought of you a lot while I was…away."

Her smile disappeared. Maleah began to fidget, another telltale sign she felt uncomfortable. He searched his mind for a topic to divert the conversation.

A two-note chime interrupted them.

Saved by the bell.

Dear Reader,

Once upon a time, my Psych 101 professor taught a lesson I've never forgotten.

"The class clown cracked a joke, and his fellow students laughed like crazy. When he repeated it, fewer laughed. He told the joke again, and no one laughed." He paused, then said, "If the same joke stops being funny when we hear it more than once, what makes us think anything good will come of dredging up past hurts over and over?"

We all have a past. But what if our mistakes still shame us to the core?

As a teen, Ian Sylvestry found himself incarcerated after his reaction to his mother's abandonment sent the dominoes toppling. Upon his release, it took time to convince others that he'd turned his life around, but Ian succeeded—or thought he had—until a chance meeting with the girl he'd left behind.

Confronted with the man he has become, can Maleah Turner forgive the irresponsible behavior that took him from her?

Why is it so hard, I wonder, to cope with the sins of our past? Perhaps we need to make this our life motto: "The future is stardust, because you can dream it; the present is clay, because you can mold it; but the past is stone, because you can never change it."

Be sure to look for the next book in my By Way of the Lighthouse miniseries. And if you enjoyed *The Man She Knew*, write me c/o Facebook, Twitter or www.loreelough.com!

Wishing you nothing but happy memories,

Loree

HEARTWARMING

The Man She Knew

—

Loree Lough

⟨H⟩ HARLEQUIN® HEARTWARMING™

Recycling programs
for this product may
not exist in your area.

ISBN-13: 978-0-373-36841-9

The Man She Knew

Copyright © 2017 by Loree Lough

Printed in U.S.A.

Loree Lough once sang for her supper. Her favorite memories of days on the road are the hours spent singing to soldiers recovering in VA hospitals. Now and then she polishes up her Yamaha guitar to croon a tune or two, but mostly she writes. With more than one hundred books in print (eighteen bearing the Harlequin logo), Loree's work has earned industry accolades, movie options and four- and five-star reviews, but what she treasures most are her Readers' Choice awards.

Loree and her real-life hero split their time between Baltimore's suburbs and the Allegheny Mountains, where she continues to perfect her "identify the critter tracks" skills. A writer who believes in giving back, see the Giving Back page of loreelough.com for details. She loves hearing from her readers and answers every letter. You can connect with her on Facebook, Twitter and Pinterest.

Books by Loree Lough

Harlequin Heartwarming

Those Marshall Boys

Once a Marine
Sweet Mountain Rancher
The Firefighter's Refrain

A Child to Love

Raising Connor
Devoted to Drew
Saving Alyssa

For more books by Loree Lough,
check out Harlequin.com.

This novel is dedicated to my family,
whose love and support make writing—even on
the tough days—so much easier.
I love and appreciate all of you!

Acknowledgments

Heartfelt thanks to those who so willingly
shared hours of time, expertise and
experiences to assure accuracy and authenticity
in this story: Attorney Dee Lawrence
(former writing student turned successful
author in her own right!) for her savvy legal
advice; Linda O'Dell (Letters for the Lord prison
ministry) for providing details about incoming
and outgoing mail in federal penitentiaries;
Marty* and George*, reformed convicts who
explained prison life and the hardships and
prejudice so often faced upon release;
Lance*, prison guard who shed light on
ex-cons' struggles to avoid recidivism;
Suzanne*, whose long-standing relationship
with a convict helped me better understand
the dynamics of supporting a man convicted
of a felony.

(NOTE: * denotes names have been changed at
the request of these helpful individuals.)

CHAPTER ONE

"MALEAH, YOU WANT to explain *this*?"

She placed the bowl of mashed potatoes on the dining room table. "Explain wh—"

When she saw what her brother held in his big hands, the words froze in her throat.

"Tell me you're not still mooning over this low-life criminal!"

"Mooning." She forced a laugh. "You're picking up old-people talk from Grampa."

"You can't distract me."

She'd made two mistakes: thinking the buffet's silverware drawer was a good place to hide the photograph, and saying yes when Eliot offered to set the table.

"It's no big deal." Maleah shrugged. And there it was… Eliot's *I'm a decorated cop and I can tell when someone is lying* look.

Maleah shoved a serving spoon into the potatoes. She and Eliot had gone round and round on this subject too many times to count, and she'd lost every round.

"Only one explanation makes sense. You've

stayed in touch with him, even though the whole family asked you not to, haven't you?"

"First of all, no one *asked* anything." Their relentless demands had been the primary reason she'd traded the comfort of her childhood room for a noisy, crowded dorm room at the University of Maryland. "How any times do I have to tell you I haven't had any contact with him in…" Years had passed since she'd scrawled *Leave me alone! Please!* across Ian's final letter. "Why won't you believe me?"

He dropped the picture into the drawer and closed it, hard. "Maybe because that creep turned you into an OCD control freak. You can't sleep with dishes in the sink. And name me one other person who alphabetizes the contents of her pantry and spice rack? Or color-codes and hangs stuff in her closet in order by length."

Maleah didn't bother to explain it was because she'd learned how much one mistake could alter a person's life—and the lives of everyone close to them.

"So I like things neat and tidy. Last I checked, it isn't against the law."

He aimed his pointer finger at the ceiling, preparing to add to his big brother tirade, but she cut him off.

"Eliot, let's not spoil Grampa's birthday dinner, all right?"

"What. Ever."

An hour later, her mom suggested getting the dinner dishes cleaned up while the rest of the Turners relaxed in front of the evening news.

"And then we'll have coffee and cake while Grampa opens his presents!"

Maleah's tension heightened; if she left the room, Eliot would invite a repeat of the for-your-own-good lectures they'd been delivering since that horrible day.

"Let's leave them." Facing her younger brother, she said, "Joe, will you get the TV trays out of the front hall closet while I—"

"Maleah, honey," her mother interrupted, "those mashed potatoes will harden like cement if you don't rinse the plates soon."

"I'll soak them overnight and load the dishwasher in the morning."

She'd tackle the job just as soon as her family left, but her mom didn't need to know that.

Joe returned with two TV trays under each arm. "Where do you want these, sis?"

"You can put them right back where you found them," her mother said. "We'll have cake and ice cream at the table, like civilized people."

He began setting up the trays. "Mom, this is Maleah's house."

Their mother's lips formed a thin line. "Fine. Do whatever you please."

"Happy birthday to me," Grampa sang off key.

"Sorry, Grampa," Maleah said, grinning. "I'll get the cake."

She'd barely had time to turn toward the kitchen when her father said, "Eliot says you have something to tell us?"

Traitor.

"As a matter of fact, I do." Maleah sat on the sofa arm beside Joe. "Got a promotion and a pay raise day before yesterday." The perfect cover-up.

Her dad beamed. "That's wonderful, sweetheart. New title, too?"

"Assistant Vice President for the School of Autism Services at Washburne-Albert Institute."

"Whew. That's a mouthful!" Joe elbowed her ribs. "Raised-print business cards and the whole nine yards?"

"*And* a private office—with a window—and my name in gold letters on the door."

"That's my girl," Grampa said. "A chip off the ol' block."

"Don't be silly, Frank. You're a retired policeman. Our granddaughter is a psychologist."

"Hey. I used plenty of psychology on the job,

Teresa. At home, too, every time you tried to talk me into getting a *safer* job."

His wife rolled her eyes. Her dad took a sip of his iced tea. "I'm proud of you, kiddo. Real proud."

"Ditto that," Frank said. "Hey, I have an idea. Let's light the candles on my cake and celebrate two great occasions with one big puff."

While Eliot poked candles into the cake, Maleah placed napkins, dessert plates, forks and a book of matches on a big wooden serving tray.

"Grab the ice cream, will you?"

"Nice try out there," he said, opening the freezer door, "but you can't keep me quiet forever."

She'd had about enough of his superior attitude. Maleah faced him head-on.

"Look. I know you mean well. And I appreciate that you think you're protecting me from my once-fickle self. But trust me. I don't need your protection. Besides, there's a time and place for everything, and this is *Grampa's* night."

His mouth formed a thin, grim line as he lit the candles. Then he picked up the tray, and marched into the living room singing "Happy Birthday." The others joined in, and although her heart wasn't in it, so did Maleah.

Eliot didn't say much—and neither did

Maleah—as they devoured cake and ice cream. Fortunately, no one seemed to notice the tension between them. Or, if they did, had decided to keep the observation to themselves.

"You guys are great," Grampa said after unwrapping his last present. "But y'all went to way too much trouble and spent way too much. Especially you, Maleah."

He'd been dropping hints since last Christmas about wanting an e-reader, so Maleah had ordered one and downloaded half a dozen books onto it.

She patted his bony knee. Would he ever gain back all the weight he'd lost during his chemo treatments?

"It was no trouble at all."

"Speaking of trouble," Eliot said, "there's something important we need to discuss as a family."

Maleah's mouth went dry. "Eliot. Please. Don't…"

He held up a hand. "They have a right to know. It affects them, too."

Mom's eyes widened and her husband's brow furrowed.

"What affects us?" they asked together.

"Quit beating around the bush, boy." Grampa scooted to the edge of the sofa cushion.

Eliot used his chin as a pointer. "Li'l miss

party maker over there is still sweet on that felon."

Maleah's cheeks went hot and her heart beat double-time. Which of them would be the first to take her to task for holding on to that photograph? Her father, if she had to guess.

Her mom said, "Maleah, what on earth is he talking about?"

She glared at Eliot.

"It's nothing, really. He found an old picture hidden away in a drawer, and as usual, jumped to conclusions and decided it means I'm still involved with Ian." Maleah threw back her shoulders. "I'm *not*, and that's the truth. But you know Eliot…"

"True or not," her grandfather said, "you have to admit that boy is trouble. Even after all these years, the mere mention of his name is enough to get everybody's bloomers in a knot. *Told* you he was no good."

"But would you listen?" Eliot put in. "No-o-o. You hung in there like a suckerfish, right up until the sheriff's deputies dragged him away."

Those final moments in the courthouse were as vivid now as it had been that dreary morning: Ian, looking like a terrified boy as one guard slammed the prison van's side door and another put the vehicle into gear. He'd raised a hand to wave goodbye, but the chain connecting handcuffs to leg irons stopped him. Tears had filled his eyes, and unable to watch, she'd closed her own. By the time she opened them again, the driver had already made the first turn onto Lombard Street and started the hour-long trip to Lincoln Correctional of Central Maryland.

Joe squeezed her hand. "It's okay, sis. I believe you." He faced the family to add, "So she saved one lousy photograph. Big deal. It doesn't mean she'll do anything stupid. We're supposed to be her support system, for cryin' out loud. If an institution like Washburne-Albert can put their faith in her, why can't we?"

She might have hugged him if her grandmother hadn't said, "Joe's right. Maleah is a smart girl. She knows what life would be like with…" She wrinkled her nose. "…with a man like that."

"Then why is she still single?"

"Same reason as you, maybe?"

Grampa laughed and Eliot said, "Shut up, Joe."

"Person can't earn college degrees and work her way up the corporate ladder if her mind is on guys and dating and whatnot…"

"Joe's right again," their grandfather said. "There's no denying our girl has worked hard to get where she is." He turned toward Maleah.

"Tell your newly-confirmed bachelor brother that there isn't anything going on between you and that ex-con."

She raised her right hand. "There isn't anything going on between me and that ex-con." Neither Eliot nor her father seemed satisfied.

"Okay, but just to clarify...when was the last time you were in contact with him?"

Joe heaved a frustrated sigh. "Aw, Dad. *Really?*"

"I know you feel like we're picking on her, son, but Eliot is right. We need to get to the bottom of this, for her own good."

Her younger brother had earned more department commendations than Eliot and their father combined, yet had somehow managed not to turn hard-hearted and suspicious, especially of those closest to him.

"It's okay, Joe," she said. "I brought this on myself by not getting rid of that picture years ago. I don't want you putting your neck on the chopping block to defend me." She looked her father square in the eye. "There's nothing to get to the bottom of, Dad. I was still living at home after Ian's sentencing, so you know as well as I do that I returned his letters, unopened. *All* of them. And after I wrote 'leave me alone' across the back of that last envelope, you mailed it. And the letters stopped coming."

Her grandmother was stuffing her husband's gifts into a plastic bag. "It's late. We should all be getting home."

Her actions and tone reminded the family that she'd always detested family discord, and one by one, they stood and made their way into the foyer. Amid a flurry of uncomfortable hugs, they complimented Maleah's dinner and thanked her for having them over.

Her mom hesitated. "You sure you don't want help with the dishes, honey?"

"Thanks, Mom, but I'll be fine."

Arm in arm, her grandparents led the way to the semicircular drive.

"Looks like snow," Frank said, pulling up his collar.

Maleah wished for summer temperatures, so Gramps could enjoy balmy breezes without needing to bundle up. The cancer that had nearly killed him refused to loosen its grip. But at least the family had remission to be thankful for.

Maleah stood on her bungalow's covered porch, shoulders hunched into the wind as the family started up their cars, waving as they drove away. She loved them dearly, even at their annoying worst. Sometimes, though, it was difficult trying to protect them from bad news—

like Ian's return from prison years ago—to ensure nothing would upset them.

After bolting the door, she leaned against it and exhaled a relieved breath.

Reminding herself that self-pity never got anyone anywhere, she walked purposefully into the living room. There, Maleah collected cake plates and flatware, and after loading them into the dishwasher, started clearing the dining room table. Halfway through the job, she noticed the corner of the photograph protruding from the buffet's silverware drawer.

She couldn't remember the last time anyone had mentioned Ian or her involvement with him. Now thanks to Eliot's mistrustful nature, the entire family would start watching her every move…again.

"Thanks a bunch, big brother, for opening Pandora's box."

A rush of memories rained down on her as she removed the picture…

When he'd called that night, Ian's trembling voice described how his mother and new husband were expecting a baby. Hurt, confused and angry, he'd pleaded with Maleah to meet him. "I just need to talk it out. I promise not to keep you out late." She'd wanted to comfort him, but homework, chores and three generations of disapproving Turner cops prevented it. Her refusal fueled his fury, and he'd hung up without saying goodbye. Months passed before she saw him again, slump-shouldered and chained to the defense table like a rabid dog.

Now, staring at his likeness, Maleah wondered for the thousandth time: If she *had* met him that night, would Ian have made a different choice?

"Enough!" She slammed the frame onto the table. "*You* destroyed your life, Ian Sylvestry, not me!"

Glittering shards of glass crisscrossed his once-carefree face, and that was fine with her.

CHAPTER TWO

"HEY, BOSS, WHAT should I do with this?"

Ian inspected the document in his assistant manager's hands. "I suppose we oughta frame it, hang it near the registration counter."

"*Si.*" Sergio shifted his weight to his good leg. "Good place for patrons to see they are dining in A-plus *restaurante.*"

Terri, *Sur les Quais*'s hostess, peered over Sergio's shoulder.

"Oh wow, Ian. That's so fantastic! I'll bet I can find a frame downstairs in the storeroom…"

"Think you can find a good place to hang it once it's behind glass, too?"

"Probably…" She started for the stairs, turning to add, "But I'll check with you before I drive a nail into the wall."

Such a timid little thing. "No need for that. I'm sure any spot you choose will be fine."

She gave that a moment's thought. "Okay then, if you're sure."

As she hurried down the stairs, he pictured

the abusive husband who'd made her afraid of her own shadow. He'd tangled with plenty of bullies at Lincoln, and quickly figured out that defending himself would only tack extra years onto his sentence. It had taken time and careful planning, but he'd found ways to end the harassment…and earn the grudging respect of fellow inmates.

And the Turners called me *a thug.* Unlike his parents, Ian believed in marriage, in sticking it out when times got tough. But in his opinion, Terri and her boy would have been better off if Steve had fulfilled his numerous threats of leaving. He'd done nothing to hide his disappointment at having a special needs son, not even from Avery. Despite it all, Avery seemed as determined to overcome the limitations of his disorder as his mother was to keep him enrolled at the Washburne-Avery Institute. A lot to admire in those two—the mother in particular, who was partially deaf. If only Terri believed in herself as much as Ian did.

Alone in his office, Ian took a knee and rotated the dial on the safe, and as he slid the big checkbook from the bottom shelf, an envelope fluttered to the floor. He recognized it instantly as the last letter he'd sent Maleah from Lincoln. Oh, he'd written others after that one came back. Dozens. A hundred, maybe.

But he hadn't mailed them.

He picked the letter up and, without reading the message scrawled across the envelope's back, buried it under last year's tax return, the titles to his pickup and Harley and his release papers.

"You in there, Ian?"

"C'mon in, Aunt Gladys."

He sat behind his desk and folded both hands on the checkbook.

"I can't believe you're still doing things the old-fashioned way. Surely you know how much time you'd save, banking online."

"I served time with guys who could hack an account like that." He snapped his fingers. "I don't trust the internet. Last thing we need now that we're in the black is identity theft."

"That's what firewalls are for, silly man. Why, I've been doing my banking online for years, and I haven't had a smidge of trouble."

He owed Gladys a lot. Everything, in fact. Gratitude inspired him to devise ways to divert her when she got into one of her "I know best" moods.

Striking a Zen pose, he said, "I enjoy doing things the old-fashioned way. It calms me."

Gladys sat back and tilted her head.

"What."

"You look…weird."

She'd earned the right to nag him about his beard and earring, or his insistence on writing checks instead of banking online, and he'd endure it. She'd earned that much, and more.

"I'll shave soon. Promise."

"No, that isn't what I mean. You look…sadder than usual."

"Than usual?" He laughed. "You make it sound like I walk around wearing a big mopey frown on all day, every day."

"You have a charming, handsome smile, but your mouth rarely sends the 'happy' message to those big brown eyes. It's that bratty girl's fault. If she hadn't been so afraid to buck her family…" Gladys pursed her lips. "She knew you better than anyone. Should have known you didn't deserve ten years for driving a car. Should have known you weren't in on the planning of that robbery, too."

She was right about one thing: Maleah had known him better than anyone. But she was wrong about the rest of it.

"I love you for defending me, and I realize hearing the truth is tough, but I knew what the guys were planning, and went along with it, anyway. What happened afterward is on me, one hundred percent."

Gladys cringed. "Boy. When you tell it like it is, you don't fool around, do you?"

Ian answered with a one-shouldered shrug.

"Well, for what it's worth, I love you, too, nephew. And I'm proud of you. It couldn't have been easy, overcoming the stigma of having served time. But you did it without complaint, without shirking your responsibility in it. If I'd been blessed with a son, I'd want him to be exactly like you."

She'd said it before, and Ian believed every word.

His aunt pointed at the wall behind him. "Is that new?"

He swiveled the chair. "Sort of. I finished it about a month ago."

"It's gorgeous, but then, so are all of your paintings. I love the colors of the sky. And you really captured the grandeur of the *Constellation*." She sighed. "It's so unfair…"

"What is?"

"That you sucked up all the artistic talent in this family."

"You don't give yourself enough credit. I can't even sew on a button, but you've designed your own clothes for years. And need I remind you that big-deal cooking show asked permission to use your recipes?"

"Two. Two recipes. And sewing is just a matter of manipulating the machine's needle."

Gladys glanced around his office. "Just look

at this place. I'm sure people are impressed when they sit here to discuss booking the banquet room. No wonder there's a waiting list."

"Dan and Lee earned the credit for that. Their menus are what draw people in, and keep them coming back."

"Now who isn't giving himself enough credit! I ran this place for twenty years before you, so I know what it takes. It's because of your leadership that the bistro runs like a well-tuned machine."

"Keep it up and I'll start blushing like a schoolgirl. How will that look when I check on tonight's holiday party?"

"All right. I know you're uncomfortable with compliments. But I just have to say…you saved my wrinkly old butt and my pride, too."

He'd agreed to accept her gift of ownership, provided she accepted a cut of the profits. "Why, just yesterday," she continued, "one of my sorority sisters said she and her family celebrated her anniversary here. You wouldn't believe how she went on and on about the ambiance, the food, the service. And she isn't the only one! Putting you in charge was the smartest business decision I ever made." Laughing, she added, "I'm making more money now than I did when I ran the place!"

He was about to thank her for sharing that with him when Terri stepped into the doorway.

"Sorry to interrupt, but a gentleman asked to see you. He's with the holiday party."

Ian shoved back from his desk as Gladys got to her feet.

"How's that boy of yours?" she asked, falling into step beside Terri.

"He's fine. Made a rocket—and launched it—yesterday."

"Amazing." Terri handed him a pink While You Were Out slip.

"Brady called a little while ago. Said there's no hurry."

His father lived in the apartment beside his, right upstairs. So why the phone call? He scanned the note and tucked it into his shirt pocket, hoping it wasn't one of *those* days.

"You think he's in one of his moods?" Gladys asked.

"Nah. Probably just didn't feel like putting on shoes and coming downstairs."

Gladys wasn't buying it. In truth, Ian didn't believe it, either. When tempted to drink—which happened every six months or so—his dad turned to Ian for some straight talk. So now Ian had a decision to make: meet with the would-be customer, or head upstairs to check on his dad…and risk losing a future booking.

He slid a business card from his pocket and scribbled his cell number on the back.

"See if the guy can give me a few minutes," he said, handing it to Terri. "And if he can't, ask him to call me in the morning."

She faced Gladys. "Good to see you, Mrs. Turner."

"You, too. Give that kid of yours a big hug for me."

Once the hostess was out of earshot, Gladys said, "You're going upstairs, aren't you?"

"Do I have a choice?"

"You always have a choice."

After the life he'd lived, didn't he know it!

"Why don't I go up, see if there's anything I can do for him?"

Ian started to protest when she tacked on, "No sense losing a booking just because your dad needs another pep talk."

"Can I trust you to go easy on him?"

She did her best to look offended.

"Seriously, Gladys…"

"All right. I'll put on my kid gloves. By the time I'm through with him, he'll be so sick of TLC he'll wish he hadn't left that message."

With that, she began climbing the stairs, stopping halfway to the top.

"Answer a question for me, nephew."

"If I can."

"Who has a holiday party before Thanksgiving?"

Ian shrugged. "A busy rich guy who's going to surprise his wife with a world cruise planned for Christmas?"

"Oh, to have a husband like *that*," she said, and continued up the stairs.

Grinning, Ian made his way to the banquet room. He had to give it to his staff. The place looked great. Linen tablecloths glowed bright white under hundreds of tiny lights covering the ceiling, and the napkins matched each poinsettia centerpiece. The DJ leaned over his equipment to take a request, and soon, Toni Braxton's version of "The Christmas Song" drew guests to the parquet dance floor.

Ian scanned the crowd. *Should've asked Terri which guy wanted to see me.*

"Mr. Sylvestry?"

He shook the man's extended hand. "Ian. Please."

"Luther. Luther Sanders," he said, pumping Ian's arm. "Real nice room you've got here. Perfect for my son's bar mitzvah next March… if you have an opening."

"I'll need to look at the book, but if memory serves, that won't be a problem."

"The boy is big into basketball, so the wife

and I were thinking maybe a March Madness theme?"

His wife called to him and he patted his pocket. "Your hostess gave me your card. Okay if I call tomorrow to set up an appointment?"

"I'm in the office by eight."

"Good. Good."

Again, his wife called his name. "Be right there, dear." Lowering his voice, he put his back to her. "Tell me…are you married?"

"No."

He studied Ian's face. "But you're thinking about it?"

"No…"

"The little woman is right. I give far too much credence to my people reading skills. And now if you'll excuse me, I need to find out what she needs…this time. Great party," he said, walking toward his wife. Ian wondered what had prompted the *are you married* question.

Another partygoer led his lady onto the dance floor. The woman bore a slight resemblance to Maleah, from her long glossy blond hair, to the way she moved, to a waist so slender that her partner's fingertips nearly met when he wrapped his hands around it.

Her stiff-backed posture told him she wasn't comfortable. Just a date, Ian decided, not a committed relationship. So why not tell the dude to knock it off?

The question reminded him of how, a few weeks earlier, his dad pointed at a couple of teenagers necking near the mall's food court: "Disrespectful Roman idiot," he'd complained.

"No way he's Italian," Ian had said. "Swedish or Danish maybe…"

"Just look at those ham hocks, roamin' all over the poor girl." Grinning, he'd faced Ian and winked. "Roman? Roamin'? Get it *now*, Einstein?"

They'd had a good laugh over it, but Ian found no humor in what was going on under the twinkle lights tonight. He'd seen plenty of couples on his dance floor, so why couldn't he take his eyes off this one?

It hit him like a slap…

After thumbing through her copies of *Baltimore Magazine*, Gladys passed every dog-eared issue to Ian. This month's cover featured Roman, feet propped on a massive mahogany desk, with a caption that read, MEET KENT O'MALLEY, CHARM CITY'S MOST ELIGIBLE BACHELOR.

He'd scanned the article just long enough to learn that O'Malley had parlayed a small inheritance and an interest in finance into the largest investment firm in the Mid-Atlantic region.

Well, how's that working out for you, he thought as Kent led his date nearer the DJ and turned around.

Heart pounding, Ian swallowed. Hard.

He hadn't seen her in what, thirteen, fourteen years? From where he stood, it didn't appear she'd aged a day. More than before, he wondered why she didn't whack Roman a good one, tell him to keep his mitts to himself. Wondered why, despite every fiber in him bellowing *Get the heck out of here, before she spots you!* his shoes seemed nailed to the hardwood. She stood twenty feet away, if that. Back when things were good between them, she'd called him Spider, an affectionate reminder to slow down as they walked "...because your legs are twice as long as mine!" If he could unglue his feet, he could reach her in half a dozen steps.

And then what? Tap her on the shoulder, say something brilliant like "Hey there, fancy meeting you here" while she reared back to whack *him* a good one?

Ian stood behind a support post, hoping to watch without being seen. Like the song lyrics said, she looked beautiful.

Thirteen years was a long time. Maybe she'd changed in other ways, and these days, wealthy successful guys were her preference. *As opposed to ex-cons who rob convenience stores...*

But who was he—the guy whose immature tantrum on that night sent him straight to a jail cell—to question who she did or didn't like?

Lady Luck must have decided to smile upon him, because so far, Maleah hadn't noticed him, while he tried his best to emulate a potted plant. He'd slink out of the hall, let Terri know that if she or the staff needed him, he'd be upstairs, checking on his dad. In all these years, he hadn't seen her anywhere except in his dreams. What could it hurt to take one last glance?

It could hurt a lot, he discovered as her gaze locked onto his.

For an instant, Maleah looked puzzled, and he could almost read her thoughts: *That isn't Ian Sylvestry, is it?* Confusion changed to mild interest as her gaze traveled the length of him, taking stock of the small gold hoop in his left earlobe, tattoos, his ponytailed, gray-at-the temples hair.

Something told him that if he didn't walk away, right now, he'd have to add *revulsion* to the flurry of emotions that had flickered across her pretty face.

CHAPTER THREE

THE SCENT OF fresh-brewed coffee greeted Ian. He'd grown accustomed to finding his father or aunt making themselves at home in his apartment. It didn't usually bother him, but on nights like this, he just wanted to be alone.

Brady held up his mug. "Care for a cup?"

"Thanks, but I'd better not. I'll have enough trouble falling asleep."

His dad's eyebrows rose. "Oh? Something went wrong at the bistro?"

Ian dropped onto the seat of a ladderbacked chair. "If only." He scanned the room. Gladys had been after him to update the space, but the homey, old-and-stable look reminded him of happier days, spent in his maternal grandparents' kitchen, where rising bread dough and fresh-baked pies welcomed family, friends and country-born neighbors.

"So where's Gladys?"

Brady shrugged. "How should I know. She was in here not ten minutes ago, lecturing me, reminding me that with all I have to be thankful for, I have no right to behave like a moody teenager." He nodded toward the hall-way. "Wish I could say she went home, but she's probably in the head."

Nearly thirty years since Brady's honorable discharge, and he still used Navy terms to refer to things like the bathroom.

"So what's eating you, son?"

"Aw, it's nothing I can't handle." *Eventually...*

"Lay it on me, so I'll have something to think about besides my own pathetic life."

They'd been down this road before, and Ian wasn't in the mood to cover the same ground yet again. His dad had a good job. A safe place to live. Food on the table and clothes on his back. And a family that loved him. Would it ever dawn on him that when Ruth left him, she'd left her only son, too?

Her self-centered move drove her husband to cheap whiskey and her only son toward a bunch of wild hoodlums that made him feel like part of a family again. Those first few years in lockup, he'd found plenty of reasons to lay everything rotten in his life at her feet. Additional years—and a lot of maturity—led him to the conclusion that he, alone, was re-sponsible for the state of his life. Seemed to Ian his dad could benefit from the same atti-tude adjustment.

Brady lifted the mug to his lips. "So…?"

Ian leaned back and, arms crossed over his chest, said, "So I saw her tonight."

The mug hit the table with a *clunk.*

"Yeah, that's pretty much how I felt."

"Jeez, son. I… I don't know what to say."

Of course he didn't. Good advice—advice of any kind for that matter—wasn't in Brady's parenting manual. At least it hadn't been since Ruth ran off with the professor.

"Man." Brady ran a fingertip around the rim of his mug. "That had to be tough."

"Yeah. Tough." Particularly that last moment, when those huge blue eyes traveled from the top of his head to the toes of his boots and back again.

"So how did you two leave things?"

"Leave things?"

Brady shifted in the chair, clearly uncomfortable playing Good Dad.

"Was she civil, at least?"

"We didn't speak. And that's fine with me."

"What's that old saying? 'You sucker your friends and I'll sucker mine, but let's not sucker each other.'"

"If that's an old saying, why haven't I heard it before?"

Grinning, Brady gave Ian's bicep a friendly

punch. "Maybe because you're just a young whippersnapper."

Brady had exceeded his fatherly concern limit. Ian could put responsibility for Brady's me-me-me mind-set on Ruth's shoulders, but common sense told him that, hard as it was to admit, his dad had always been this way; put to the test by his wife's betrayal, he'd simply shown his true colors. As a teenager, the role reversal thing caused resentment that revealed itself in dour expressions and whispered complaints. But Lincoln had taught him that it didn't pay to waste time wishing for the impossible, and he'd taught himself to accept things—and people—at face value.

"Whippersnapper," Ian echoed. "You're not old enough for language like that."

Gladys breezed into the room. "Who's a whippersnapper?" she asked, pouring herself a cup of coffee.

"This boy of mine. I recited an old adage, and he'd never heard of it."

She joined her brother and her nephew at the table. "What old adage?"

Brady got to his feet, stretched and yawned, then said, "I'm beat. See you two in the morning."

Gladys sized up the situation in two seconds flat: "So the kid laid something on you that you couldn't handle, and you're off to escape to dreamland, are you?"

Ian had developed a talent for sizing things up, too, and unless he was mistaken, his dad was about to retaliate. He'd been on the receiving end of the man's sharp tongue often enough to know that Brady didn't play fair. Only the good Lord knew what awful thing from her past he'd dredge up to even the score…if Ian didn't intervene.

"Hey auntie…who you callin' kid?"

In one blink, he got a taste of the glare she'd aimed at his dad. In the next, her expression softened.

Gladys clutched her throat and wrinkled her nose. "Auntie?" she repeated. "*Auntie?* Real funny, nephew, but fair warning— Call me that again and…" She leaned closer and patted his forearm. "…and I'll wait until the bistro is filled to capacity to give you a big juicy kiss, right on the lips, and call you sweetheart!"

She'd do it, too! "Fat lotta good that'll do ya," he said, snickering, "when everybody knows I'm nobody's sweetheart."

Brother and sister exchanged a questioning glance.

Brady shrugged. "Don't look at me. I don't have a clue what he's talking about."

"Yeah, well, he's your son."

"Yeah, well, you played a bigger role in raising him than I did."

"Only because you're such a—"

Ian made a big production of shoving back from the table. Grabbing a mug from the drain board, he filled it to the rim and said, "Knock it off, you two, or I'll send you both to bed with no supper."

Gladys's left eyebrow rose. *"Sweetheart,"* she said, accentuating each syllable, "it's nearly one in the morning."

"And I had supper at six."

"Way past your bedtime, then," he told them. "Don't forget to say your prayers…"

He'd just provided his dad with the perfect opportunity to leave the room—and the conversation. How many seconds before he took advantage of it?

"Alarm's set for five. Think I'll turn in."

Half a second later, the door slammed behind him and Gladys said, "All right. Out with it. What's eating you?"

She'd keep at him until he told her something, so Ian said, "Same old stuff."

"Baloney."

"Come again?"

"Here's an old adage you'll recognize. 'You can't fool an old fool.' Now spit it out, buster, or I'll go next door and get my guitar…"

Ian reared back as if she'd smacked him and feigned terror. Hands up, he said, "I'll talk!"

Folding his hands on the table, he shared the true story of an incident that had taken place years ago when, after recognizing the prison tattoo on his forearm, a fast food clerk refused to serve him. A humiliating experience, since everyone in the restaurant stopped what they were doing to see how Ian would react.

"They expected a fight," he told Gladys, "but they left disappointed."

"Good for you. After all these years of walking the straight and narrow, you don't have to prove yourself to anyone."

Almost word for word what he'd told himself as he left the place...without so much as a French fry.

She folded her hands, too. "First of all, how'd that self-righteous fool know it was a prison tat, unless he'd served time, too?"

Leave it to Gladys to find the needle in the haystack.

"And second of all?"

"You're a good man, and I couldn't love you more if you were my own son."

Wrapping her hands with his, Ian said, "Don't make me start into another rendition of 'you saved my sorry hide' tale."

"Tale? Hmpf. It's one hundred percent true.

Why would I mind hearing it again?" Their companionable laughter blended, producing a warm smile on his aunt's face. A smile that quickly diminished as she withdrew her hands.

"You aren't all down in the mouth because some wiseacre burger pusher gave you a hard time…"

"Well, silly me," he kidded, "thinking I could fool you."

"'Bout time you wised up. For the last time, out with it."

What did he have to lose?

"I saw Maleah tonight."

"Oh my. Oh wow. Holy smokes." Gladys sipped her coffee. "Good grief," she said, wincing. "Who taught that father of yours how to brew a pot?"

"Ruth."

"Still can't bring yourself to call her Mom, can you."

Ian shook his head. She hadn't earned the title.

"So did Maleah see you, too."

"She was a little busy, hanging all over her cover-model date."

The left brow rose again.

"Kent O'Malley. *Baltimore Magazine's* Bachelor of the Year?"

"Oh yeah." Nodding, she said, "Oh my. Oh

wow. Holy smokes." Then she slapped the table, making Ian jump. "No way you can convince me she's serious about that blowhard."

"Wasn't aware you and Kent were acquainted."

"Don't need a personal introduction to know he's all shine, no substance. Not Maleah's type at all."

A lifetime ago, *he'd* been her type. "A lot of water has flowed under the bridge since that day in court. "I've changed. She has, too."

"Not that much. I'll bet my diamond tiara it was a work-related date and nothing more. Now tell me *everything*."

"She seemed…she looked…" Ian didn't know how to describe how she looked as she stood, entangled in O'Malley's arms, comparing the once clean-cut boy he'd been to the scarred, tattooed ex-con he'd become. "I think it surprised her, seeing how *much* I've changed. Scared her a little, too, I think."

"That's natural. Man doesn't spend ten years doing hard time without it taking a toll." Unable to come up with a suitable response to that, Ian only nodded.

Gladys got up, put her mug in the sink, then emptied what was left of the coffee into the drain. "Promise me you'll teach that brother of mine how to use a coffeemaker, will ya? Grounds are too expensive these days."

She stood behind him and gently tugged his foot-long ponytail. "Oh what I wouldn't give for a pair of scissors right now..."

"If I had a dollar for every time you told me you love my hair, I could buy that newfangled icemaker I've been drooling over."

This time, she wasn't so gentle when she jerked the ponytail. "Small talk is not your forte, Ian Sylvestry. You can try to distract me with ice makers and coffeemakers and—"

"You're the one who took a side trip, talking about coffee."

"You've got me there, too." She kissed the top of his head. "Feel better now?"

He wouldn't feel better until he could blot Maleah's image from his memory.

"My advice?" she said, walking toward the hall.

Ian braced himself.

"Call her. Put all your cards on the table. Trust me, she's not involved with Mr. Owns-the-East-Coast."

He wouldn't reach out, not even if O'Malley told him directly that he had no interest in Maleah. He'd already put her through enough. What if she'd been with him that day at the fast food place? No way he could live with seeing her humiliated because of her association with him.

"I know what you're thinking."

"Do you, now?"

"You think you hurt her, hurt her so much that she can't forgive you for something you did when you were a stupid, naïve, impressionable boy. But let me remind you that Maleah has a big loving heart."

It was the first nice thing she'd said about Maleah since he got out.

"She loved you, for a while anyway, and that tells me she's not all bad." Gladys rearranged the salt and pepper shakers. "Because in those days, you weren't easy to love."

One of a hundred reasons he wouldn't call her.

"Promise me you'll think about it," Gladys said from the hallway. He took a moment, just long enough to let her think he'd seriously consider making that call. "G'night, Gladys. Sleep tight…"

"…and don't let the bedbugs bite."

Her all-knowing expression told him she believed he'd take her well-meaning advice.

But he wouldn't. Ever.

A WEEK AGO, to the day, her brother had found the silver-framed photo of Ian and unearthed every memory she'd carefully and deliberately buried.

The photo itself had been taken with her metallic pink pocket camera, his second birthday gift to her that year. "Sorry it's such a mess," he'd said as she'd removed wrinkly, balloon-festooned paper, "I'm all thumbs." After showing her how to use it, Maleah posed him in front of the Blue Poison-Dart Frog enclosure at the Tropical Rain Forest exhibit. (Tickets to the National Aquarium had been his first birthday gift to her.) Some girls claimed their sixteenth birthdays were the best, but for Maleah, the magic number would always be seventeen...

...because at the end of that remarkable day, Ian surprised her with a third present: a thin silver band that held what he'd called the smallest diamond on Planet Earth. "Before you put it on, you should know this isn't one of those goofy friendship rings your girlfriends are showing off." They needed to graduate from college, find stable employment, and save their pennies for a safe place to live, he'd recited in an oh-so-grown-up voice. Until then, the ring symbolized the promise between them: Someday, they'd become husband and wife.

Maleah eased the picture from its new hiding place. *I dare you to find it at the bottom of my underwear drawer, Eliot!* She returned the picture to the drawer. If Eliot snooped and found it, no doubt he'd retaliate in his typical tough cop way: "If you'd thrown it out, like I told you to, there'd be no need to worry about snagged panties or bloodied knuckles."

She'd tried. Several times. Once, she got as far as placing it atop an empty cereal box in the kitchen trash can before rescuing it. Of all the memorabilia, why did this photo hold such significance?

Knock it off, idiot. Memories like that were the reason Eliot didn't trust her.

She kicked off her heels, hung up the little black dress, and slipped into her PJ's. Hair piled loose atop her head, Maleah scrubbed lipstick, mascara, and eye shadow from her face, loaded her toothbrush, and leaned into the mirror. "If you could see me now, Kent O'Malley," she mumbled.

"You're the sexiest woman on feet," he'd whispered into her ear.

"Just because I'm blonde," she'd whispered back, "doesn't mean I'll fall for a tired old line like that."

"Oh? What line *would* you fall for, then?"

He'd chosen that moment to spin her around. And that's when she saw Ian, all alone at the edge of the dance floor, looking as stunned and confused as she felt. Somehow, she managed to follow Kent's lead while they danced, praying all the while that he wouldn't turn her again, because she wanted—*needed*—to see more of Ian.

She'd often wondered how much he'd changed after ten years in prison, and now she knew. Poets might describe him as ruggedly handsome, and Maleah had to agree. The close-cropped beard and silver strands threading through nearly-black hair gave him the distinguished look of a college professor, but the muscles bulging from his formerly reed-thin frame were anything but professorial. The biggest difference, Maleah decided, were the worry lines, etched between still-dark brows. That, and a sad, almost pleading look in those oh-so-serious eyes. *Go to him*, was the crazy, unbelievable thought that popped into her head. If Kent hadn't stopped dancing, hadn't said, "You're white as a bedsheet. What's wrong?" would she have done it?

She checked her calendar on her phone. Two back-to-back meetings, both before ten, both with the parents of severely autistic kids, followed by a volunteer stint at Johns Hopkins Children's Oncology, to paint Batman and Superman and Pokémon characters on the patients' faces. If she didn't get a few hours' sleep, no telling what nonsensical things she'd say—or do.

Maybe a cup of chamomile tea would settle her nerves...

But an hour later, she was still wide awake.

Tucked under a downy comforter, she closed her eyes and pictured the teacher of the yoga class, "Breathing to Relax," that she'd signed up for years ago.

"It's like counting sheep," the petite redhead had instructed. "Inhale for a count of four, exhale for a count of four—all through the nose—and repeat until you feel the tension and stress floating away."

Even after twenty reps of four, sleep eluded her.

Angry, flustered and exhausted, she tossed the covers aside.

The power went out often enough that Maleah taught herself how to get round the century-old town house in the dark without stubbing toes or bumping into furniture. Surprisingly, it took very little time to memorize every square inch of the old house...

Sixteen steps across the velvety Persian rug put her at her dresser, where she flicked on the light and jerked open the top drawer.

Twelve stairs led her down to the first floor, and twenty-seven paces brought her into the kitchen.

This silly ceremony could just as easily have been performed upstairs in the master bathroom. But knowing what nestled at the bottom of that waste basket would have guaranteed a fitful, completely sleepless night.

Bare toes depressed the pedal that lifted the stainless trash can's lid.

"This one's for you, Eliot," she said, and released Ian's picture.

In the morning, after she'd stuffed the bag into the big bin out back, she'd find out what it felt like to be free of Ian Sylvestry, once and for all.

CHAPTER FOUR

FIRM DECISIONS MADE in the middle of a long night, Maleah discovered, didn't always deliver positive results.

Ian's picture shouldn't actually go to the curb because…what if one of the garbage men cut his hand tossing it into the truck? Besides, it seemed a shame to throw away a perfectly good silver frame when an inexpensive 8x10 piece of glass would fix it up, good as new.

Maleah shrugged into her ski parka and tiptoed down the back porch stairs, taking care to avoid that squeaky third step…the one that always alerted her nosy neighbor.

She'd never had occasion to go outside at this hour, and now understood what her grandfather meant when he said, "Dark as pitch out there!" But what had she expected? It was three in the morning. And Channel 13's Marty Bass predicted rain. As usual, he'd been right.

Right as rain, she thought, shivering as cold drops pelted her cheeks, the backs of her hands.

Biting down on a mini flashlight, she aimed the narrow beam at the trash can, eased off its lid, and laid it handle-down in the grass— miraculously without making a sound. *Good job*, she thought, poking a hole in the plastic bag. Unless the frame had slid deeper into the sack during the trip out here, it should be right on top.

Without warning, the tiny yard was flooded with light. Bright, white, blinding light.

"Dumpster diving, eh?"

"Vern!" The very person she'd hoped to avoid. "You scared me half to death!"

"Better than scaring you all the way there…"

A joke? At this time of night? She liked him better when he was grumpy.

Forearm over her eyes, she squinted over the fence separating his property from hers.

"How many watts is that bulb, Vern? Ten thousand? Twenty?"

"It's a two-fifty LED," he said matter-of-factly. "Why bother havin' a floodlight at all if it ain't a-gonna, y'know, *flood* the place with light?"

He tightened the belt of his corduroy robe. Did he own any real clothes? she wondered.

"What're you doin' out here at this ungodly hour, anyway?"

She might have come up with a suitable retort…if he hadn't continued with "Kids these days. Inconsiderate. Dumb as a box o' rocks. *Noisy…* Why, in my day, young folks had respect for their neighbors. It's them dad-blasted liberal college professors, I tell ya, fillin' kids' heads fulla 'me-me-me-I'm-so-special' bunkum all the live-long day."

On second thought, she didn't like Grumpy Vern better, after all.

"Well?"

She turned off the flashlight. Why waste the batteries when Vern's porch light was more powerful than the sun?

"Well what?"

"What. Are. You. *Doing*. Out. Here?"

Maleah clutched the photo to her chest and replaced the trash can lid. "I threw this away by mistake," she said, showing him the frame, "and didn't want the trash guys to haul it away in the morning."

"And you couldn't wait 'til then to paw through your garbage?"

Why hadn't she thought of that?

Because you've got Ian on the brain, that's why.

She had a notion to turn right around and put the troublemaking thing right back into the trash.

"Sorry if I woke you," she said instead.

"You didn't. Haven't slept a whole night through in...can't remember when."

"Sorry to hear it."

"Don't be. I'm used to it."

Vern seemed in a mood to chitchat...the last thing Maleah wanted to do. There were a lot of things not to like about this night: Kent, behaving like they were a couple when he had no right to. Frosty winds. Sleety rain. Grouchy, nosy old neighbors. Eliot, for starting the whole picture debacle in the first place. And Ian Sylvestry, for looking sad and wounded earlier tonight.

She took hold of the icy screen door handle. "I'm off tomorrow afternoon." They'd been neighbors since Maleah bought the town house, eight years ago, and doubted they'd said more than a hundred words to one another in all that time. "Why don't you come over, say, two o'clock. I'll make us some coffee and we can get better acquainted."

One eye narrowed. So did his lips. "Why?"

"Because I want to prove to you that I'm not an inconsiderate, dumb as a box of rocks, noisy, educated by liberal professors kid. And I want you to prove to *me* that you're not as mean and cantankerous as you seem."

"Yeah? Well, you'd seem mean and cantankerous, too, if you caught your neighbor digging through her trash at…" He pulled back the cuff of his robe to read his watch. "…at fourteen minutes after three."

Ought to be an interesting chat, Maleah thought, hiding a yawn behind her free hand. If he showed up.

"You like cheesecake?"

"Love the stuff." He squinted the other eye this time. "Why?"

"I know a little bakery. Cheesecake is their specialty. I'll pick one up after my last meeting so we can—"

"—get better acquainted."

"Right."

"Just so's ya know, I don't do coffee." He patted his chest. "Bad for the ol' ticker."

But of course…

"Two o'clock," she said. *And please, wear something other than that ratty old robe.*

Maleah locked up, then shook rain from her waterlogged parka. Some landed where it was supposed to…on the mudroom rug. The rest soaked her favorite flannel pajama bottoms.

Now, if she hoped to get any sleep at all before the alarm chimed at six, she'd have to change.

This horrible, never-ending night was Ian's fault. One hundred and ten percent.

And if she ever saw him again, that's exactly what she'd say.

OVER CHEESECAKE AND DECAF, even Vern asked to tag along with Maleah to help serve breakfast at Our Daily Bread. "Must be something a grumpy old geezer can do." He was amazingly good with on-the-spectrum kids.

Moments after introducing him to the rest of the volunteers, Berta, who managed the place, tossed him an apron and put him to work scouring pots and washing dishes.

Maleah delivered another huge tray, piled high with dirty dishes. "I forgot to warn you, this is where she starts all the newbies. She says if they can handle this back-breaking chore, they're in it for the right reasons. Sorry…"

"The woman is right, so there's nothin' to be sorry for. What's up with that, anyways? Did your folks knock you around when you were a kid?"

"Of course not. I was raised in the least dysfunctional family you'll ever meet."

"Good reason to quit apologizing, then. Don't want people thinkin' less of them, do you?"

Odd, she thought, because Ian had been the first person to ask why she said sorry so often.

"Mashed potatoes to serve up," she said, leaving the steamy kitchen.

She'd no sooner plopped a scoop into a partitioned tray when the gray-bearded gent on the other side of the counter said, "This is my cousin, Ian. He's a little shy, or he'd tell you himself…he thinks you're real pretty."

Maleah thanked the cousins for the compliment and ladled a double serving of gravy onto each tray.

Yet another Ian reference. Yesterday, a little leukemia patient asked Maleah to paint a wolf on her brother Ian's cheek. And on the way home from Hopkins, the guy who gave her change for a twenty at the Harbor Tunnel toll booth wore a name tag that said Ian. How was she supposed to stop thinking about him if the universe insisted on throwing reminders in her lap?

During the drive back to Ellicott City, Vern talked nonstop about how fulfilling it was, working at the soup kitchen.

"I have a car, y'know. Ain't been driven in a year, maybe more. Gonna have it serviced, so's I can go downtown more than once a week."

"That's good of you."

"Nah. I have my problems—who doesn't?— but I'm better off than a lot of people. Seems only right to give a little, after all the taking I've done in my lifetime."

He'd said much the same thing in her kitchen, but she hadn't pressed for details. If he wanted to tell her about his past, he'd do it with no prompting from her. She pulled into her drive-way as Vern said, "You know what I think?"

Already she knew him well enough to real-ize he'd tell her, no matter how she answered.

"I think you've got man troubles. Big ones that go way back." She couldn't very well deny it, now could she?

"You wanna talk about it? I'm told I'm a pretty good listener."

"Thanks, but maybe some other time. I have a bunch of chores waiting for me inside. And then I have to go back to the office."

"Crazy workaholic. What's so important it can't wait 'til Monday morning?"

"The Washburne-Albert Institute is about to launch its annual month-long winter fund-raiser."

"I've heard about that. 'Kids First,' right?"

"Yup. Maybe you'll have time to go to the craft fair or the antiques auction."

"Maybe..."

"And if you have a lady friend you'd like to impress, I might be able to wrangle a couple of tickets to our good old-fashioned Baltimore bull roast, or even the grand finale...the black tie dinner."

"Black tie? No way I'm rentin' a monkey suit to eat rubber chicken."

Not overly enthused.

"You're a Ravens fan, right? And wasn't that an Orioles banner I saw on your front porch last season?"

"Yeah, so?"

"So a couple guys from each team—and a coach or two—have said they'll participate in the autograph session. We signed a couple of top ten recording artists and half a dozen or so movie stars, too."

Vern shook his head. "My, my, my. You're a walking, talking sandwich board, aren't you? I hope they're paying you extra for this off-duty PR."

Laughing, Maleah got out of the car. "I enjoyed working with you today, Vern. It's been a real pleasure seeing the jovial, generous side of you."

He slammed the Jeep's passenger door and knocked on its red roof.

"Feel like talkin' about that man trouble today?"

Was the universe conspiring against her?

"Back in high school, I had a boyfriend. He got involved with some rough characters, and one night, they robbed the convenience store on Route 40. One of the guys had a gun. Loaded. And used it on the clerk. The two that robbed the store and the one who shot the clerk got fifteen years for armed robbery, aggravated assault and attempted murder. Would have been longer if they hadn't been minors."

"And your boyfriend?"

"Ten years at Lincoln for driving the get-away car."

"How long ago?"

"A lifetime." She sighed. "Seems like a life-time ago that he was released."

"And no contact between you two since he got out?"

"Nope. None." Until the other night. Al-though she wouldn't exactly call that contact...

"Then why the big sad eyes? You're not still sweet on the guy I hope."

Maleah honestly couldn't say.

"Was it altar-bound serious? Or just your typical kiddie romance?"

"Serious enough. He asked me to marry him."

"Tough break for you, and I pity the fool."

"Pity him? Why?"

"He chose a gang of thugs over a life with you?" Vern shook his head. "Can't imagine havin' to live with a mistake that big."

Her dad, Eliot, even kindhearted Joe had said similar things. What they failed to realize was that *she* had to live with it, too.

"Nobody's caught your eye since?"

"Oh, I accept a date every now and then." *But*...

"But the guys aren't *him*."

If anyone had said her spotlight-blazing, opinionated old grouch of a neighbor would be the first person in her life to get it, *really* get it, she'd have called them crazy. *Goes to show*, she thought, *you can't judge a man by his robe*.

They said their goodbyes in the driveway, and as he unlocked his front door, Vern looked at the sky.

"Uh-oh...better dig out the ice scraper, girlie. It's gonna snow tonight."

"Snow?" She looked up, too. "I hope you're wrong. I hate driving in that stuff."

"So do I. But mark my words. We'll be sweepin' white stuff off the steps come mornin'."

He was about to step inside when Maleah stopped him with, "Hey Vern? Where are you from, originally?"

"Texas." Laughing, he added, "What, did my pointy-toed boots give me away?"

More like your pointed turn of a phrase, she thought.

"Something like that." She waved. "Hope I won't see you in the morning."

"Oh, you will. And Maleah?"

"Hmm..."

"Have your friends hook you up with some

blind dates. Talk to your preacher about eligible bachelors in the parish. Ask your mother if any of her friends have unmarried sons. Sign up with one of those internet dating sites."

"Sorry, but I've been there and done *all* of that. They were nice guys, for the most part. Just not...not my type." Hopefully, she'd caught herself in time, and Vern hadn't noticed that she'd nearly said *just not him.*

"If you're gonna be sorry about anything, it ought to be that you're wasting time mooning over an ex-con."

Mooning? *Really?* When had it become the latest go-to word of men?

"Your teeth are chattering, you adorable moron, you. Get inside before you catch your death and let me do the same. I can't afford to heat all of Oella, y'know."

Once his door slammed and its bolt slid into place, Maleah went inside and changed into fleecy sweats, then brewed herself a mug of tea and carried it to the living room. Is that what she'd really been doing? Comparing all her dates with Ian?

You're a shrink, girl; shouldn't you know?

CHAPTER FIVE

AT THE FIRST planning meeting for the gala, Maleah saw Ian's name on the volunteers' list. Could this be Eliot's idea of a sick joke? Was he trying to catch her in the act of searching the facility for her first love?

More likely it was a name-related coincidence. Not that his name was like Joe Green or Tom Smith, but… She'd worked for Washburne in one capacity or another for years, and not once had Ian appeared at any Kids First events.

Maleah carried the clipboard to the sign-in table. "Hi, Darcy," she said, reading the young woman's stick-on name tag. "I wonder if you can help me with something…"

The girl smiled up at her. "I'll try."

Maleah pointed at Ian's name on the list. "I've never worked with this guy before. What do you know about him?"

Nodding, Darcy said, "Oh, yeah. He's Terri Hudson's boss." She handed the clipboard back to Maleah. "Ms. Hudson's son goes to school here. You've probably seen her around, working with the hearing impaired kids. She has a hearing impairment herself." She blushed slightly when she added, "Mr. Sylvestry is a sweetie. When Avery—that's Terri's son—needs a dad substitute, Mr. Sylvestry fills in."

She didn't know what to do, now that Darcy had confirmed that Mr. Sylvestry was indeed Ian.

"Now that you mention it, I do know her." They'd had a few brief interactions at Washburne, and a slightly longer exchange on the night the woman hostessed Kent's holiday party. "A very pleasant, efficient lady."

"Yes, she is."

Maleah tucked the clipboard under her arm. "Thanks, Darcy. Need anything? Water? Soft drink?"

"I'm good, but thanks."

Maleah walked away wondering if Terri knew about Ian's background. Surely not, or she wouldn't allow her special needs son to spend so much time alone with him.

What do you care? It's none of your business.

Fortunately, in her capacity as Assistant PR director of the banquet, Maleah could delegate any tasks or activities that might require her to work with him directly...or reject him as a volunteer.

A deep booming voice interrupted her thoughts. "Maleah! Just the person I was looking for."

Stan Howard, generous donor to Washburne and personal friend of the director, said, "There's somebody here I'd like you to meet."

His ear-piercing whistle turned every head within her line of sight. The blast must have alerted his intended target, because he smiled and waved. Maleah, too short to see over others' heads, waited for Stan's "someone" to appear.

"Don't look so nervous. You're gonna love this guy. Everybody does. He's real easygoing, and no matter how menial the task, he gives it his all."

"Haven't met a Washburne volunteer that I didn't like." *Yet...*

He took a step closer and lowered his voice. "Fair warning…at first he appears a little rough around the edges, and you might hear some rumors, but trust me, not a one of 'em is true."

"What kind of rumors?"

"Spent a few years in the slammer. Poor guy served his time and cleaned up his act. He deserves a break. But you know how judgmental people can be." He pointed. "Speak of the devil… Ian, hey, good to see you, buddy! This is the li'l beauty I was telling you about. You'll answer to her while you're working on the gala." Stan smiled at Maleah. "Maleah Turner, meet Ian Sylvestry."

"Pleased to meet you."

She gave his extended hand a quick shake-and-release. "Likewise."

"So where do we start, boss?"

"I'm not sure yet. Let me talk with a few of the event chairs and see what they need help with." She focused on Stan. "You have his contact information?"

"Well yeah." Stan gave her a sidelong glance. "But so do you." He looked at Ian. "It's on your registration form. Right?"

He answered with a nod, then tacked on, "It's a requirement of anyone volunteering to work with—or around—kids."

"And you passed the background test?"

"And I passed the background test."

His voice, last time she'd heard it, had been shaky and almost timid. Not so anymore. Given the opportunity, he could easily find work recording voice-over commercials or substitute for a radio DJ instead of Avery Hudson's stand-in dad. His "I'm meeting you for the first time" act was flawless, too, a talent no doubt honed at Lincoln. A slight shiver zipped up her spine: What else had he learned there?

Stan gave Ian's shoulder a brotherly squeeze. "This place is a madhouse." He drew Ian and

Maleah closer in a three-way hug. "So here's what you two are going to do…" The only thing separating them was Stan's ponderous belly. That, and years of artificial indifference. Ian's dark eyes bored into hers, exactly the way he had when they were younger—and in love.

Quiet laughter rumbled from Stan's chest. "You're going to leave here, right now, for someplace quiet. So you can discuss how best to put Ian to use. He's a talented artist, and knows his way around a kitchen, too."

He leaned forward to glance at his wrist-watch, and in the process, moved Maleah closer still to Ian.

"What time does your place close on Sunday nights?"

Ian's voice was guarded when he said, "Six."

"Why so early?"

"Most of my employees are married, with kids. Tomorrow is a school day."

So Ian hadn't been a guest at the bistro on the night of Kent's party? He *owned* it?

Stan winked at Maleah. "See there? Didn't I tell you he was a good guy?"

He didn't give her a chance to respond. Instead, Stan released her, then Ian.

"Here's an idea… I'll have my driver take you over there. You can take a look at his paintings, maybe even get a bite of his famous cheesecake." He gestured, bringing their attention to the crowd. "Lord knows you can't make plans here."

"Plans?" Maleah echoed.

He looked at her as if she'd grown a second nose.

"Finding out which of your volunteers is best suited to do what needs doing, of course." He chuckled. "You're pullin' my leg, aren't you?" And looking at Ian, Stan added, "This gal has pulled off some of the best functions I've ever attended."

He frowned as an announcement crackled through the overhead speakers.

"See what I mean? You can't make any good decisions with all this going on. So how about it? Can I have my driver run you over there?"

"Curious as I am to see the inside of that presidential-looking SUV of yours, I rode my Harley," Ian said. "I need to balance the checkbook. And I haven't made up next week's schedule yet." Eyes on Maleah, he added, "The bistro is closed on Mondays. Maybe tomorrow, when you get off work?"

She didn't want to be alone with him, not tomorrow, not ever. But Stan and the facility director had been college roommates. Rejecting his idea was the equivalent to an insult, to him and her boss.

"We don't need a face-to-face meeting, Stan. That's what telephones and email and text messages are for."

Stan waved the idea away. "Later, maybe, once you've got things nailed down. But I didn't get where I am by taking the easy way out during the planning phases of any project." He looked from Maleah to Ian and back again. "Neither of you strikes me as the type to take shortcuts."

His challenge hung in the air between them. From the look on Ian's face, Maleah realized Stan's pull extended beyond facilities like Washburne.

Another notice blared from the overhead speakers.

Ian winced. "You make a good point, Stan, but so does Ms. Turner. We can accomplish a lot through texts and emails."

"Nonsense."

His jovial demeanor turned coolly professional, as quick as the flip of a switch.

"Look. Kids. I don't like to throw my weight around," he said, "but when I funnel a six-figure donation into a project, I expect things will get done correctly. And leaving contrails through cyberspace is *not* my idea of efficient."

Ian shifted his weight from the right foot to

the left. Nodding slowly, he stared at the floor between his polished black biker boots. Hands pocketed, he lifted one shoulder in a casual shrug. "Stan, c'mon. Be reasonable. Even you have to admit this whole in-person planning idea was kinda last minute. Give us a day to shift things around on our calendars at least. Can we get back to you?"

He met Maleah's eyes. "Don't mean to be presumptuous. In your position as Assistant VP of…" Grinning—but only barely—he said, "Sorry, but I forget the rest of your title."

It stunned her to learn he knew anything about what she did for a living. Stan must have filled him in…

"Point being," Ian continued, "you have other department heads to deal with. Autistic kids' parents. The kids themselves. And since I don't have that problem over at the bistro, how about if you call me when you find a hole in your calendar, we'll discuss a convenient time to get together."

Thanks a bunch, *Stan.* If she said yes, Maleah had to meet with Ian. And if she said no, Stan might get the impression she wasn't up to the job. And it galled her that, either way, it was a win for Ian.

"Might as well get it over with."

Instantly, she regretted her choice of words.

"That didn't come out quite the way I intended it." A nervous giggle punctuated her sentence. "What I meant was…it seems both Mr. Sylvestry and I have time, right now. So if you're amenable, I'll meet you at your restaurant in—"

The switch flipped again, and Stan's boisterous laughter all but drowned out the drone of yet another broadcast.

"What's with all this Mr. and Ms. Stuff? You're going to be working together. *Closely.* For at least the next three weeks, minimum. Read my lips and repeat after me: Mah-lee-ah. Eee-yen." When they didn't respond, he grabbed their jaws and repeated his instructions.

"Okay, all right," Ian said, taking a step back from Stan. He met Maleah's eyes. "I'll head over to the bistro and wait for you… *Maleah.*"

He'd said something eerily similar on the night he presented the little silver band…

If Stan hadn't been there, waiting and watching, she might have suddenly remembered an important appointment.

"I have a few things to finish up in my office, and then I'll be right over."

"See? Now was that so hard?" Stan smirked.

"Do I know how to make things happen, or do I know how to make things happen!"

If only she could hold him accountable if things went sideways—and they probably would—and she ended up firing Ian?

CHAPTER SIX

"It's a lovely old building," Maleah said, leaning into the deck rail. "And the view, well, it's priceless."

He'd half expected her to berate him for agreeing with Stan. And for every awful thing that might have happened to her since the guards carted him off that day. During the drive from the Institute to the bistro, he'd made up his mind to take it on the chin. She had a right to vent some frustration. God knows he'd done his share during his ten years at Lincoln. Her polite behavior seemed too good to be true...

He nodded toward the *Constellation*. "Ever done a tour of her?"

"I'm embarrassed to admit it, but no."

She smiled. Not the big loving smile that he'd seen in his dreams. But close enough.

Considering.

"It's on my bucket list, though. Along with the Science Center. The National Aquarium. Poe's house, and Babe Ruth's, too. The B&O Railroad Museum..." She faced the water again. "Not sure why it seems like I never have time for things like that. I have friends— married with kids—who've seen all of Charm City's sights."

Married. With kids. If he hadn't screwed up, *she'd* be married with kids. *His* kids. Eyes shut tight, Ian lowered his head, hoping what he'd done to her wasn't the reason she'd remained single.

From the corner of his eye, he could see her, watching as a sailboat floated silently by, its navigation lights reflected by the dark Inner Harbor waters. If not for the motorcycle, roaring by on Thames Street below, she could have heard the quiet clank of rigging lines hitting the mast, too.

Arms crossed and shoulders hunched, Maleah shivered.

"Let's go inside," he said. "I'll make us some coffee and we can get our Stan talk out of the way."

Nodding, she followed him. A lifetime ago, she would have reached for his hand, given it a loving squeeze as they walked down the wide-planked hall. Lord, how he missed things like that. Missed *her.* It hadn't been easy, picking up the Sunday *Sun* and reading about her involvement in one fund-raiser or another, or turning on the evening news and seeing her respond to reporters' questions about improvements to Washburne. It hurt like crazy, knowing she was literally minutes from him, yet completely out of his reach. That seemed fair punishment for what he'd put her through, but he didn't have to like it.

She'd stopped to admire sketches of the building as it had looked a century ago, and photographs of the changes it had undergone through the decades. Hands pocketed, he stood beside her.

"Looks like the former owners took great pains to preserve the historical integrity of the place."

"It was a mess when my aunt bought the place." He pointed to the collage of snapshots, showing each phase of construction. "She has a good eye."

She stepped up to a more recent collection of pictures. "Who's responsible for these?"

"I am."

Even looking apprehensive, she was gorgeous. If he'd known how hard it would be, standing this close to her, Ian never would have suggested a one-on-one meeting. Not even for Stan, his dad's boss.

"Feel free to wander around while I get the coffee started."

Yet again she followed, this time to the kitchen.

"Wow. Nice setup." She turned slowly, taking in polished stainless appliances, countertops, and shelving lined with pots, pans and kettles that shone under the fluorescent lights. "I know a few people who own restaurants who'd turn green with envy if they saw this place."

Pleasant as all this small talk sounded, Ian tensed, wondering when the proverbial other boot would drop. He hid the uneasiness by stepping into the cooler.

"How many chefs do you have?" she called out.

"Two, right now." Ian emerged carrying two slices of cheesecake. "Of all the things I used to do around here," he said, kicking the big door shut, "I miss that most."

She pulled out a stainless stool and sat down. "So you still like to cook, huh?"

No fewer than a dozen times, he'd made good old-fashioned country breakfasts for her, his dad and Gladys. As he filled two big white mugs with coffee, Ian wondered if she could still pack away meals like a linebacker...

He slid a mug across the counter and grabbed forks and napkins from bins near the industrial dishwasher. "It's decaf, so..."

"Good." She flapped a napkin across her

knees and picked up a fork. "So there are a few things I have to say," Maleah began.

Ian braced himself and waited for that other boot to drop.

Maleah said, "I get the impression you and Stan go way back…"

"He was my dad's college roommate. Bought the company where Dad works. And since it's cheaper to ship things in and out, here on the coast, Stan made Baltimore his corporate headquarters." He paused. "I get the feeling you have some history with him, too."

"Not as far back as your association with him. Stan is Washburne's biggest donor, so like it or not—and for the most part, I do *not*—I'm expected to defer to his whims."

"Bummer."

"Make no mistake, Ian. *I'm* in charge of the Kids First events. Put me on the spot that way again, and I'll have a new assistant like *that*. And you'll just have to find a new way to help your hostess and her little boy."

Who'd told her about Terri and Avery? he wondered.

"I, ah, I didn't mean to step on your toes. It's just…when Stan issued that Do It My Way order, I tried to find a solution that would appease everybody, equally."

"Uh-huh." Chin up and shoulders back, she

used her fork as a pointer. "But for future reference, I've been on my own for a long time.
I don't need or want a hero."

She'd always been spunky, but not like this.
"Message received."

He took a bite of cheesecake, and so did she.

"Which chef came up with this recipe?"

"Gladys. She taught me everything I know
about running a restaurant."

"I always enjoyed spending time with her."
After taking a sip of coffee, she asked, "Did
she visit often when you were…"

Eyes closed and blushing, she waved a hand
in front of her face. "Sorry. That was rude."

"Nah. It's only natural that you have questions. Ask me anything. Really."

Maleah sighed. "I honestly wouldn't know
where to begin."

He didn't like seeing her uncomfortable.
Liked it even less that he, alone, had made
her feel that way.

"Kind of a convoluted story, my ending up
owner of *Sur les Quais*. Gladys banked every
dollar I earned in lockup, so when I got out,
I had a tidy nest egg waiting for me. She insisted that I move into the furnished apartment
upstairs," he said, thumb aimed at the ceiling.
"When I'd racked up a couple dozen 'Thanks,
but we don't hire ex-cons' rejections, she put

me to work here, washing dishes, mopping up, scrubbing bathrooms… Couple years later, on my birthday, she made me the manager. Then one year, on *her* birthday, she retired, and handed over the deed."

"I'm not surprised. She always struck me as a bighearted lady."

"A year ago, I'd paid her back, in full and with interest." Ian didn't know why it was so important for her to know that. "To answer your earlier question, no, she didn't visit me at Lincoln. Neither did my dad. Because I told them not to."

"Wow. A scary place like that, all alone at your age? That couldn't have been easy."

"Would've been harder, seeing their reaction to the place. So I kept my head down and my nose clean, so I could get out sooner, rather than later."

"Does it bother you? Talking about it, I mean?"

He'd always been open and honest about his stint at Lincoln, mostly in the hope of preventing others from making the same reckless gaffes. Discussing it with Gladys and his dad hadn't posed a challenge, and when his staff at the restaurant good-naturedly ribbed him about his "time in the pen," he'd laughed right along with them. But sitting here, not two feet from the only woman he'd ever truly loved? Not easy. Not easy *at all.*

"Let's just say certain things are easier to talk about than others."

Her eyebrows rose, a telltale sign that he'd piqued her curiosity. Didn't he owe her better than to force her to drag it out of him?

"It was noisy, for one thing. I doubt there were five minutes when the place was quiet. Walking on eggshells, not knowing when a look or a word or even a gesture might set somebody off was kinda crazy-making. The lack of privacy took a while to get used to."

Chin resting on a fist, Maleah shook her head. "Those things," she said, pointing at the rough-looking tattoos on his forearms. "Did you do them yourself?"

Ian inspected the rough, faded gray-blue letters that spelled GOOD LIFE. "My penmanship lacks style, even on paper." Linking his fingers, he said, "Yeah, I did them myself."

"What materials did you use?"

"Burnt match heads, crushed and mixed with ink from a broken Sharpie, and the innards of a blue ballpoint pen, mixed up in a toothpaste cap…rubbed into scratches."

"Open cuts?"

"You, better than just about anyone, know I never was the sharpest tack in the box."

"But...did they get infected?"

They had. To the point of getting him out of laundry duty for two solid weeks.

"Nah, not really."

"Were things really so bad that you felt it necessary to resort to...to self-mutilation?"

He forced a laugh. "Didn't do it because conditions were bad."

"Then *why*, Ian?"

If a couple of innocuous inscriptions could inspire a frown like that, how would she react to the garish markings fellow inmates inflicted during his first weeks at Lincoln? Lucky for him, she'd never see those.

"Maybe we should get to work. I'm guessing Stan will expect a report first thing in the morning."

"You're right." Maleah shoved the half-eaten cheesecake aside and, picking up her gigantic purse, withdrew a small laptop. "I think we should start by designing a flyer," she began, firing it up. "Something that, if we don't go overboard with phrasing, can double as a press release or a mailer."

"Good idea."

She felt bad, asking about his days in the penitentiary. Prison movies and the stories her grandfather, dad and brothers told about how miserable life in prison was had almost inspired sympathy toward Ian.

Almost.

Maleah carried the laptop to his side of the counter, and as her fingers flew over the keyboard, she began a flurry of rapid-fire talking. Better to have him think she was the same silly chatterbox she'd been at eighteen than risk Ian finding out that despite it all, she wanted what was best for him. And unless she'd misread his penetrating eye contact, raspy-soft voice, and sad smile, he felt the same way,

Ian made a few suggestions about placement of the Washburne logo, highlighting the names of the stars who'd be present at the gala, and adding a color photos of the headliners. One by one, Maleah incorporated them all.

"It's a great start," she said, saving the file.

"And to think it only took us half an hour."

Maleah closed the laptop. "Well, it isn't like I haven't done this before."

"Couple dozen times, according to Stan."

She returned the computer to its slot in her bag as he added, "I have a few friends in the media who can help publicize the event. I can make some calls, if you like."

"Friends, as in TV and newspaper reporters?"

"Yeah."

He rattled off a few names, and Maleah recognized each. In the past, all but one had ignored her voice mail and email messages.

"That'll be a big help," she admitted. "How do you know those people, if you don't mind my asking."

He gave a nonchalant shrug. "Helped Tom Scottson with a documentary about kids in prison he did a few years back. One thing led to another. Before I knew it, I was the go-to guy for a couple of similar TV series he filmed here in Baltimore." He shrugged again. "The directors and a couple of the producers still call every now and then."

So, Maleah thought, he'd committed a felony and served time for it, and instead of being shunned, the media had turned him into a silent hero of sorts? She didn't know how to feel about that.

"Guess I'd better go," she said, zipping up the big bag.

"Right. Four o'clock always comes earlier than I think it will when I set the alarm."

"That's early."

"Earlier I get to the farmer's market, less likely things will be picked over."

"You do that yourself? I thought that was the chef's job."

"Sometimes. But Dan's wife just had a baby— what a set of lungs that kid has—so Lee and the rest of us are picking up the slack for a few weeks." Ian grinned. "Just until he adjusts to his new no-sleep schedule."

Had his association with TV types taught him when and how to polish up his *I'm a changed man* veneer? Or was this the new Ian?

"Very nice."

"Dan's good people. We're happy to do it."

Maleah reached for her jacket, but Ian beat her to it.

"Where'd you park?" he asked, helping her into it.

"In the lot across the street."

As he led the way to the side door, Ian said, "You want to call Stan in the morning, or should I?"

"If it's up to me, I say we let him call us. I don't appreciate being pushed around like that."

He smiled. "You'll let me know what he says?"

"What makes you think he'll call me? *My* dad and Stan aren't best friends."

Unlocking the door from the inside, he stepped onto the sea-blue porch. "Okay, if I hear from him, I'll let you know." He pointed to the narrow lot on the other side of Thames Street.

"Which is yours?"

"The silver SUV, right next to that gigantic motorcycle."

"That's Harriet the Harley. Bought her years ago, when she was hardly more than a bucket of rusty bolts."

"How many trips does it take to get produce here on that thing?"

Laughing, Ian took her elbow and escorted her across the street. "I use the black pickup beside Harriet for that."

She unlocked her car and eased the briefcase onto the passenger seat, and as she slid in behind the wheel, he leaned on the driver's door.

"Sorry if my Lincoln stories upset you."

"Upset me? Why would they upset me? *You're* the one who served time, not me."

Had he stepped back because of her curt tone, or the smug expression that no doubt accompanied it? *You've become a cold, heartless woman.*

"You never were one to beat around the bush, were you?"

"It's a confusing waste of time, and unnecessarily hard on the shrubbery."

One side of his mouth lifted in a wry smile. "It's been good, seeing you. Even better knowing you don't hate my guts."

She'd tried hating him, but the good times

they'd shared made it impossible. "Harboring ill feelings...another waste of time."

Oh, aren't you *the philosopher tonight!*

"Uh-huh," he said. And after a moment, "So...once we get Stan's approval, we'll have those flyers printed up?"

"We're not waiting for his approval. He insisted that we meet and make some plans, and we did far more than that. I'll print the flyer and email you a copy. Once you've made contact with your reporter pals, let me know, so we can work out a good time for interviews and whatnot."

He leaned a forearm on the car's roof. "I'll have them get in touch with you."

"With me? But you're their go-to guy..."

"Why would they want to feature this ugly ol' mug when they could film your pretty face?"

Grateful for the darkness that hid her blush, Maleah buckled her seat belt.

"Good work tonight," she said, reaching for the door handle.

He took the hint and stood back. "How long will it take you to get home from here?"

"Now? Half an hour."

Ian nodded as she shut the door.

"Good. Drive safely now, hear?"

Maleah aimed the SUV toward South Caroline. With any luck, the traffic lights would be on her side and she really would be home in thirty minutes.

If it took longer, she wouldn't complain. She'd always done her best thinking behind the wheel, and the meeting with Ian had given her a lot to think about. How to explain to her family that she'd work with "that bum Ian Sylvestry" until the night of the gala, for starters. And how he'd parlayed life as an ex-con into respectable relationships with the media… something she'd hadn't accomplished in her years with Washburne. At least, not to the degree Ian had.

On the other hand, she hadn't yet seen proof that he could arrange the interviews. For all she knew, the promise was all part of a well-rehearsed act. If so, would Stan place the blame where it belonged? Because one thing Maleah didn't need at this point in the gala's schedule was another reason to resent him.

CHAPTER SEVEN

THE CHRISTMAS TREES of the World display that opened the Kids First event was one of the best Ian had ever seen. Hundreds of them, all shapes, sizes and colors, adorned with ornaments depicting the traditions of each represented country. His assignment? Make sure the lights stayed lit and the decorations stayed in place.

"Too bad they're fake," said a deep voice.

Turning, Ian looked into the eyes of Maleah's older brother.

"Eliot. Long time no see."

"Ten years, plus what, another fifteen?"

Ian chose to ignore the sarcasm. "Give or take."

He gave Ian a quick once-over. "You're rougher around the edges than I remember, but you didn't age near as much as I thought you would."

Ian saw two boys, perhaps six and eight, hovering nearby.

"Your kids?"

"Yeah, poor poor Dad," said the taller of the

two, "it's his weekend with us. We're doing stupid stuff until he can drop us off."

If Ian had ever seen a man look more hurt or embarrassed, he didn't know when. A lot of life had happened to Eliot during Ian's years on the inside...marriage, kids and divorce. The guy had never gone out of his way to be friendly—quite the opposite, in fact—and yet he felt bad for him.

"I read someplace," Ian told the older boy, "that dads aren't as good at the one-on-one stuff as moms because they're too busy protecting their kids from the dangerous stuff in the world." He glanced at Eliot. "Especially dads that are cops."

The smaller kid piped up with "Dad is always, *always* telling us to keep our wits about us, because there are crazies around every corner." He looked up at his father. "Can we go to Dairy Queen after this?"

"Sure, sure." Eliot slid a ten from his wallet, handed it to his oldest son. "There's a gift cart right there. See if you can find something your mom might like."

In one blink of the eye, Eliot looked as grateful as someone who despised him could look.

In the next, his expression reverted to the no-nonsense tough cop Ian remembered so well.

"I don't need any parenting help from the

likes of you, Sylvestry. My boys and I get along great."

"I'm sure you do." Ian glanced at the kids, squinting at the price tags attached to delicate, hand-blown glass ornaments. "They look a lot like you. Seem like good kids, too."

Eliot's frown deepened. "I didn't come here seeking your compliments *or* your approval."

"Yeah? Then why *are* you here?"

"In a word, Maleah. She said over Sunday dinner that some Washburne big shot pressured her into working with you. And *I'm* here to say if you know what's good for you, you'll do your job and nothing more."

He didn't like Eliot's tone. Or his ready-to-fight stance, for that matter. He tried to put himself in the man's shoes. What red-blooded loving brother would stand idly by while his only sister dated an ex-con? Understanding the man's behavior was one thing, but he didn't appreciate being raked over the coals in front of paying customers and other event volunteers.

He was about to say all that when the sound of shattering glass stopped him. "Wasn't us, Dad," said the little guy. "It was that kid." He pointed. "The one who's been running around."

"I know," Eliot said. "Saw him out of the corner of my eye."

"We bought Mom an angel ornament," his older son said, holding up a small white box.

"Good. Zip up your jackets. We're leaving."

"Can we still go to Dairy Queen?"

"Sure. Why not?"

He faced Ian, pointed a finger and narrowed his eyes. "Remember…do your job. That's it. Or else."

Or else what? he wanted to ask.

"One question," Ian said instead.

"Yeah…"

"Did Maleah put you up to this?"

"Absolutely not. She doesn't even know we're here. And if you know what's good for you, you'll keep it that way."

Again with the "if you know what's good for you" garbage. To avoid regular beatings, like those he'd been subjected to that first year at Lincoln, Ian had learned to endure a certain amount of bullying. But he saw no reason to tolerate Eliot's intimidation now, even if his intentions were more or less good. He put himself in Eliot's path, effectively blocking his exit. "Look. Eliot. I get it. If my sister was cavorting with a known felon, I'd wig out, too. But *you* need to know that I have no interest in Maleah." Too much time had passed, time that changed them. Yes, he liked her even better now, maybe, grown up, feisty and independent, than he had all those years ago, but that didn't mean things could ever be the same. "So save your threats for somebody who *doesn't* have her best interests at heart, okay?"

The boys ran up and, grinning, flanked their father. "We're ready for ice cream!" the little guy said.

Ian watched them walk away, hand in hand, Eliot nodding and smiling as the boys chattered all the way to the main entrance. Despite the older one's surly comment earlier, it was clear father and sons really did have a good relationship.

And for the first time since meeting Eliot, Ian envied him.

Just then, Ian spotted Maleah an aisle away, giving directions to a visitor. When she looked up, he waved. He hadn't intended it as an invitation, but when she started moving toward him, he thought, *Two birds with one stone.* Find out what, if anything, she wanted him to do, and—

"I see you had a visitor."

It surprised him to learn that she'd watched all that and hadn't intervened. "Yeah. A real fun reunion."

Maleah didn't respond, and Ian decided she hadn't heard him as she turned to straighten a crystal angel on Finland's tree.

"Maybe next time you guys have a Turner

family get-together, you can set your brother straight. Make sure he knows you're safe from the big bad ex-con."

She took half a step back. "No need to shout, Ian. I'm standing right here."

"Sorry."

"So is that what Eliot told you? That he thought you were threatening me in some way?"

"No. He's concerned I'm trying to pick up where I left off. Pretty much told me to do my job and keep my distance…or else."

"Or else what?"

"That's what I wanted to know. I didn't ask him, of course, because his kids were with him."

She lifted her chin. Crossed both arms over her chest. Took half a step *forward*.

"If you're waiting for me to apologize on his behalf, don't. Eliot has always been protective, and under the circumstances, you can hardly blame him. I was a mess, for months, thanks to you. And he was right there, helping pick up the pieces."

A two-by-four to the head couldn't have hurt worse.

"I get it. In fact, I admitted to *him* that I get it. Doesn't mean I like being taken to task in front of a bunch of strangers."

She shrugged again, as if to say *That's the*

price you pay for participating in an armed robbery.

If that's what she truly felt, he couldn't blame her. That hurt, and riled him, too.

Every time the prison mailman handed him a Return to Sender envelope, his heart shrank a bit more; when Turtle poked that last one through the chipped gray bars, Ian all but gave up. Lincoln's chaplain, having heard that he wasn't eating or sleeping much, made an unscheduled visit to cell block D, during which the old priest said something Ian had never forgotten: "Self-pity is the most destructive of human emotions. Get involved in activities that put you last, not first." The advice had served him well...until he saw her on the bistro's dance floor. Since then he'd flip-flopped from wondering if what they'd once had could be revived, and wanting to protect her from *him*. He reminded himself how important family had always been to her. If it came down to choices between their feelings and even the most casual business relationship with him, she'd choose them.

As she should, since—as she'd pointed out—they'd been there to pick up the pieces after he went away.

"Just so we're on the same page," she said, standing as tall as her five-foot frame would allow, "we both know that Eliot has nothing to worry about…right?"

"Right. And neither do you. Soon as this Kids First stuff ends, you'll probably never see me again."

"No need to back away entirely. Washburne needs all the capable volunteers it can get. I'm sure they can find ways you can continue helping out that don't involve working with me."

She must have realized that her curt words rattled him, because Maleah smiled. Not the big happy grin that once lit up her entire face, but Ian preferred it to the way she'd been looking at him since Eliot left.

"Have you had a chance to see the entire exhibit yet?"

"Not yet. Too busy fixing what these curious visitors mess up. My mom used to say 'You look with your eyes, not your fingers.' Guess they never heard that one."

"Funny. My mom said the same thing."

It'd be nice if it meant she was looking for common ground, but Ian knew better.

"Too bad I can't make a couple of signs, post 'em around the auditorium."

"Why can't you?"

"I, ah… Well, where can I find paper, markers and tape?"

She pointed. "You'll find everything you

need in the storeroom. Can't wait to see if your artistic abilities held up after all those years…"

Her voice trailed off. Blushing, she said, "Sorry. That came out wrong."

"Hey, it is what it is. No need to walk on eggshells around me. My name isn't Eliot."

The smile vanished like the smoke from a spent match. In its place, the same look of disapproval that had furrowed her brother's brow moments ago.

"I need to make a few phone calls. If you need anything, text me."

Ian couldn't think of a thing he might need, but she'd walked so quickly away, he didn't have a chance to say so.

On his way to the storeroom, she cut a glance his way before ducking into the main office. Part of him wished he could read her mind. Was she wondering how big a mess he'd make of the posters, and who she'd have to answer to once he distributed them throughout the hall? Ian made up his mind to do her proud, and create the best "Please don't touch the merchandise" signs this facility had ever seen.

At least then he'd have the satisfaction of knowing his actions wouldn't cause her any grief.

Because God knew he'd already caused her plenty of that.

SURELY THERE WERE better ways to avoid Ian than by hiding out in the office, shuffling papers and scanning her phone's contacts list.

She hadn't been close enough to hear the exchange between the men, but the look on her brother's face had told her what she'd needed to know. When Eliot put his mind to it, he could be downright abrasive and, having been on the receiving end of it too many times, she felt sorry for Ian. Ridiculous, considering all he'd put her through. What he'd put *everyone* through. Yes, he'd been young, and of course it had been a hurtful shock, hearing that his mother's life continued to tick along swimmingly, even as his dad was drowning at the bottom of a whiskey bottle. But not even pent-up anger and bitterness excused what he'd done. He'd earned a stiff punishment, but *she* hadn't!

Maleah had lost track of the times she'd wondered how things were going for him in prison. Was he being abused? Or had he become an abuser? When they let him out, would he be the same gregarious, kindhearted Ian she'd fallen in love with? Or would life behind bars harden him?

In her weaker moments, she'd hoped he would return to her, healed and whole, so they could pick up where they left off. The immature, futile dream of a silly schoolgirl. But she'd grown up, chosen a career in the psychiatric field. Coupled with the dozens of articles she'd read about recidivism, Maleah came to the only conclusion she could: what she'd shared with Ian ended when that prison van drove away from the courthouse, and nothing could change that. She picked up her phone and scrolled to Eliot's name.

"Hey sis," he said on the first ring.

"Am I catching you at a bad time?"

"Nope. I'm on second shift today. What's up?"

"It's great that you brought the boys to see the Christmas trees. Did they enjoy it?"

"Seemed to. Even bought an ornament for Amber."

"Which they could have shown me, if you'd bothered to stop by and say hi."

"I, ah, promised to take them for ice cream. And you know how Amber gets if I bring them home late."

"Yes, it's a shame she isn't a little more flexible. Maybe a civil conversation is all it would take to accomplish that."

"Doubtful…"

"Speaking of civil conversations, I noticed you had one with Ian earlier that was anything but."

"Big fat tattletale. I made it clear he wasn't to bug you with it."

"He didn't. I *saw* you."

Silence.

"Tell me, big brother, just how long were you planning *that*?"

"Since Sunday, when you showered us with the good news that he'd volunteered to work with you."

"He didn't volunteer to work with *me*. He volunteered to work for Kids First."

"Oh, so you're defending him now."

"Our association is strictly business. And it's going to stay that way."

"Uh-huh."

"Eliot, stop it. You need to see, once and for all, that I'm not the simpering little girl who cried herself to sleep for weeks after he left. I'm older and wiser now. A self-supporting, self-made woman who's perfectly capable of running my own life. Save your concern for your impressionable boys, why don't you?"

"You wouldn't talk that way if you weren't still in love with him."

"Stop it," she said again. "I have no feelings for him, whatever. He said himself, after I hammered at him to find out what you two talked about, that when Kids First is over, he'll fade into the woodwork. His words, not mine."

"And you believe that."

"I have no reason not to. He's been out of Lincoln for years, and hasn't once tried to contact me."

"Timing, as they say, is everything."

"Please. He built a good life for himself. Why mess it all up by digging up the past *now*?"

"You know I don't believe in coincidence."

"What does that have to do with anything?"

"If you think for one lousy minute that he didn't know you were in charge of this Kids First stuff, you're sadly mistaken."

"You're wrong. Ian was more surprised than I when he realized we'd be working together."

"I don't believe that for a minute."

"Now why doesn't that surprise me?"

Following a lengthy pause, Eliot said, "Hate to cut this short, but I have some chores to do before I head to the station."

"Be safe out there. I love you."

"Love you, too."

CHAPTER EIGHT

MALEAH THOUGHT IT would be easy, delegating tasks to other volunteers to avoid Ian, but she'd been wrong.

She hadn't expected him to produce much in the way of publicity and marketing for the events, but she'd been wrong about that, too.

It meant talking to him nearly every day, if not to schedule TV, radio and print media interviews, then to arrange photo shoots. It shouldn't have been a problem, since most of their conversations had been on the phone.

Wrong again. Because his efficiency roused grudging admiration. Maleah didn't want to admire him—or anything about him. The reason was simple: if she allowed herself those positive reactions, how great a leap would it be to affection? At the end of that road lay nothing but a repeat of the heartache and disappointment that would come when he abandoned her again.

Once, while passing the conference room that served second duty as the volunteers' office, she'd caught a glimpse of him on the phone, big booted feet propped on the radiator and a pencil behind one ear as he cited all the reasons a segment about Kids First would make a perfect news feature. Ian's back had been to her, but she didn't have to see his face to know that those long-lashed dark eyes were shining with wit and enthusiasm. The gray in his hair gleamed bright under the overhead fluorescent fixtures, and reflected from the white gold-and-onyx initial ring she'd bought for his eighteenth birthday. He wore it on his right pinky finger now. No surprise there, considering how much he'd bulked up in the years since she'd seen him last. The fact that he still wore it after all this time…

That was the image that popped into her head every time he called with an update, and it worried her more than she cared to admit, because the very sound of his voice took her back to those sweet, whispered conversations that lasted long into the night…

"Maleah?"

Startled, she turned toward the door.

"Stan. It isn't like you to pop in unannounced, especially at this hour."

"It's after 9:00 a.m., kid. How long have *you* been here?"

Laughing, she said, "Since seven. A little before, actually. I get more work accomplished in the couple hours before the place starts jumping than I can the rest of the day. Too many distractions and interruptions. But I'm sure you know all about that."

"A good secretary is what you need." The laugh was as big as the man himself. "I just stopped by to tell you that your dedication is paying off. I'm hearing some good things. Seems I made a wise decision, partnering you with Ian."

If he'd made the same statement a few weeks ago, Maleah would have disagreed, wholeheartedly. She didn't ask who Stan had been talking to, because any minute now, he'd offer up the information on his own.

"Have a seat, Stan. You're giving me a crick in my neck."

"No, no, can't stay. Have a meeting with the mayor in half an hour. Thought as long as I was in the neighborhood, I'd see if you need me to cut a check."

"A check? For what?"

"Advertising. Decorations. Catering. That all takes money, remember."

"Yes, I'm well aware." She opened her laptop, pulled up the Kids First file and clicked on the Donations tab. Stan stood behind her, reading the screen as she said, "We're doing well. Really well. Better than we have in years, in fact. I think that's due in large part to all the publicity Ian generated...free publicity, I might add."

Straightening, Stan rubbed his double chins. "Hmm... Is that grudging admiration I hear in your voice?"

"Not grudging at all. He's doing a stellar job, promoting the events. Contributions are coming in from all over the state."

"You don't mind working with him, then?"

"Why would I?"

"Well, with your history..."

"History?"

"He told me everything. And if I know Ian, he exaggerated on the 'what I'm guilty of' side, not the other way around. I'm well aware that he put you through your paces. So a little... a little bitterness would be perfectly understandable."

"We've established a comfortable working relationship."

"You're sure?"

His words said one thing, his expression something else, and yet again, Ian had put her in the position of convincing someone that their relationship was strictly business.

"Yes, Stan, I'm sure."

Shaking his head, he made his way to the door. "If you say so." Turning, he aimed a stubby finger at her. "Just promise me that if anything develops, you won't let it interfere with the work. There's a lot riding on these events, don't forget."

"Have a good day, Stan. And don't worry. I've got this."

"You might want to revisit the 'who's the boss' subject."

"What? Why?"

Stan stepped into the hall. "Because that's exactly what Ian said."

She waited until the elevator dinged, signaling Stan's final departure, to grab her cell phone. After scrolling to his number, she hesitated to press Call. To date, Ian had initiated every call, and without exception, had been prepared, always efficient. She wanted to project the same professionalism, even while arranging an in-person meeting to find out how Stan got the impression Ian saw himself as the boss.

It occurred to Maleah that she didn't need an explanation to set up a get-together.

"Maleah. I was just about to call you. What does your afternoon look like?"

"Wide open. Why?"

"CBN wants to send a team to film you, talking about Washburne, Kids First, what it's like, leading your volunteers... Don't worry,

I've checked with the administrator. He says he trusts you to do 'em all proud."

As usual, he'd considered all the alternatives.

"So you're okay for today, around three o'clock? I could push this off until tomorrow if that works better for you."

"No, today is fine. I hate doing these things, but I might as well get it out of the way."

"Are you kidding? You're a natural."

She didn't say more, for fear of sounding like a compliment-me-seeker.

"Are you planning to be here? When the news crew arrives, I mean?"

"Wouldn't miss it."

"Good. After they wrap up, I'd like to talk with you for a few minutes."

"Sure, sure. It'll probably be late. Why don't you meet me at the bistro afterward. I'll buy you dinner."

Maleah had hoped for a quiet place, her own turf, for when it came time to say "Let's get this clear: *I'm* the boss."

"We'll eat in my office. More privacy in there."

Considering her indecision, his take-charge attitude should have come as a relief.

It did not.

And yet she said, "All right. See you after the interview, then."

"Oh, you'll see me sooner than that," he said, stepping into her temporary office. The breath caught in her throat at the sight of him, smiling and bright-eyed in snug jeans and black boots. The hint of tattoos peeked from the cuffs of his crisp white shirt.

"I was on TV Hill, finalizing tomorrow's interviews, and since I was so close, I thought I'd stop by, see if you needed me to do anything."

Close? At least six miles separated the station from the facility...

He placed a takeout cup of coffee on the edge of the table.

"Still drink it easy on the sugar, easy on the cream?"

Maleah had already exceeded her coffee quota for the day. "Yes. Thanks."

"Would've brought a bagel or something, except I know you're not big on breakfast. At least, you didn't used to be."

She still wasn't, and yet thoughts of a toasted bagel smothered with cream cheese made her stomach growl. She hoped he hadn't heard it.

"I saw Stan in the parking lot," Ian said, settling onto the chair across from hers. "What did he want?"

"He stopped by to compliment us on a job

well done." Since the subject opened itself, she saw no point in putting off the "boss" discussion. "And ask some pointed questions about who's holding the reins."

"You're in charge. But I thought he knew that."

"Evidently, when you were bringing him up to speed on all you're doing to publicize Kids First, he got the impression I'd handed control over to you."

"Whoa." He held up his right hand. "Don't know what he *thinks* he heard, but I didn't say anything like that."

Well, Ian certainly looked sincere...

"Truth is, I have more than enough to keep me busy. Between running the bistro and SAR training sessions and keeping my dad in line, believe me, I have no desire to wrestle control away from you. Besides, you're doing a bang-up job. Only a fool would try and get in your way."

Maleah wanted to believe him, but years of suspicion and resentment got in the way.

A knock on the door interrupted them.

"Mr. Ian?"

"Avery!" Smiling, he crouched and held out his arms. "What're you doing here, kiddo?"

One arm slung around Ian's shoulders, the boy perched on Ian's knee.

"Mom is making signs. I came to help."

"Is that so?"

Hands flapping and head bobbing, Avery showed every tooth in his head.

"When they're finished, I get to hang them. And I get to use one of those big staplers, all by myself!"

His mother appeared in the doorway.

"*There* you are." She faked a stern expression. "You're supposed to tell me when you're going off somewhere without me," Terri said, speaking and signing at the same time.

"I did tell you," her son signed back. He lowered his voice and, leaning closer to Ian, said, "Is it my fault if she was looking the other way?"

Ian touched a finger to the boy's nose. "Now, you know better than that, don't you…"

Avery rolled his eyes and hopped down from Ian's leg. "Yeah, yeah, I know."

Maleah had never seen Ian interact with a child before, let alone one with special needs.

She had to admit, it was an impressive sight.

He looked at Terri. "I know it's your day off, but are you two coming to the bistro tonight?"

"Wouldn't miss it."

Ian faced Maleah. "Have you met Maleah Turner? She's in charge of the Kids First fundraiser."

"Yes, of course," she said, extending a hand. "Good to see you again, Ms. Turner."

"Please. Call me Maleah."

"I'm sure you're busy." Terri looked at her boy. "Has Avery been bothering you?"

"No, not at all. Did you get your ticket to the big gala yet?"

Terri's smile waned slightly. "Not yet."

"You're a volunteer, so your ticket is free."

"Thank you, anyway, but..." She grasped her son's hand. "Time to go, sweetie. We have lots of signs to hang!" Terri met Ian's eyes. "See you tonight."

"You bet." He ruffled the boy's hair. "Have fun, but be careful with that big stapler, y'hear?"

Excitement and anticipation intensified the boy's hand movements.

"I will!" he said, hugging Ian's knees.

When they were out of earshot, Ian said, "That's some kid right there." The look on his face echoed the fondness in his voice.

First chance she got, Maleah would look into the boy's file. Several times, Maleah had seen him in the halls at Washburne's school; he'd entered the program before she accepted her first position with the facility, and so far, hadn't had an opportunity to meet one-on-one with him and his mother. A casual conference would help her better understand Avery's progress, and perhaps suggest additional ways to improve his treatment.

"Sometimes, I don't know how Terri does it."

Ian returned to the chair facing Maleah's. "Divorced her abusive husband a couple years back. Her cousin was a part-time waitress, and Terri took a few of her shifts at the bistro. When I noticed that some diners were having trouble communicating with her, I put her at the hostess station. She mans that post like a sentry!"

Ian's expression underscored his admiration for Avery's mother. Had the relationship evolved into something more than boss and employee?

"Just between you and me," he said, "Avery is my favorite."

"Favorite what?"

"Favorite Washburne kid. We've worked together for a couple years now. Saturdays here and there, the occasional camping trip…"

Maleah had seen several such outings on the calendar. Volunteers nearly outnumbered kids, so she hadn't felt it necessary to sign up. How many times, she wondered, would she have found Ian's name on the lists?

"Well, I'd better get out of your hair." Ian

stood and made his way to the door, pausing to add, "Will we see you at the bistro tonight?"

They'd already solved the "who's the boss" problem, so there didn't seem much point in it.

"You didn't see the notice I posted near the storeroom?"

She hadn't, and said so.

"It's a get-together for the volunteers, but since you're in charge of them, I'm sure they'd enjoy seeing you there, too. Nothing fancy… fried chicken, mashed potatoes, green beans… ice cream bar for dessert. The kids love making their own sundaes."

The kids again. If only Eliot could see Ian now.

"They'll all be disappointed if you aren't there."

"I'll think about it…" She'd planned to complete a few household chores. If time allowed, Maleah would place an order with her favorite nursery, too, to ensure delivery of the prettiest plants for her gardens and flower pots.

He stepped into the hall, turning to say, "I hope you can make it. Like I said, it's no big deal. Just a chance for the volunteers to get to know one another better, since not all of them have a chance to work together. Come as you are. Six o'clock in the banquet room."

"I'll try."

"You have to eat anyway, so why not save yourself the bother of cooking and cleaning up?"

"Frozen pizza and TV dinners don't require either," she said, grinning.

"Well, it's up to you." He shrugged. "But just remember...fried chicken...my very own recipe."

"I'll try," she repeated.

"'Do or do not,'" he said, quoting a movie line, "'there *is* no try.'"

And with that, Ian disappeared, leaving Maleah to wonder why she couldn't wait until six o'clock rolled around.

CHAPTER NINE

IAN HAD BEEN bent over the bistro's checkbook for half an hour when a soft knock interrupted his concentration.

"Sylvestry!" said a booming baritone voice. "Why haven't we seen you down on Russell Street?"

He endured the wide receiver's powerful handshake. "Working on this Kids First stuff," Ian said. "Fun. Fulfilling, too. But time-consuming."

"Ain't that the way it is with all fund-raisers?" Angus Miller, known as Marshmallow—Marsh for short—slapped Ian's back.

Ian had worked with the team, raising money for a variety of the players' favorite charities... including one that helped find jobs and living quarters for recently released convicts.

"Hungry? I could wrestle you up a sandwich or something..."

"Thanks, but I can't stay." He took an envelope out of his shirt pocket and held it out. As Ian reached for it, Marsh said, "Why isn't your name on the list of people attending the gala?"

In a word: Maleah. He'd promised her—and himself—a strictly business association.

"Too much to do," he said. "This place doesn't run itself, y'know."

"Yeah, well, I talked with Gladys today. She's a live wire, but you probably know that better than I do."

Ian failed to see what his aunt had to do with anything.

"She wants to attend the shindig, but doesn't have a date."

Surely this giant of a guy wasn't asking permission to date his elderly aunt!

"I can't go," Marsh said, handing over the envelope. "Paid big bucks for these tickets, and even though the money is for a good cause, I'd hate to see them go to waste."

"Ah. So you want *me* to escort my aunt. To a black-tie affair." Ian laughed. "Can you see me in a monkey suit—cummerbund and ruffled shirt—with all these tattoos, an earring and this hair?"

"Hey. If I can squeeze all two hundred forty pounds of me into a tux, you can wear one, too." He punctuated the statement with another slap to the back. "Besides, don't you owe it to your aunt?"

Not many people knew the extent to which Gladys had helped him. The truth came out early in their friendship, when Marsh's no-nonsense lecture changed Ian's attitude from self-pitying to self-motivating. And anyway, the only thing she liked better than getting all gussied up was rubbing elbows with big shots like Marsh.

"You make a good point." Grinning, Ian said, "But I'm still gonna look like a freak. I don't own a pair of patent leather shoes."

"You can rent 'em. I'll throw in an extra twenty bucks."

"Don't add insult to injury, Marsh. Okay. Fine. I'll go." He peeked into the envelope.

Only two weeks until the gala…his last legitimate excuse to see Maleah. "Well," he muttered, "all good things must come to an end."

"What's that? You're not trying to worm your way out of it already, I hope."

"Nah. It's just…" Ian pocketed the tickets. "There's this girl. We were tight, real tight, before I was sent away. Hadn't seen her in years, and then…" He snapped his fingers. "There she was, on the banquet room dance floor, in the arms of another guy."

"Life goes on, huh? Bummer. But help me understand, bro. What's this girl have to do with the gala?"

"Everything. She's Maleah in-charge-of-all-things-Kids First."

Marsh nodded. "But I don't see the problem."

"Neither of us expected to work together. She was nice enough about it, but made it pretty clear that when things wrapped up, she expected me to disappear again."

"And you took a vow or somethin'?"

"Not exactly."

"You're obviously still boots over Harley helmet in love with her. You know the old saying, 'All's fair in love and war.'"

"I so much as *think* about starting things up again, there *will* be a war…between her family and me. And before you say I'm nuts, you need to know that her grandfather, father and two brothers are cops."

Marsh winced. "Gotcha. They don't want their girl fraternizing with a known felon. Ex-felon."

"Something like that."

"Wait just a minute… The two of you were a thing before you went to Lincoln?"

"Yeah. So?"

"So she isn't a girl, Ian. She's a full-grown woman. You don't need anybody's permission to start things up again. Except hers, of course."

As if Ian hadn't thought of that a couple thousand times over the years. He didn't feel like getting into it with Marsh. Or anyone else for that matter. Maleah deserved a guy with a clean slate, who could make her proud. Ian wasn't that guy. Not by a long shot. Not in her eyes, anyway. Could he change that? Memory of how it had felt every time his letters were returned, unopened, made him wonder why he even wanted to.

"Thanks for these, Marsh. But just so you know, Gladys is likely to bake you a couple thousand chocolate chip cookies to show her appreciation."

Laughing, Marsh patted his stomach. "Tell her I'm on a diet until the season ends. She's a fan. She'll get it." He gripped Ian's hand again, and gave it a good shake. "Good to see you, Sylvestry. Don't be such a stranger downtown. You know the team schedule."

From halfway down the hall, Ian heard "And don't wait until the last minute to get fitted for a tux."

He took out his phone searched for "Tuxedos, Fells Point, Maryland." As the list populated, his chef appeared in the doorway.

"Hey," Dan said. "We're ready in the banquet room. What time should I have Lee write on the cake?"

It had been a last-minute decision to add cake to the menu. If Maleah showed up, Lee could pipe Happy Birthday in pink icing. If not, well, dessert was dessert, right? He'd put a lot of thought into the cake's design. Three layers of chocolate separated by raspberry jam and white buttercream icing, topped off with more buttercream and trimmed with a decorative frosting rope. Too bad he hadn't come up with a way to explain why he'd decided to add Early Birthday Party to the volunteer get-together. *Sure doesn't go with your arms' length strategy...* "I'll let you know once we have a head count."

Dan smirked. "Once you find out if the birthday girl is gonna show up, you mean."

Ian had worked hard at being above-board with everyone, his staff in particular. But sometimes—and this was one of them—he wished he'd held his cards a little closer to the vest. A whole lot closer.

"Hope the DJ can play something besides rap," Dan said. "Took me three days to kick the headache from the last shindig."

"Made a point of hiring a guy that plays a variety of styles."

"So everything is set up, huh?" Dan checked his watch. "Folks will be here soon."

Bad idea to hope that included Maleah, and yet...

"Okay. I can take a hint." Dan headed for

the kitchen. "Should I text you when people start showing up?"

"Nah. I have to finish paying the bills. Stamping envelopes. Filing the statements."

"You could save a lot of time doing all that online, y'know."

"So I've heard." Half an hour later, he stood in the mirror, trying to decide whether or not to fulfill Gladys's "When are you going to shave that beard!" request. He opted for a trim, since the whole reason he'd grown it was to hide the vicious scar inflicted when he'd defended a new guy from four hefty prisoners.

He'd changed his clothes three times. Polished his bike boots. Opened the pricey aftershave his dad had given him for Christmas the year before last. All that in preparation for seeing someone who probably wouldn't be coming. *Y'big dope.*

An hour after that, nearly forty guests sat around the banquet room, laughing as they munched crispy chicken and creamy mashed potatoes. As instructed, the DJ kept the sound turned down to encourage conversation. There was just one thing missing…

And then, as if in response to an unspoken wish, she appeared in the doorway, wearing jeans, knee-high brown boots, and a waist-hugging sapphire sweater. She'd twisted her hair into a bun, and the golden, windblown curls hiding her ears made her appear ten years younger—as if she needed any help in that department.

He crossed the room to welcome her, and saw that she'd applied a light coat of shadow that exactly matched her blue eyes. For an instant, Ian didn't know what to say.

"You trimmed your beard," she said, breaking the awkward silence. "Looks nice."

"I, ah, thanks. You look good, too."

He took her elbow. "There are a couple seats over there," he said, leading her away from the DJ booth. "Close to the food, not too close to the speakers."

Terri and Avery waved and smiled as she approached their table.

"Good stuff," the boy said, waving a golden drumstick. "Better get some before it's gone!"

Coral-tinted lips spread in an easy smile that made his heart thump.

Ian pulled out her chair. "Have a seat. I'll fix you a plate."

"I'm perfectly capable of—"

"Of course you are. Just humor me, okay?"

Why are you doing this? was the question in her big eyes. To be honest, Ian had no idea. He only knew that if he hadn't found a valid excuse to walk away, right then, he might have kissed her instead.

How would he walk away—and stay away when the Kids First festivities ended—when it hurt like crazy, just being across the room from her!

Ian handed her the plate, a napkin and flat-ware. "What can I get you to drink?"

"Water will do."

"You're sure? We have sodas, sweet tea, lemonade, wine and beer…"

"You must really want her to like you," Avery said, snickering.

Maleah laughed. Oh how Ian loved the sound of it. If he thought for a minute he could inspire that, every day for the rest of her life…

"Aren't you going to eat?" Terri asked.

There was just one available chair, right beside Maleah's. "Maybe later. Let me check on a few things first."

Ian made the rounds, picking up empty plates, asking if the guests needed refills… far enough away to pretend he was busy, close enough to hear Avery asking questions: How long had she worked at Washburne? Did she have brothers and sisters? Could she cook, and was her chicken as good as Ian's? Maleah held her own, answering as if being interviewed by a TV reporter... Until the boy said "Are you divorced, like my mom?"

She blinked. Pressed a palm to her throat. Ian held his breath, half expecting her to say something like *a criminal ruined me for men and romance forever.*

Instead, Maleah said, "I'd make a terrible wife."

"Why?" the boy wanted to know.

"I work too many hours, for one thing. And I'm oh-so-fussy about...about everything."

Nodding, Avery said, "Just like Mom. Put something where it doesn't go, and hoo-boy."

Terri laughed. "I'm not that bad, am I?"

"Worse!" her son teased.

"You just need the right man to come along," Terri said knowingly. Maleah shook her head.

If this wasn't one of those *if only the floor would open up* moments, Ian didn't know what was.

On the off-chance she looked up, looked at *him*, Ian put his back to her. It would be hard enough, hearing her agree with the boy. Seeing her face when she did...

"Hey, Ian!" Dan called from the kitchen. "Time for dessert?"

The chef winked and pointed to the cake, balanced on his big palm.

"Sure." He didn't much feel like going through

the motions of announcing her birthday, grinning while everyone sang. Too late to get out of it now, he thought. In minutes, Lee would add the birthday message to the cake. Minutes after that, the wait-and kitchen staff would gather, waiting for Ian to make a brief speech in her honor.

Ian groaned under his breath and headed for the DJ's booth. "Need to borrow your mic for a minute," he said. "Get the Happy Birthday song queued up…"

He grabbed a butter knife from the nearest table and, clinking it against the rim of the DJ's tumbler, waited for the crowd to quiet down.

"Hope you're all having a good time," he said. And when the group finished complimenting the food, the chef, the wait staff, Ian continued with, "Glad you've had a chance to get to know one another a little better. You're all working hard to make the Kids First events a big hit. I have an announcement to make…"

Oohs and ahhs were followed by inquisitive chatter, which ended when Ian said, "There's a very special person here tonight. And we want to help her celebrate a very special event."

Everyone glanced around.

Ian signaled Dan, who sent Lee into the banquet room, carrying a candle-lit cake emblazoned with Happy Birthday Maleah.

"Maleah, we'd like to thank you. Without

your leadership, Kids First wouldn't be such a roaring success."

Her cheeks glowed bright with an embarrassed blush. In the old days, she'd hide behind her hands when caught by surprise. Instead, she rested her chin on folded hands.

Ian signaled the DJ, who started up the birthday song. Within seconds, everyone joined in.

Ian only mouthed the words. Because one week to the day after they celebrated her birthday, all those years ago, two burly cops slapped cuffs on him and tossed him into a paddy wagon…yet another reason she belonged with a good man, and not a guy whose past could rise up to haunt her, shame her, at any given moment.

The song ended with a round of applause and several men yelling "Speech! Speech!"

To his surprise, Maleah grabbed the microphone.

"My birthday isn't for another week yet," she began, "so I'm touched by this sweet surprise. Thank you, not only for the cake, but for everything you're doing to make Kids First a huge success. Your hard work shows, and I think we're going to see quite a profit when all is said and done. Already, we've banked more contributions than ever before, and I don't have to tell you what a big difference the donations will make in the lives of kids on the spectrum. You're wonderful. All of you. And I hope to have the pleasure of working with you again."

Her hand was shaking when she handed the mic back to the DJ. She made a beeline to her chair. *That's* when she hid behind her hands, as she had when he called her pretty, or smart, or sweet…or told her how much he loved her.

Who was he kidding? He loved her, still, and always would. Ian hadn't felt this sorry for himself in a long, long time.

He ducked into his office and hoped he could get his emotions under control before anyone noticed he was missing.

CHAPTER TEN

MALEAH HADN'T SEEN Ian since the night of the party. A good thing. But it wasn't like him to miss meetings, or send someone in his place to perform assignments and deal with the media. Had he caught one of the viruses that had been floating around?

"A decent person would pick up the phone and ask," she muttered.

"What's that?" Vern wanted to know.

"Nothing. Just talking to myself."

Her neighbor laughed. "Again?"

"It's one way to ensure someone's listening," she joked back.

"I'd listen…if you talked louder. And didn't mumble."

Just a few months ago, their exchanges amounted to little more than the courteous waves and nods of strangers. These days, it seemed Maleah talked more to Vern than to any of the Turners.

"So what brings you outside on this cold dark night?" he wanted to know.

"Just needed a little fresh air."

"Ah, the boyfriend again, eh?"

She'd never called Ian a boyfriend, not even in the past, and no matter how many times she stressed the point, Vern insisted on referring to Ian that way.

"He hasn't shown up for anything Kids First—related in over a week and I'm concerned he might be sick. This close to the gala, we need all hands on deck at Washburne."

"Your phone only takes incoming calls?"

Maleah pulled her coat tighter around her.

"You're in charge of things down there. If you're afraid to make the call yourself, assign the task to an assistant."

"I suppose I could…"

"Sure. That way, no need to get all lovey-dovey and personal, but you'll have your answer."

Maleah nodded again.

"And then you can quit worrying about ol' lover boy, and concentrate on more important things."

"Are you wearing your watch, Vern?"

He unpocketed the gold timepiece, inherited from his grandfather, and popped its lid.

"Ten-oh-eight," he said, and snapped it shut again.

Too late to call Ian, she decided.

"It's never too late, y'know..."

Laughing, Maleah said "Get out of my head, Vern Malachi!"

A moment of companionable silence passed before Vern said, "Smells like snow."

She looked up at the cloudless sky, at the crescent moon and a thousand stars, winking from the darkness. "Goodness, I hope you're wrong. Last thing we need this close to the gala is a snowstorm."

"Aw, don't sweat it, kid. It's only mid-November. Even if we get a couple-a inches, it's too early in the year for it to stick around for very long."

He'd made a good point. Still...

"Are you ready for the big jamboree this weekend?"

"Ready as I'll ever be."

"Who's your date?"

"This isn't 1965, Vern. Women go solo to things like this all the time."

"Yeah, yeah, yeah. But you young'uns could learn a thing or two from the way we did things in the old days."

Some changes, Maleah thought, were for the best.

"If I got you a ticket," she said, "would you go to the gala as my date?"

"I'm flattered, but...not on your life."

Vern managed quite well on his fixed income, but what if the prospect of shelling out a hundred dollars for a dinner suit had inspired his answer? He was too proud to let her rent one on his behalf, and too smart to believe she had a coupon tucked in a kitchen drawer. He appeared to be about the same size as her grandfather, whose tuxedo had likely been in mothballs for a decade...

"Would you come with me if I could arrange for you to borrow my grandfather's tux?"

"Why isn't he going?"

"He's a bigwig with the Fraternal Order of Police. Some of the members and their wives are getting together in Ocean City to plan the annual Maryland convention."

Vern nodded, and for a minute there, Maleah thought he'd changed his mind.

"Sorry kid, but you're on your own."

"It's just as well," she said. "My jitterbug skills are mighty rusty."

"I've had about all the fresh air I can take."

He jerked open his screen door. "Remember... it's never too late to do the right thing."

Translation: Call Ian.

He didn't give her time to agree. She heard his dead bolt click into place, and when his huge spotlight went out, Maleah decided to test his theory.

It was nearly ten-thirty by the time she hung up her coat and brewed herself a mug of herbal tea. Phone in hand, she scrolled to his number and began second-guessing Vern's suggestion. During her moment's hesitation, Maleah accidentally pressed Call.

"Everything okay?" he said.

"I was wondering the same thing. And by the way, I hope I'm not calling too late."

"Nah. I never turn in before midnight. So…"

So…if everything is all right, why are you calling me at this hour? she finished for him. "People have been asking where you've been. I think they're worried you might have picked up a flu bug."

He didn't answer right away.

"It's nice to be missed."

"They'll be happy to hear you're feeling fine."

Another pause, and then, "Who's 'they,' if you don't mind my asking."

He might as well have said *Gotcha!*

"I didn't take names, Ian."

She heard the smile in his voice when he said, "I've missed them, too."

"Well, it's late. I'll let everyone know you're all right."

"Thanks."

"Where have you been, if you don't mind my asking?"

"Man. Sorry. Could've sworn I told you. I offered to run some SAR workshops. Plus, we had two wedding receptions and a couple of bachelor parties here at the bistro."

Now that he mentioned it, Maleah did remember something about seminars...

"SAR?"

"Search and Rescue. Training the dogs, actually. Couple night classes with the handlers, workbook stuff, mostly, followed by a weekend of in-the-field training."

Maleah had read articles and watched documentaries about the dedicated individuals who, along with their well-trained canines, helped locate scores of lost and missing children and adults. Given his dedication to the kids at Washburne, it shouldn't surprise her that Ian was involved with a group like that.

Eliot's warning gonged in her head: *It's not a matter of if he'll backslide, but when.*

"How long have you been doing this?"

Either he'd just yawned, or she'd asked a question he didn't feel comfortable answering.

"I, ah, I first got involved at Lincoln. Liked it," he said, "and stuck with it after my release."

Eliot believed Ian would never amount to

anything and that, under the right circumstances, he'd revert to his old ways. Because
in her brother's jaded opinion, "People don't
change."

But Ian had turned a failing restaurant into a
thriving business, earned the respect of every
volunteer he'd worked with, including Stan, a
hard man to impress. "Remarkable," she said,
meaning it.

"Not really. All the credit goes to the dogs.
They're smart. Hardworking. Capable. And
love what they do."

He could have been describing himself.

"I've had the good fortune to work with
some of the best canines and handlers." Even
after completing a Kids First task alone, he'd
given credit to others. She hadn't retained
much information about Search and Rescue,
but Maleah knew enough to believe the dogs
were only as good as their trainers. Despite
Eliot's prediction, Ian *had* changed—for the
better—from the guy who once blamed his
mother for replacing him and his father with
another man and another child, blamed his father for allowing whiskey to destroy what little
was left of the Sylvestry family, blamed his
friends for talking him into participating in
the armed robbery.

She had a feeling if she asked who he blamed for his years at Lincoln, Ian would say, "Me."

Yet another positive change.

He broke into her thoughts with "You should meet my mutt."

"I didn't realize you had a dog. But of course you have a dog. You're a dog trainer. And a Search and Rescue guy. What's her name?"

"Cash, a hundred pound, black-and-gray German shorthaired pointer who thinks he's a teacup poodle."

"Maybe you can bring him to Washburne sometime."

"But…you're afraid of big dogs."

She'd never forget the day they'd gone hiking in Patapsco Park. A couple, picnicking near one of the trails, had tied their slobbering mastiff to a metal ground spike. All it took to snap it like a dry twig was the sight of a squirrel, racing down the path.

"I think the name Brutus is branded into my brain," she said, laughing.

He laughed, too. "Don't think I ever saw anyone run as fast as you did that day."

"I climbed that tree pretty fast, too, for a girl in shorts and flip-flops."

After the danger had passed that day, Maleah's giggling had nearly turned to tears of joy.

Right now, though, she felt like crying.

"Well, it's late. I'm glad you're okay. I'll pass that on to the others...unless you're planning to come to Washburne tomorrow."

Ian cleared his throat. Had the memory choked him up, too?

"One last class," he said, "and a bridal shower in the banquet room. So no, not tomorrow."

Just as well.

CHAPTER ELEVEN

"How many people do you think are here?" Gladys wondered aloud.

"I read someplace that this room holds five hundred, and it's packed," Ian said.

"Then the gala is a hit, thanks in no small part to you."

"Me? No way. I made a couple phone calls, arranged a few interviews. Maleah's personality...*that's* what sold the event."

His aunt rolled her eyes. "It isn't against the law to take credit for what you accomplished, you know." She glanced toward the wall of French doors, then pointed toward the bar. "Be a sweetheart, will you, and get your parched old auntie something cold to drink."

"Root beer or ginger ale?" he teased.

"Surprise me." Gladys winked. "I think I spotted an old friend. You'll find me near the entrance."

It was Maleah she'd spotted, greeting newly-arriving guests.

"Hi there," he heard Gladys say. "You probably don't remember me but—"

"Of course I do. You're Ian's aunt. We were almost on the same committee for the Kids First swim club."

"Ah…the year I broke my hip. Bad memories. Let's change the subject, quick!"

Laughing, Maleah said, "It's good to see you've completely recovered."

"You call that changing the subject?" Another wink and then, "Love your gown. Don't tell me…it's from Sweet Elizabeth Jane's."

"Yes. It is. But…how did you know?"

"Why, it's only my favorite shop in Ellicott City. I make the trip from Fells Point to Main Street every couple of months, just to see what's new over there."

Gladys waved Ian over.

"Look who I ran into," she said, relieving him of both goblets.

"Will you listen to that?" Gladys shouldered Maleah into Ian's arms. "They're playing your song."

Ian steadied Maleah, then frowned at his aunt. "What are you talking about?"

"People are starting to stare. Dance, you two, dance!"

He led Maleah to the center of the floor.

"Don't know what gets into her sometimes. Sorry."

"No apology required. I'd have ended up on the floor if you hadn't caught me."

He'd forgotten how good, how *right* she felt in his arms. If she kept looking up at him that way…

"You look pretty good in an evening gown."

"And you look good in a tux."

"Good thing it didn't snow, like Marty Bass said it would."

"In his defense, he said *might*."

"So he did…"

"But you're right. If it had snowed, I'd break my neck in these shoes."

Ian disliked small talk almost as much as the foot and a half separating them.

An elderly couple plowed into his back, driving his bearded chin into her forehead.

"Sorry," he repeated.

"Any plans to shave it someday? Not that you don't look handsome."

"It serves a purpose," he said cautiously.

"Oh?"

"There was this new guy at Lincoln," he began. "Skinny li'l fella with thick glasses and buck teeth. He looked crossways at a couple of the tough guys one day, and they started in on him. Three against one wouldn't have been fair, even if he'd been the size of a linebacker."

"So you stepped in…"

"Yeah, and one of the guys whipped out a shiv." Ian took her hand in his, guided her finger along the scar. Maleah snapped her hand back fast. "Sorry you asked?"

"No."

She looked into his eyes. *Deep* into his eyes. "I'm sorry that happened to you."

He waved her sympathy away. "Good crowd," Ian said, surveying the room. "How much do you think Washburne raked in tonight?"

"Why? Are you going to round up your buddies and rob the ticket counter?"

The comment cut to the bone, surprising Ian so badly that he nearly trod on her toes. But really, what did he expect? What he'd done had turned her life completely around.

"That was completely uncalled-for," she said, "and didn't come out at all like I intended it."

He couldn't imagine how she'd intended it, because the only thing Ian could think of was an article he'd read in the Sunday *Sun* about how the brutal truth was often hidden behind sarcastic humor. If that's how she really felt…

If—biggest li'l word in the English language.

It had never been more clear than right now: for the rest of her days, she'd see him as a semi-reformed prisoner. And the worst thing about it was, he couldn't even dislike her for it. On the off-chance that she'd look into his eyes again, Ian pulled her close, so close she couldn't see his face at all. With any luck, the song would end soon and he could leave the dance floor without looking like an inconsiderate jerk.

Eliot hadn't said it in so many words, but the guy believed that misery was the only thing Ian could give Maleah; he probably hadn't given a thought to the fact that his sweet, innocent sister could mete out her own brand of misery.

She had a good life, a great job, a loving family. The Washburne big shots didn't mind having Ian around to do the heavy lifting and grunt work, and didn't complain when his PR contacts brought much-needed attention to the institute's fund-raisers. But their Maleah, associating with a known felon? The last thing Ian wanted was to jeopardize her credibility with those same bigwigs, or cause strain in her family.

The song ended, finally. It wasn't easy letting her go. He'd just have to take comfort from the fact that it was best for her.

Maybe someday, if he kept living an upright life, it'd be best for him, too.

"I WAS BEGINNING to get the idea you'd decided to work through the night," Brady said.

Living above the bistro made it easy to work late without the dreaded long drive home. But now, again, Ian wished he hadn't given his dad and aunt keys to his apartment. Cash trotted over and sat at his feet, waiting for his customary hello scratch on the forehead. Ian dropped his keys into the hand-carved bowl beside the door, hung the tux jacket on the hook above it, and stooped to greet the dog.

"Hey buddy. Did ya miss me?"

Grinning, the dog loosed a breathy bark.

"Yeah, well, I missed you, too."

Standing, Ian whipped off the bow tie and added it to the wooden bowl.

"So what's up, Dad?"

"Just killin' time." He dropped the recliner's footrest. "I'll move to the couch so you can enjoy your La-Z-Boy."

"Don't worry about it. Gonna grab something to eat." He moved to the other side of the island. "I've got ham and cheese. Rye bread, too."

"Sure. Why not?"

Ian leaned into the fridge and grabbed two bottles of root beer…the closest thing to real beer he kept in the house. It had been an easy decision thanks to the times he'd come home to find his dad, passed out cold and surrounded by empty cans. Side by side on tall swivel stools, father and son assembled sandwiches in comfortable silence.

Ian speared a tomato. "Want one?"

"I'll pass."

"Lettuce?"

"No thanks."

Normally, his dad enjoyed the works. Tonight's bare minimum attitude made Ian wonder which ugly memory had inspired the visit.

"Pass the mayo, will ya? And then tell me what's going on."

Brady stopped chewing. "What makes you think there's anything going on?"

He wasn't in the mood to recite his dad's something's-up indicators: Dour expression, growly one-word responses, slouched shoulders...

"Let's just call it ex-con-tuition."

Brady winced. "I wish you wouldn't do that.

He took a swig of root beer. "So how was the party?"

The mention of it was enough to awaken the image of Maleah, all dressed up like a storybook princess.

"Good turnout," Ian said. "Food was decent. So was the music."

"See anybody you know?"

"Just the usual suspects. Reporters from the *Sun*, TV anchors, that balding host from the news show…"

Brady nodded. "I can't stand that guy. In my day, reporters were objective. John Q. Public had no idea how they felt about things."

"Which is as it should be," Ian finished with him.

That, at least, inspired the hint of a smile.

"Did Gladys have a good time?"

"Seemed to." Her smug expression came to mind. First chance he got, Ian intended to give his aunt a piece of his mind; if she hadn't forced Maleah into his arms, her cutting remark wouldn't keep him up tonight—for God only knew how many more nights. On the other hand, he wouldn't have the memory of how wonderful she'd felt in his arms, either…

"So where is that sister of mine?"

"I offered her a ride, but she decided to call a cab." He struck out his pinky finger and said in a shaky falsetto, "As one of the high muckety-mucks, you're expected to hang around until the bitter end."

That got another grin from his father.

"When I left, she was schmoozing with a couple of the big league guys."

"That's no surprise. She's all wrapped up in

another team fund-raiser, though for the life of me, I can't remember which charity this time."

"She loves it." He met his dad's eyes to add, "Wouldn't hurt you to get involved." He recited Father Rafferty's advice: "Doing for others is a surefire way to get your mind off yourself and your troubles." He'd consider himself lucky if focusing on his dad right now helped him get his mind off Maleah later.

"Troubles? What makes you think I've got troubles?"

Only everything, Ian thought.

"So what's bugging you?"

"Leave it, son. Just leave it, okay?"

"No can do. The longer you stay in this mood, the more likely you are to go back to your old ways." He paused long enough to let that sink in. "It'd be a shame. You just earned your five-year chip, don't forget."

"Thanks to you and Gladys, I *can't* forget."

How much time had to pass before the man let go of this defeatist mind-set?

"Heard from your mother lately?"

So *that's* what caused this latest bout of down-in-the-mouth: He'd bet anything that his dad had been looking through the photo albums again. "She sent a card for my birthday, with a $25 gift card to Applebee's."

"Yeah, I remember. Cheap, self-centered

witch. You'd think she'd pick up the phone once in a while, see how you're doing. You *are* still her son, even if she did run off with The Uppity Professor. Bet that boy of theirs is a royal pain in the you-know-what."

To see how *he* was doing? He almost laughed out loud.

"She makes one stupid decision," Brady continued, "and you and I pay for it for the rest of our lives."

One stupid decision.

The years had tamed his animosity toward Ruth. Seemed to Ian his dad would be a lot happier and more productive if he'd do the same.

"If you ask me, our lives are pretty good. What's that old saying…we've got three hots and a cot. And each other, too. What more do we need?"

"Good grief, boy," Gladys said, satiny skirt rustling as she swished into the room, "are you quoting *The Old Hobo's Handbook* again?"

She stooped to pet Cash.

Ian grinned. "Thought the mutt and I might have to suit up to find you."

"Don't waste your SAR talents on the likes of me," she teased, sliding onto the stool beside his and helping herself to a bite of Ian's sandwich. "So how was it, being back in her arms?" she said around it.

He wanted to say horrible. Terrific. Painful. Outstanding. Instead, Ian told Gladys what Maleah had said.

Eyes wide, she inhaled a sharp gasp. "Why, the coldhearted little brat!" Dusting bread crumbs from her fingers, she added, "Oh, is *she* gonna get a piece of my mind next time I see her."

Brady looked past Ian to say, "I wouldn't if I were you. It isn't as though you have much to spare."

She aimed a steely glance in her brother's direction. "When I want your opinion, I'll ask for it." She faced Ian. "How did you react?"

"I didn't. Good thing, too, since it didn't take long to figure out she was joking."

"Jokes are supposed to be funny, nephew." She aimed a red-taloned finger at him. "You can pretend she didn't hurt you until the cows come home, but I know better."

"Why didn't you say something, son, instead of putting up with my selfish mood?"

For one thing, his dad's mood distracted Ian from his own.

"I'm fine, you two. It isn't like I haven't heard stuff like that before. In a day or two, I'll have forgotten all about it."

It wasn't true, but they didn't need to know that.

Gladys yawned and stretched. "Much as I

hate to admit it, I'm pooped. I'll see you down-in-the-dumps dudes in the morning." After giving Cash a last pat on the head, she zeroed in on Brady. "Well?"

Both dark eyebrows rose. "Well what?"

"Are you going to sit there all night, or go home and let this boy get some much-needed shuteye?"

Brady glanced at the clock. "Gee. How time flies—"

"—when you're feeling sorry for yourself," Gladys finished, *"again."*

Fortunately, Brady chose to read the comment as a joke, and following noisy kisses, bear hugs, and sweet dreams wishes, he and his sister went home—Gladys to the apartment to the left of Ian's, Brady to the right.

Ian cleaned up the sandwich fixings and changed into flannel PJ bottoms and a T-shirt, grateful for the tick-tack of Cash's toenails filling the quiet, semidark rooms.

The dog nudged his fingertips, putting an end to his musing.

"Time for a treat?"

The dog answered with a huffy bark and, after handing him a small bone-shaped biscuit, Ian plopped into his recliner. It didn't surprise him at all when Cash lay the treat beside the chair and leaned his chin on its arm.

"You're welcome, buddy," Ian said, scratching the soft fur between the dog's floppy ears.

Satisfied, Cash lay down and began gnawing on the bone.

"We've got a pretty good life, don't we?"

The pointer stopped chewing long enough to aim a doggy smile at his master.

"Only one thing missing…"

Cash's eyebrows rose, first one, then the other, as if to say, *But…you just said we have a good life. Make up your mind!*

"Good point," Ian said, grinning. He kicked back in the chair. "Should-a seen her tonight. Man." Ian exhaled a sad sigh. "You'd like her… when she isn't spouting pent-up rage."

Cash walked away from the treat, put his paw on Ian's knee. The moment of intense man-to-dog eye contact compelled him to lean forward and kiss the top of Cash's head. "No need to worry about me, buddy. I'm okay."

His calm reassurance was enough to send the dog back to crunching on his treat.

Ian grabbed the remote and turned on the TV. While flicking through the channels, he stopped on Channel 45's late news broadcast. When the screen filled with Maleah's gorgeous face, he turned up the volume. The icon in the corner said WASHBURNE KIDS FIRST GALA DIRECTOR MALEAH TURNER.

"Oh yes," she was saying, "this has been one of Washburne-Albert's most successful fund-raisers to date, thanks to hard-working volunteers like Ian Sylvestry."

He caught himself grinning. "Well, what do you make of that?"

Cash cocked his head and looked at the TV, and promptly went back to chewing. Had a guilty conscience prompted the compliment? Or did she really believe he'd contributed heavily to the campaign's success?

If he thought it possible to live a normal happy life with Maleah…

Ian shook his head, and when the station switched to another feature story, he flipped to a black-and-white Western.

It had been a ridiculous thought. In order to move forward with a plan like that, he'd first need to earn back her trust. But for that to happen, he'd have to earn the trust of the rest of the Turners, too. Both objectives seemed too far out of reach, and promised to sap him of more time and patience than he possessed.

"What do you think, buddy? Am I a fool to think I should I go for it?"

A bored sigh whooshed from the dog's lungs.

"My sentiments exactly."

But even as he said it, Ian started thinking

about things he could do to work his way back into her good graces.

He'd start with an early-morning visit to see what she needed from him now that the gala was behind them.

His cell phone rang, startling him and Cash.

Dropping the footrest, his heart beat harder at the sight of the familiar SAR number in the caller ID screen.

"Sylvestry..."

"We can use you and Cash," the incident commander said. "How soon can you be here?"

"Be where?"

"Building collapse in Cherry Hill. Dangerous neighborhood; make sure you and the dog wear the Kevlar vests..."

"Wouldn't leave home without 'em. See you in twenty."

Cash, sensing he had a job to do, stood, tail wagging. And Ian didn't bother changing clothes since he'd step into protective gear once he arrived on site. "When was the last time we gassed up the truck?"

The dog blinked and smiled as Ian buckled the SAR collar.

"Think we have enough in the tank to make the twenty-minute drive to Cherry Hill Road and home again?"

More canine smiling and blinking as Ian secured Cash's pocketed vest.

As it turned out, they arrived in fourteen minutes flat. He didn't need a street address, thanks to search lights, police and fire vehicle strobes. Nearly midnight, and the place was lit up like high noon on a California beach. And oh what a place…

He'd watched news coverage of a sinkhole in the Cherry Hill neighborhood, crushing a storm drain and flooding the area, putting additional stress on the already crumbing stone foundations. Seventy-five, eighty years ago, this two-story bungalow had probably been a gorgeous home. But decades of neglect had faded the red brick to a dull rust color and peeled white paint from the window and door frames. The roof teetered on the porch, all but obliterating the wood stairs and wrought iron railings that once led to the front entrance. Somewhere beyond this jumble of smoking wood, a family had once celebrated Thanksgiving dinners and grandkids' birthdays.

"Glad you're here, Sylvestry."

Ian shook Alex McDougal's hand.

"So what's the deal, Mack?"

"Neighbors say it's a husband and wife in there. In their eighties." He pointed at a young family, huddled behind the police tape. "They gave us this. Belongs to their mother. Lucky for us, the lady forgot her coat in the daughter's car."

Real lucky, Ian thought, bending to allow Cash to get a snout full of the scent.

After donning a thick fireproof jumpsuit, gloves and helmet, Ian checked Cash's gear. Satisfied that his partner was protected, he said "Let's get 'er done, buddy."

As always, the dog trotted alongside Ian.

"Take care in there," Mack called after them.

Oh, he'd take care, all right. A couple thousand gallons of water swirled around fallen, still-sparking lines, and that wasn't good. Not good at all.

Firefighters had prepared a pathway of sorts, using axes and pry bars to move lumber aside. It was small comfort, knowing they'd stick close by, ready to deal with sparks that might flare into flames as Cash's nose led them to the elderly couple.

The men walked in a crouch, their flashlight beams crisscrossing the darkened interior.

When they'd been inside about ten minutes, the guy out front said, "Missing floorboards here." Then, the near-silence was shattered by Cash's barking.

He'd found the couple.

The team followed the steady yapping to the stairs, and halted their approach.

"No way that'll hold all of us," one of the men said.

"Probably won't hold any of us," said another.

Ian moved forward. "I'll go."

The others didn't argue. It made sense, after all, since Ian knew best how to read Cash's signals.

Concerned as he was about the condition of the people trapped up there, Ian made his way up cautiously. If they were alive—doubtful, since neither had called out for help—he'd need help carrying them back downstairs and outside to the waiting ambulance, one at a time. If they weren't, they'd still have to make the same trek.

Cash met him at the top, tail straight out and ears up. The ceiling height made it necessary for Ian to crawl as the dog led the way. He'd only gone a few feet when he heard soft moans, a woman's voice, weak and thready.

Despite being blanketed with plaster, splintered boards and loose nails, she managed to croak out, "Oh thank God. Thank *God.*"

"Don't talk," Ian said, crawling up beside her. He took her pulse. It, too, was weak and thready. No surprise there, considering the amount of blood she'd lost.

He grabbed his radio. "Top of the stairs," he

said into it, "eight feet back, six to the right. Woman alive; still looking for the man."

A voice crackled a reply: "Sending up a backboard."

Ian carefully removed debris from the lady's chest. With her hands and arms now freed, he said, "Ma'am, can you point out where your husband is?"

One knobby-knuckled finger aimed left, toward a huge mound of rubble in a corner. Sure enough, a bloodied hand poked out from beneath the mess. If the guy survived that, it would be a miracle.

Creaking floorboards interrupted the morbid thought.

"The place is weaving and bobbing like a drunk," the firefighter said, "and there's barely a breeze outside."

Ian had felt it, too. If they didn't get out of here, and fast, they'd all perish in this dismal place.

Working together, the men eased the woman onto the backboard. "Husband's over there against the back wall," Ian said. "But we can't risk bringing another guy up here."

"Right. Let's take her down and come back for him."

Their bulk, added to the weight of the now-unconscious woman, caused the staircase to squeal and screech. Ian knew the sound…nails, working their way out of the boards. The men kept moving down the failing staircase, Cash close on Ian's heels.

"Took you long enough," Mack teased when they reached fresh air.

"Bite me," a firefighter joked back. "That place is like a house of cards. Somebody so much as sneezes, it'll flatten like a pancake."

Once he and Ian handed the woman off to paramedics, Cash sat beside Ian. "You're done for the night, buddy," he said, squatting to scratch the dog's ears. "Good job. Real good job." Straightening, he faced Alex. "If I don't make it out, take him to my dad's place."

Mack winced. "Aw, shut up. You're coming out."

But everyone within earshot knew that wasn't a given.

The firefighter made a move to lead the way inside, but Ian stopped him.

"You've got a wife and kids at home, dude. Besides, I know right where he is."

"I'll wait here until you reach the top."

Ian read the message loud and clear: no sense taking the chance that their combined pounds might rip the already-loosened nails from the ragged risers and bring down the entire staircase.

As before, he moved slow and steady, making sure his steps didn't cause more damage to the already unstable treads. At the top, he got onto his hands and knees, and crawled until his pant leg got caught on a shard of wood. He pulled gingerly, praying with every tug that his movements wouldn't finish what the collapse had started.

The beam of his flashlight landed on the mound in the corner. The bloodied hand was in the same position it had been earlier...palm up and fingers curled inward, like a spider on its back. Fingertips pressed to the wrist, Ian hoped for a pulse.

Nothing.

He sat back on his heels, thinking *This is no way to leave the world.*

"All clear up there, Sylvestry?"

Ian took a moment to collect himself. Yeah. Poor ol' guy's gone." The floor trembled slightly when his partner's boot hit the bottom step. Trembled again on the next one. "Take your time. The whole place is rockin'. And go easy when you reach the top. There's sharp stuff pokin'—"

A loud, terrifying groan drew his attention up, just in time to see the ceiling careening toward him. Crooking an elbow over his eyes, Ian braced himself for the impact. It hit hard and fast, and in the seconds that followed, he thought of the elderly man—barely a foot away—killed by his own home.

...no way to leave the world...

It didn't hurt nearly as bad as he'd expected. The hardest part was remembering to inhale, exhale, inhale...

How ironic. Because he'd come close to meeting his maker a time or two at Lincoln. Had a few near misses while riding the Harley. Pulled through a couple of close calls during other SAR missions. Heck, he'd even survived losing Maleah, the most painful, regrettable experience of his life.

It was ironic, all right; just a few hours ago, he'd decided to figure out how to win her back.

"Sylvestry... Sylvestry?"

He tried to open his eyes, and failed. "You're in the ambo, on the way to Hopkins."

Whose voice is that?

"Hang in there, kid. Hang in there."

Ah, it's Mack...

"Get his phone, find his dad's number."

Hey, you're supposed to hook Cash up with him, not separate them...

The light was so bright, he could see the glow through his closed eyelids.

Voices, half a dozen or more, merged into one.

A needle prick. Feeling woozy.

Was this it then? The end?

When they tell her I'm gone, will she cry?

Ian hoped not. He'd only seen her cry once, on the day they carted him off to Lincoln. Because he'd caused her tears, and the admission shamed him, even now.

If the powers that be decided to give him one more chance, he'd make things right.

Somehow, I'll make things right...

CHAPTER TWELVE

Sore muscles and achy bones had kept him awake most of the night.

That, and thoughts of Maleah.

Ian rolled onto his side and bit back a groan. Last time he'd checked, the bedside clock read five forty-three. Now, as steely gray light glowed through the blinds, it said seven thirty-seven.

He'd pulled a lot of all-nighters over the years. Ordinarily, after two solid hours of deep catch-up sleep, he'd wake refreshed and raring to go. But lying immobile for that long had intensified every ache and pain. Tempting as it was to remain huddled under the covers, he levered himself up, tossed back the covers, and eased his legs over the side of the bed. Cash stirred, then got to his feet, eyebrows raising and lowering as Ian struggled into his faded flannel robe.

"Don't look so worried, buddy," he said, leaning into the walker, "I'm okay."

The scent of coffee lured him to the kitchen, where he found Gladys, reading the morning paper at the big island that separated the rooms.

"Thought I'd have to bang a ladle on the spaghetti pot to rouse you." She folded the paper and hopped down from her stool. "Hungry? Pancake batter is ready to go. And I bought a package of your favorite sausage links."

The pain meds had all but obliterated his appetite, but she seemed eager to do things for him. Besides, if he didn't eat, recovery would take twice as long.

"Sounds good."

"Sit down before you fall down, nephew. You can watch the news while I get breakfast on."

Nodding, he inched toward the recliner and, setting the walker to its left, slowly lowered himself onto the leather cushion.

Gladys delivered a steaming mug of black coffee. "So how was it," she said, placing the newspaper beside it, "sleeping in your own bed for the first time in over a week?"

"Real nice. Quiet. And I sure as heck didn't miss being shaken awake every half hour so those nurses could check my vitals…"

His aunt crossed to the window wall and pulled back the gauzy curtains.

"Is that…is that *snow*?" he asked.

"Started falling last night around eleven."

Baltimore had seen its share of mid-winter snowfalls, but they'd rarely lasted very long. Evidence of this one would likely disappear in a few hours, too. Not that it mattered if it decided to hang around; he had nowhere to go. The surgeon made it clear that Ian was to stay put, eliminating any chance that he might fall on his way downstairs to the bistro. A visiting nurse would stop by daily to give him a once-over and supervise five minutes' worth of laps around the apartment. Seven to ten days of that, and the doctor would give the go-ahead for physical therapy, three times a week, working his way up from ten-minute sessions to hour-long workouts. Ian wasn't looking forward to any of it.

"Guess you're glad you didn't take my furniture arranging advice, aren't you?" Gladys said, flipping a big flapjack.

Ian thought of the way she'd insisted the fireplace ought to be the focal point, not the water view. But it wasn't like her to so easily admit a mistake, so he let it slide.

"Where's Dad?"

"At work." She winked. "I only know *one* person who can afford to sleep half the morning away, then loll around in a lounge chair."

"I ought to order some kind of thank you gift to show my appreciation." Cash rested his chin on Ian's knee. "Dad took real good care of this boy," he continued, scratching behind the dog's ears. Ian planned to get something for Gladys, too. It would have meant three, maybe four additional days at Hopkins if she hadn't volunteered to move in here and keep a watchful eye on him.

"I prefer gift cards, myself," she said, wiggling her eyebrows.

She carried a big tray into the living room and rested it on the recliner's arms, then unceremoniously stuffed one of the bistro's linen napkins into the collar of his sweatshirt. It reminded him of the time his car was in the shop, and Maleah offered to drive him to work.

On the way, they'd stopped for burgers and fries and, as usual, he'd smothered his with ketchup. "Your boss will pitch a fit if you walk into the computer store with red stains on that white work shirt," she'd said, gently tucking a paper napkin into his collar. A sweet and simple gesture, motivated by sweet young love...

"Need anything else?" Gladys asked.

And without even thinking, Ian said, "Just Maleah."

His aunt studied his face for a moment.

"More sausage, another pancake, even buttered toast," she said, shaking her head. "I can deliver any of that. But Maleah?" Grabbing the remote, she turned on the TV.

Subtle, he thought as the weather channel appeared on the screen, but not even news of an oncoming blizzard had the power to keep his mind off Maleah. He hadn't seen her since the night of the gala…when a house literally fell on him. He'd only been away on SAR business for two days, and she'd called to see if he was all right…

He bit into a sausage link, washed it down with a gulp of coffee.

"Did she call?"

"Yeah, day after the accident. Said she heard about it on the news."

"Did she say if she might stop by?"

Gladys frowned. "Your breakfast is getting cold."

In other words, *no*.

"Your nurse will be here in half an hour, so eat up."

Oh, he'd eat, all right. Eat and exercise, and do his level best to get a decent night's sleep from here on out. He might be down for the count, but he wasn't out, at least not yet. Once he'd recovered, he'd go to her, healed and whole, and tell her to quit behaving like a spoiled brat and get over herself.

No doubt she'd give him a piece of her mind, and maybe then, he'd finally get over *her*.

CHAPTER THIRTEEN

THE DAY DRAGGED, mostly because Maleah couldn't concentrate on anything but the fact that Ian had nearly been killed while volunteering to save others. She'd nearly dropped the hot curling iron when the morning news anchor stated Ian's name in the intro to the story about the deadly house collapse. He'd saved an elderly woman at great risk to himself.

She glanced at her briefcase, where she'd stuffed the letters between her laptop and wallet.

"You will *not* read them," she muttered, slapping the steering wheel.

Maybe a big green plant, delivered to his house, would serve much the same purpose…

Indecision had never been a problem for her, so why couldn't she make up her mind about anything related to Ian Sylvestry!

Quarter-sized snowflakes continued to fall. Thankfully, the forecasters had been right, predicting the ground was too warm for it to accumulate. It made for dicey driving, though, as commuters jockeyed for position on I-95.

When at last she arrived home, Maleah hung her coat and keys on hooks in the front hall and headed straight for the kitchen. Her rumbling stomach demanded some attention. A can of soup and a sandwich should quiet things down. She'd seen *Casablanca* in the TV guide's list. A glance at the clock confirmed she had just enough time. With the flame turned low under her smallest pot, she headed upstairs to change into sweats.

The letters, still hidden deep in the briefcase, came to mind. How odd that Ian had tied them up with the now off-white satin ribbon attached to the corsage he'd pinned to the wispy shoulder of her pale pink gown. Wide-eyed and smiling, he'd looked so handsome in his rented white tux. Far more handsome than any other boy at the junior prom.

If she was honest, Maleah had to admit that he'd grown into a man who'd earned the respect and admiration of others. If only her family could accept how much he'd changed.

Hypocrite, she thought. *If you had the courage of a flea, you'd set them straight.* And sparing them the so-called bad news because Grampa had cancer wouldn't play into it at all.

The image of Ian, bruised, battered and bandaged, flashed in her mind. She blinked away the tears that stung her eyes. Things always looked worse in a person's imagination than in real life. Sending a plant sounded better and better…on the off-chance her picture was more real than fantasy.

Downstairs, she looked up the florist's number and gave them a call. She settled on the Southwest Garden green plant arrangement.

The cactus and succulents in a blue-gray ceramic bowl wouldn't require much attention, so it might last through his recovery period.

"Let's add a couple of Mylar balloons," Maleah said, "and a box of truffles." Hopefully, his doctor hadn't listed chocolate as something to avoid.

"And the card?"

Maleah didn't even have to think about it. "How about 'While you rest and recover, I'll be thinking of you, and praying you'll be back on your feet soon. Fondly, Maleah.'"

"Nice," the woman said. "I might save that, in case a future customer has no idea what to write." She collected Maleah's credit card information and Ian's name and address, and promised the gifts would arrive by noon the following day.

That got her out of the in-person visit, but what would she do when he called to say thank you?

Maleah tuned into the movie and sat, soup and sandwich balanced on a tray on her lap. She'd missed the first ten minutes, thanks to the phone call. But having seen the beginning half a dozen times, she could recite the dialog by heart.

Nearly two hours later, she sat dry-eyed and confused. Always before, the ending left her teary-eyed. Why not this time? she wondered, putting her supper dishes into the dishwasher.

Afraid she might be tempted to read those letters, Maleah locked up, turned out the lights, and headed upstairs, intent on going straight to bed. But a sudden thought interrupted her as she reached for her favorite pajamas. The photo of Ian that she'd rescued from the trash... She picked it up and looked into those big, dark, smiling eyes. Would they be bruised and swollen, she wondered, after his ordeal? Should she call to find out? Perhaps stop by to see for herself? *You can pretend you're just making sure the plant arrived...*

When in doubt, her grandfather liked to say, it was best to sleep on things. So she put the picture back where she'd found it, brushed her teeth and climbed under the covers.

But sleep wouldn't come. She blamed it on the awful news about Ian. His photograph and the tiny bale of envelopes, secured by a satin ribbon.

Maybe if she moved the letters, she could put them out of her mind...

Downstairs, she clicked on the light beside her overstuffed flowery chair and unsnapped her briefcase. For a moment, Maleah stared at the envelope on top: her parents' address perfectly centered. In the upper left corner, his name, prisoner ID number, and Lincoln's address. Atop it all, her angry command, printed in bold black letters: RETURN TO SENDER.

She didn't know what compelled her to do it, but Maleah slid it from the stack and turned it over. Still securely closed, even after all this time, she noted. It didn't take much effort to break the seal...

Now what?

Well, she'd come this far...

Maleah slid the letter from its envelope and, tucking her legs under her, read the first line.

"My sweet Leah..."

He said very little about life at Lincoln, save to explain the courses he'd signed up for. English Lit. Psychology. Trigonometry. Physics. "Too much paperwork," he'd written, "but it beats reading the beat-up novels on the library cart."

In letter after letter, Ian described volunteer

projects, such as tutoring inmates in English, science and math. Most of the high school dropouts, he explained, were just happy for the excuse to spend a few hours a day outside their cells. Others, though, planned to take the GED test when they got out. "Makes me feel better about myself, knowing they have a chance at landing a decent job after they leave this miserable place."

The line stood out, because it had been the first time he'd admitted just how unpleasant life at Lincoln had been.

The last letter touched her most deeply, because in it, Ian talked about the SAR courses, working with a variety of dog breeds to prepare them for search and rescue missions. She could tell how enthusiastic he was by the size and slant of his handwriting. "First thing I'm doing when I get out," he'd written, "is signing up with one of those teams." He'd punctuated the sentence with a clumsy smiley face, followed by "Make that the *second* thing. First thing I'm gonna do is wrap you in the biggest hug you ever had."

As she restacked the letters, tears filled her eyes. If she'd given him half a chance… *Water under the bridge.* She'd hold on to the letters until Ian recovered. In the meantime, they'd remain in her briefcase—no chance Eliot would find them there, since he didn't know the code to unlock it.

Back in her room, she huddled into the covers while images painted by his letters flitted through her head. All this time, she'd told herself that he'd ruined her for other men, even though everything learned in psychology classes said otherwise. Feeling sorry for herself provided the perfect excuse to stay angry with Ian...and avoid commitments, even with the many standup guys her friends and family had introduced her to.

They said that a woman like her, with a big, caring, unselfish heart, shouldn't spend her life alone. If any of that was true, why hadn't she considered what *Ian's* life had been like? For the first time in many years, Maleah cried herself to sleep.

THE EFFORT OF making his way from the bedroom to the living room left Ian shaky and out of breath. Oh, how he hated feeling so weak and helpless!

Gladys peered over her reading glasses and shoved her phone aside. "Don't know how people read articles online," she said. "The font is so small!"

Ian eased into his recliner. "You can enlarge it, y'know."

"Give me a good old-fashioned, inky fingers newspaper any day."

"Wasn't the paper delivered today?"

"I'm sure it was. I just haven't had a chance to run downstairs and pick it up yet."

"Thought Dad usually did that."

Gladys shrugged. "He'd already left for work when I got up."

"What's up with that? He hates that job."

Another shrug. "Special project, or so he says."

"Whew." He raised the chair's footrest. "I was beginning to think he was avoiding me."

"Don't read more into it than what's there. You know as well as I do that brother of mine will do anything to avoid adversity." She made her way to the fridge. "Hungry? I'm in the mood for poached eggs on toast."

"Sounds good."

His cell phone buzzed. He checked the caller ID screen and tossed it back onto the side table. Evidently, Maleah had no plans to check in with him.

"Feeling better this morning?"

He stretched out in his recliner. "Better than yesterday."

"That scowl says otherwise. You didn't take your pain meds, did you?"

"I don't like the way they make me feel, all

dizzy and sleepy." That's why he'd decided to take the pills only at bedtime. A good decision, since in addition to curbing achiness, they guaranteed deep, dreamless sleep. At least so far.

"Don't look so disappointed, nephew. She might reach out, eventually."

He might have responded with *yeah, right* or *fat chance*...but he was tired. Tired of wondering and waiting. Tired of putting his life on hold for maybes and mights. Tired of never knowing where he stood with Maleah—who played Pollyanna one minute, then Ice Queen the next.

He'd never asked much from life. Just what every guy his age wanted. A wife, a house with a yard that his kids and Cash could run around in. And he might have it, too, if he hadn't turned a blind eye to every woman who'd seemed even remotely interested. It had been stupid to think that someday, after he'd made something of himself he could show her all he'd accomplished as proof of how sorry he was and how much he'd changed.

And he'd done it all *for what*? To hear her wonder aloud if he might rob a children's charity?

Ian blamed the surly attitude on lack of sleep, sore bones, feeling out of control over...

everything. Soon after his release, he'd learned to let "can't trust an ex-con" insults roll off his back by employing the old "Don't let others' opinions distort reality" quote. If it worked then, it'd work now.

"Stop beating yourself up, Ian. If she doesn't come around, well, it's just proof she isn't good enough for you."

Weird. And all this time I thought it was the other way round.

Cash whimpered and looked up at him.

"What's the matter, buddy? Did Auntie Gladys forget to feed you this morning?"

"I fed your precious boy," Gladys said. "Took him out for a potty break and gave him a treat, too. In all fairness, Brady did what he could to cheer Cash up, but I guess there's just no replacing the irreplaceable Ian Sylvestry."

Whether or not he'd earned it, Ian believed he had the full support of Gladys and his dad, the bistro employees and fellow SAR volunteers, the people he'd worked with on Washburne projects. He glanced at Cash and grinned. *And the undying devotion of my faithful sidekick.*

Why wasn't that enough? Why did he want so badly to add *Maleah* to that list? "He isn't accustomed to seeing you this way," Gladys continued, cracking eggs into boiling water.

"Don't know what would become of him if anything happened to you…"

The hint wasn't lost on Ian. He reached down and petted the dog's head. "Love you, too, buddy. Don't worry. I'm gonna be fine."

She dropped four slices of bread into the toaster. "When you're on your feet again, first thing you should do is take him for a walk to Henderson's Wharf. He loves sniffing the air down on the docks."

Six city blocks, minimum. Ian shook his head as Gladys buttered the toast.

"I dunno." He watched her plate the toast. "Could be a good long while before I'm ready for that."

"Are you kidding?" she asked, spooning an egg onto each slice. "Took you nearly ten minutes to get from the bedroom to the chair yesterday. Today, you did it in half the time. Keep up with those exercises, and you'll be back to normal in no time."

Palming his fork, Ian smiled up at her as she put his breakfast in front of him. "Thanks, Gladys. You're the best. And I really mean that."

"Wouldn't be here if I didn't believe that. Now eat up. Few things yuckier than cold eggs."

He could think of one thing yuckier than that. Life without Maleah.

Soon after Gladys collected his tray, Ian dozed off. If not for the repeated peal of the doorbell, he might have saved the old guy and himself, too…at least in the dream…

"Well, well, well. Look who's here," Gladys said.

Using his good hand, Ian knuckled his eyes and finger-combed his hair. He couldn't be awake, he decided, because unless hallucinations were a side effect of the meds, there stood Maleah, looking like a cover model in a long black coat and snug knee-high leather boots. "Go on in and make yourself at home," his aunt said, taking her coat, "and I'll put on a pot of coffee."

"No deliveries yet?" Maleah asked.

Gladys's brow furrowed. "Deliveries?"

Leaning closer, Maleah whispered something that put a smile on his aunt's face. Both women looked his way, and when Maleah's gaze locked on his, Ian did his best to sit up straighter.

"Well, it isn't noon yet…"

And then she began walking toward him. Cash got up to greet her and happily accepted a pat on the head. Ian grinned. She sure did look cute, snuggling up to the dog's muzzle. Sounded cuter still, telling him what a pretty boy he was…in high-pitched baby talk. *Good ol' Cash*, he thought, watching the dog lap it all up.

Any minute now, he'd come to. It would take a concerted effort not to be in a bad mood, considering who'd starred in his dream, but—

"Does it bother you to talk about it?"

She moved to the couch, and Cash followed her.

"Talk about it?"

"The building collapse that put you in this condition."

He'd take last night's pain pill earlier, so it had an extra hour or two to wear off before morning. This was bordering on a nightmare.

"You look better than I expected."

Meaning, she'd thought about him? Ian shook off a sudden urge to grin and said, "What do you want to know?"

"Were you scared?"

Ian rubbed his eyes again, then picked up his coffee mug. She looked genuinely concerned.

"No more than during any other rescue," he said, "until the ceiling caved in." Cash, chin resting on one of her knees, used a paw to tap the other. His way of saying *It's okay to pet me some more, lady...*

And she did.

Now that the fog had lifted, he wondered how she'd heard about the accident.

"Did Gladys call you?"

Maleah glanced into the kitchen and, seeing what he saw—his aunt, busily putting cookies on a plate—she bent nearer to him to say, "I heard about your…accident…on the morning news the day after the house collapse."

"Ah, so you already know the details."

"Actually, the broadcast barely touched on the 'what happened' aspects of your…" Her compassionate gaze slid from his swollen face to the bandage wrapped around his head, the sling that protected his left arm, the cast on his right thigh. He must look a sight. "So really, all I know is that you and Cash had been dispatched to a search and rescue mission, that you saved one of the people trapped in the house, and ended up in the hospital trying to save the second."

At the sound of his name, Cash flashed his best doggy grin. *Who knew you were such an outrageous flirt?* he thought.

"An elderly couple," he said. "Soon as I'm able, I'll make a few calls. See how the wife is making out."

"I can do that for you, if you like…"

Had the offer been prompted by her inherent do-gooder tendencies? Or was it a sign she still cared?

"I appreciate it," he said, "but by the time

I'd get you all the information, I could do it myself."

Gladys delivered her coffee. "I have laundry to fold. You two play nice now, y'hear?" she said, and disappeared down the hall.

"I'd almost forgotten what a lovely woman she is."

Ian nodded. "My dad compares her to a toasted marshmallow. Crusty on the outside, warm and gooey on the inside."

Maleah laughed, and oh how he loved the sound of it.

"Coffee's good." She took a sip.

"You're lucky my dad didn't make it." Ian winced.

Smiling, Maleah said, "Will you need much therapy?"

"In-home nurse walks me around the apartment couple days a week. For now. When she gives the thumbs-up, I'll start the real stuff."

"If you ever need a ride to the rehab center, let me know."

If he took her up on the offer, was it possible to mend fences, prove to her that he was a changed man? He'd bet patients prolonged their recovery all the time thanks to such offers from former sweethearts.

"I should go…"

In a hurry to escape, are you?

"Yeah, I'm sure you have a mountain of work waiting for you back at the Institute."

"That isn't the reason. You look tired. And unless I'm mistaken, you're in a lot of pain, too. I just don't want to wear you out."

"You aren't. I'm glad to see you. Really glad."

The doorbell rang, and Gladys called out, "That's probably for you, Maleah…" Those whispered comments earlier made sense now. She'd arranged a get-well gift of some sort. But why not save the delivery fee, and bring them over herself? *Don't read too much into it, stupid.*

A middle-aged man stepped inside, put a cardboard container and what appeared to be a box of candy onto the kitchen island, then handed Maleah three Mylar balloons. GET WELL, one said. CHIN UP! said another. And the third was a gigantic yellow smiley face.

Maleah tipped the guy, who hurried on to make his next delivery.

"Any dietary restrictions?" she asked, placing the candy box on his side table. She returned to the kitchen to get the cardboard container. "I remember how much you love truffles…"

"No restrictions," he said. "And thanks. You didn't have to do this."

"It's no big deal. Just a little something to cheer you up."

Oh, she'd done that all right, in spades.

"This is easy to care for. Just soak it well once a month, keep it near a sunny window. Don't use tap water, though. The chlorine and fluoride will kill the plants…and leave an ugly white residue on the sides of the pot. No need to buy distilled. Bottled is fine, or you can fill a pitcher with tap water and let it rest for about twenty-four…"

Another trademark Maleah Turner trait: Rambling when she felt out of place, nervous or afraid. Which of the three provoked her cactus care lecture? It didn't matter, really because Ian felt like a heel for making her feel anything but welcomed.

"You'll get a kick out of this," he said, grinning. "I was dead to the world when you first got here, and thought you were a mirage or something."

She aimed a maternal digit in Cash's direction. "Don't touch this, or you'll be sorry, okay?" She patted his head and pointing at the plants said, "No, no, no…"

Maleah moved the garden to the shelf unit beside the TV, well out of his reach. Returning to her place on the couch, she smiled at Ian.

"Better to be safe than sorry."

"Definitely."

"So…you were…you were dreaming? About *me*?"

A remark like that from the old Maleah might indicate that she felt flattered. But the new Maleah had changed a lot, and Ian couldn't get a read on what it meant now.

"I guess you could say that."

A tiny smile lifted the left corner of her mouth. "Don't know if I've ever been the star of a guy's dream before."

She'd stood center stage in hundreds of dreams during his years at Lincoln. What would she say if he admitted it now?

Only one way to find out…

"It probably won't surprise you to hear that I thought of you a lot while I was…away." The smile disappeared, and in its place, the all-business expression he'd seen her aim at people like Stan, the Institute's administrator, her supervisor.

Maleah began to fidget—another telltale sign that she felt uncomfortable. He searched his mind for a topic to divert the conversation.

A two-note chime interrupted them. *Saved by the bell.*

"I'll get it, Gladys…"

Terri and Avery stepped into the apartment, and were promptly greeted by Cash. The boy got onto his knees and hugged the dog's neck, and paid no attention to the adults in the room.

"You look awful," Terri said.

She'd baked something, and placed the foil-covered plate on the island.

"Man. Aren't *you* good for a guy's ego." Ian smirked. "I hope that's your world-famous brownies…"

"She made three batches," Avery said, looking into Cash's eyes. "One for you, one for Mom and me, and one for the teachers and aides at my school." The boy crossed the room, sat on his heels next to Ian's chair, and Cash flopped down beside him. "What did they do to you?"

Ian pointed at each injury and provided a tip-of-the-iceberg explanation for each bandage and cast.

"Does it hurt much?"

"Nah. I'm tough." He flexed his good bicep and winced, which sent Avery into a fit of giggles.

Ian faked a frown. "Make yourself useful, meanie, and get us both a brownie." He looked at Maleah and Terri. "You guys want one, too?"

"They're not *guys*, Ian." Avery rolled his eyes and got to his feet.

"Use a plate," Gladys said, joining them. "And get one for the rest of us, too."

She zeroed in on Maleah, sent what Ian recognized as an approving nod. It made Maleah blush, and she looked pretty cute doing that, too. Ian worried if she didn't knock it off, he'd say something stupid, like *I love you to pieces, Maleah Turner. Always have, always will.*

He clamped his jaw shut.

Avery handed Ian his brownie. "I'm real glad you didn't die. You're one of my best friends."

Ian laughed and clutched his aching rib cage. "I'm glad, too." He wiggled a forefinger to invite the boy closer. When Avery leaned in, Ian added, "You're one of my best friends, too."

Through all of this, Maleah had stood near the kitchen island, quietly observing. If he had to guess, he'd say the conversation between him and Avery gave her something new to consider: *Ian Sylvestry, convicted felon, enjoying a positive interaction with a special needs child; maybe he'd changed for the better, after all.* Quick as a blink, the affectionate expression dimmed. Memory of her cutting remark on the dance floor came to mind. If she believed he could steal from kids like Avery, was Maleah also suspicious of his friendship with the boy?

"You aren't eating your brownie," Avery said.

Ian took a huge bite and chewed, mostly to

buy him some time to think without *some-one* thinking he might be planning some new crime.

"Good, isn't it?" the boy said around a big bite of his own.

Nodding, Ian replied with a closed-mouth smile. He needed to quit dwelling on what she'd said. What did it matter if she'd meant it or not when there was no hope of a future between them?

Ian glanced at her. The sweet, tender look had returned. Man, what he'd give for the power to read her mind, just for a few minutes.

You'll drive me stark raving nuts, he thought.

"We have to go," Terri said, extending a hand to her son.

"Aw, Mo-o-om, do we have to go already? We just got here."

"I know, but we need to get you to school. You've already lost hours, thanks to the dentist appointment. And besides, Ian looks tired."

Avery gave Ian a judicious once-over and, shoulders slumped, trudged to the door.

"Good thing I didn't take off my coat."

"Thanks for stopping by, guys," Ian said. "It was good to see you, and I know Gladys and my dad will think so when they get hold of those brownies."

"Don't let them eat too many," the boy said. "Mom baked 'em for *you*."

Hand raised as if taking an oath, he said, "You bet."

Maleah, acting as hostess, thanked them, too, and closed the door behind them.

Gladys broke a brownie in half. "That was sweet of her."

Then she was pressing her fingertips to her lips, dark eyes wide and blinking as Maleah calmly made her way to the row of wrought iron coat hooks beside the door.

"You're not leaving already, are you?"

"Ian looks pale," she told Gladys. "I'm afraid I've already overstayed my welcome."

"No," he said, "you haven't. And I'm fine. But I understand that you're busy at work. Thanks for the gifts."

Gladys poked around in the box the cactus garden had come in. "Good grief, nephew. You didn't read the card?" She fanned her face with it. "That's the *first* thing you do when opening a gift."

"I, uh, didn't realize there was a card." He looked at Maleah. "Sorry."

"It isn't his fault, Ms. Syl—Gladys. I forgot to give it to him."

A peculiar glint sparked in Maleah's eyes.

What reason would she have to leave the card for him to find later?

Gladys slid the card from its tiny envelope and placed it on his open palm. She stood beside his chair, hands on hips.

Ian looked up at her. "What…"

"Aren't you going to read it?"

It consisted of two, brief lines. "Already did."

She snapped it from his hand.

"Holy smokes, Gladys. You trying to add paper cut to the list of the things wrong with me?"

"Oh, hush. No harm done." Moving her reading glasses from the top of her head to the bridge of her nose, she read aloud: "'While you rest and recover, I'll be thinking of you, and praying you'll be back on your feet soon. Fondly, Maleah.'"

Maleah looked at him—studied him was more like it—no doubt to see if he'd read more into her signature line than she'd intended. He couldn't very well admit that the word *fondly* stuck out like the thumb of his thickly bandaged left hand. Would've been nice if she'd written *love* instead, but he'd take what he could get.

For now.

"That's so touching, Maleah." Gladys pressed

the card to her chest, then made eye contact with Ian. "Isn't it sweet, nephew?"

Hardly the word he'd use.

Maleah hitched her purse strap higher on her shoulder and opened the door. "Thanks for the coffee, Gladys," she said. And turning toward Ian, Maleah added, "Don't eat all that candy in one sitting."

The door had barely clicked shut behind her before that day—a lifetime ago—resurfaced in his mind: He'd bought her a heart-shaped box of inexpensive chocolates. She ate one nougat-filled treat...and he devoured the rest in less than fifteen minutes. Maleah would have been well within her rights to say "I told you so!" when his stomach started churning and his head began to pound. Instead, she found a nickel-sized white tablet at the bottom of her purse, dropped it into a bottle of water, and made him drink every last drop. The vile fizzy stuff did help settle his roiling gut. Got rid of the headache, too. But nothing made him feel better than when he said "Do you know how much I love you?" and she responded with "About as much as I love you, I suppose." *There's something seriously wrong with you, Sylvestry.* Why else would something like that hurt so much after all this time?

"Think I'm going back to bed," he said, grunting as he lifted himself from the chair.

"Great idea. Maleah was right. You do look pale. A nap will do you good." Ian put his back to her as fast as he could, because one look at his face and the woman who'd been more mother than aunt to him would demand to know why there were tears in his eyes.

CHAPTER FOURTEEN

MALEAH COULDN'T GET Ian's face out of her mind. The furrows on his otherwise smooth brow told her he was in considerable pain. And his usually deep strong voice had sounded as weak as he looked. It made her wonder if he might be bleeding from one of the surgery sites. The fact that he'd smiled in that approachable way he had before the whole Lincoln incident was the only reason she hadn't picked up the phone to get more details from Gladys.

She never should have gone to his apartment. The gifts, the reasonably comfortable conversation might have given him false hope, and that wouldn't be fair. Ian had put his life on the line for total strangers, and look how he'd ended up. That wasn't fair, either.

They'd been alone at least fifteen minutes before Terri and Avery arrived. Why hadn't she asked all the questions that had been swirling in her head? Questions about life at Lincoln. Were the guards cruel? Was the food horrible? How dreary was the place? Did he have enough blankets to warm him during the cold winters? A fan to cool him in the summertime? How did he busy himself while alone in his cell? Letters in, letters out were probably the only way for him to hold onto memories from home. And from what she remembered of his father, Brady didn't write often, if at all. How sad that Gladys was the only person Ian could truly count on in life. Well, Gladys and Cash.

Even if she'd taken advantage of the opportunity, she wouldn't have asked her most bothersome question: How often had he thought of her? A silly question, since in every one of the fifty-two letters, he apologized profusely for the self-centered actions that put her in a precarious position with friends and family, and he repeatedly said that he missed her.

He'd never know the full truth.

Because she'd never tell him…

Maleah stared out the window behind her desk, across the lawn and gardens. Two swans slid across the aqua surface of the pond, leaving ripples in their wake.

Ripples…like those Ian's crime had caused.

It seemed wrong to continue punishing him for one crime that took place so long ago. A crime he'd paid for by sacrificing ten years of freedom. She hoped that eventually, the time would come when people saw his slate as wiped clean. People like Eliot, her father and grandfather. Even her mother and grandmother. And most of all, herself. "Pointless," she said to herself, stacking and restacking papers on her desk. *What's done is done, and what happened is ancient history.* She'd have to learn to live with her guilty conscience, just as she'd learned to live without him, because her family would never approve of a renewed relationship with Ian. Her family meant the world to her, and she couldn't do anything that might upset or disappoint them.

Not even if it meant there was so much as the whisper of a chance—

Her desk phone rang, and she picked up the handset, relieved.

"Hey sis."

"Eliot…what's up?"

"I'm fine, how are you?" he said, laughing.

"Sorry. I'm a bit distracted this afternoon. Everyone all right at your house?"

"We're all good."

"And work?"

"That's good too. So the reason I called… I have the boys this weekend, thought I'd take 'em to the B&O Railroad Museum. They've got the miniature Christmas garden set up…."

"Oh, they'll love that."

"I was hoping you could come with us."

"Would you believe I've never been there, despite how close it is to my place? When were you thinking of going?"

"Saturday. Early afternoon."

"Want me to make a light lunch, since I live so close?"

"No, I want to take you out someplace. Maybe Cacao Lane. Call it a peace offering."

"A peace offering? Why?"

"I've been pretty hard on you since that…" He cleared his throat. "I haven't exactly been a loving brother lately. Joe's right. You don't deserve that."

Maleah didn't know what to say. He'd almost said something snide about Ian, but stopped himself. It told her that he'd control himself in front of his sons, too.

"You're a great brother." *Most of the time.* "I haven't spent nearly enough time with the boys lately. Or had a meal at that restaurant in ages, either. This'll be fun."

"I think so, too. Better let you go or I'll be late for my shift. Love ya, sis."

"Love you, too, big brother."

"Has Mom talked to you about Thanksgiving dinner?"

"No, but I'm sure it's on her to-do list."

Eliot laughed. "That thing gets more un-wieldy every day."

"But thankfully—no pun intended—it doesn't change much. You'll pick up ice and sodas. I'll make a dessert and a side dish. Joe will get stuck with chips and pretzels."

"Maybe I'll shake things up a little this year, bring a store-bought pie."

Maleah gasped. "You wouldn't dare!"

He paused before saying, "I've missed you, kiddo."

"Ditto."

"Want to just meet us at the restaurant?"

"That makes sense. I can hardly wait."

She scribbled a note on her desk blotter. CALL MOM. On second thought, maybe she'd stop by on the way home. With her brain in a tizzy, she wouldn't accomplish much here, anyway.

Maleah stuffed her laptop and the usual file folders into her briefcase and almost couldn't snap it shut, thanks to the bundle of Ian's letters taking up so much extra room. During the drive to Ellicott City, Maleah considered other places to hide them until he healed up and she could return them to Gladys.

Ian...

With any luck, any family members gath-ered at her parents' house tonight would fol-

low Eliot's example, and not talk about him at
all. Just in case, though, Maleah came up with
a few change-the-subject lines.

Ian...

He'd tried to hide his misery behind wise-
cracks and slanting grins, but he hadn't fooled
her. Post-op pain, she believed, explained only
part of the problem: Any patient would view
a doctor's "stay home and stay quiet, indefi-
nitely" orders as a prison sentence of sorts. But
for someone with a past like Ian's...

Better to dwell on what he had that many patients didn't, a muleheaded drive to overcome
all obstacles that would speed his recovery to
the point that it surprised everyone, his surgeon included.

Her dad was out front, gathering the mail
when she pulled into the curving driveway.

Opening her car door, he said, "Well, look
what the wind blew in."

Maleah grabbed her purse and got out. Even
though Eliot the Snoop had been at work for
hours now, the briefcase, she decided, was
safer on the floor between the front and back
seats.

"What brings you here on this gloomy gray
day?" Pat said, bussing her cheek.

"Can't a girl pay her folks a visit because
she misses them?"

Arm in arm, they trudged over the recently-shoveled brick walk toward the front porch. "Mom's going to be glad to see you. Said just this morning that she wanted to call, start making arrangements for Thanksgiving."

"I figured as much." They climbed the brick steps, and as he opened the storm door, she said, "Eliot called me today, and gave me a heads-up that she's started her to-do list. He also invited me to join him and the boys on Saturday at the B&O Railroad Museum." After stomping snow onto the foyer rug, Pat hung his jacket and hers on the hall tree.

"Ah, right. I read in the morning paper they've got the Christmas garden all set up." He led the way into the sunny kitchen where her mom was at the sink, her back to them.

"You know I can't hear you when you talk to me from another room," she said over one shoulder.

Pat winked at Maleah. "It just so happens I wasn't talking to you."

"Oh dear. We've reached that age, have we?" She giggled. "Well, you know what your father says…"

"…talking to yourself is one surefire way to know someone is listening," they said together.

Pat quickly tacked on, "But I wasn't talking to myself, either."

Ann turned, and when she saw Maleah, said, "What a terrific surprise!" She dried her hands on a yellow-checked towel. "If I'd known you were coming," she said, hugging her daughter, "I'd have made dessert."

"I'll fill up on whatever smells so delicious."

Ann pointed to the Crock-Pot, nestled in a corner of the counter. "Beef stew. Didn't have parsnips, but I think we'll survive."

She guided Maleah to the long trestle table. "Sit down. Tell me all about your latest projects." Ann took three tumblers from the cabinet and filled them with iced tea.

When Ann delivered the drinks, Pat said, "How was traffic?"

"Pretty good, actually. The State Highway Administration did a great job, salting and plowing. People are still driving like maniacs, but that's nothing new."

"Joe tells me Eliot's been riding you pretty hard since finding out you reconnected with Ian."

In her head, Maleah uttered a teenage-sounding "Da-a-ad." Aloud, she said, "He means well."

"Joe and I both told him to back off."

"Because I told them to," Ann said. "You're a big girl. Smart, too. We can trust you not to do anything stupid."

Maleah sipped the tea. "Excellent as always. I've watched you make it for decades, but mine never tastes as good."

"Oh, I'm sure it does. It's all perception... mom's tea is better because mom made it."

Perception. If the family had it in their natures to exercise a little of that, maybe they'd stop being so judgmental toward Ian.

But who was she to talk? This morning, she'd considered the possibility that under different circumstances, Ian might have served more time for participating in the actual robbery and shooting.

"I've met with a long list of families," she told them, "and helped get their children into the Institute's school. A few didn't need daily intervention, so they'll attend weekly or biweekly sessions. It's so gratifying to see the relief on the mom's and dad's faces, knowing their kids will get the help they need to prepare them for everything school related."

"I don't think I've ever heard you talk about what Washburne does," Pat said.

"Initial evaluations determine whether or not kids need occupational therapy, physical therapy, speech therapy. We have some talented therapists onboard."

"And you were one of them." Ann patted

her arm. "Do you miss it? Sorry you accepted the promotion?"

"No, the added salary is helping build my bucket list account."

"Bucket list?" the Turners said together.

"Travel, mostly. I want to visit Ireland. Scotland. England. Italy. And go out west again."

"That was a great trip, wasn't it?" Pat said. " Reminded me of when I was a kid, and visited Uncle Buck's ranch when school was out."

"I'd probably start with Alaska."

Her mother laughed. "But Maleah, you've already been there, twice!"

"Wouldn't mind seeing it, myself," her dad said. Then, "So this invite from Eliot...are you going?"

"Yup. He's treating me to lunch at Cacao Lane."

"Isn't that sweet, Pat? Don't you just love hearing that our kids aren't just siblings, but friends, too?"

He smirked with affection. "Wasn't always that way."

Oh, how she adored her family.

"How're Gran and Grampa?"

"Ornery as ever," Pat said. "Dad wanted me to take him to work with me, so he could attend a few roll calls and talk about how they did things in *his* day."

"Oh, that would have stood you in good stead with everyone!"

The front door slammed and a deep voice said, "Did I hear my name used in vain?"

Ann got up and went to the sink. "Better get this table set," she said, washing her hands. "When that man pops in for supper, he expects it on the table, *tout de suite*."

Maleah stood beside her mother and lathered her hands, too. "I'll help. Which bowls are we using tonight?"

"The plain white ones." She snickered. "Frank says designs make him miss things on his plate."

"Well, it's true," Frank said, following Teresa into the room. "Why, once I left a whole bite of chocolate cake, smack dab in the middle of some confounded flower!"

"Good to see you two," Maleah said, accepting hugs and doling out kisses.

"We were driving by on our way home from Grampa's doctor's appointment." She held Maleah at arm's length. "I'll give you three guesses as to what he said."

Laughing, she drew her grandfather into a three-way hug and did her best to emulate his voice. "'Bet Ann has something good on the stove, and you know she always cooks more than she and Pat can eat...'"

Laughter filled the already bright room and the women got busy setting the table.

Moments later, all five held hands as Frank led the blessing:

"God in heaven, we thank you for the grub and the gal who cooked it, and for all gathered here. Amen."

Before everyone let go to pick up their forks, Teresa added, "And let this old man's tests come out A-Okay."

"What were the tests for, Grampa?"

Using his fork to spear a slice of bread, he grumbled, "Aw, you know doctors these days. Go in to have an ingrown eyebrow hair removed and they'll take half your blood and toss you onto an x-ray table looking for who knows what. It's nothing."

Teresa's face said otherwise, but Maleah decided to hold her questions until after dessert.

"What brought you out in the snow?" Frank asked her.

Shrugging, she smiled and said, "Just had a yen to see Mom and Dad. Lucky me, I got Grams and Grampa, to boot."

"So what's new with you, sweetie?" Her grandmother had obviously been crying.

"Nothing much, really. Things are quiet at work, and the next fund-raiser doesn't officially kick off until spring, so I'm putting in normal hours and loving it. I might use this unexpected extra time to repaint my kitchen."

Pat sat back in surprise. "Didn't you just do that last spring?"

"Fall, honey," her mother gently corrected.

Maleah answered her unasked question. "I thought the color would grow on me."

"See there?" Frank said. "It's like I always say. Sometimes, what looks like a deal, isn't." Mint-green looked great in the downstairs powder room, but didn't match a thing in her kitchen.

"When you're right, you're right," she admitted.

"See, that's what I love about this kid," he told his son. "Smart enough to know when to butter up her elders. Now pass the butter, will ya?"

"What's the theme of the next fund-raiser?" Teresa wanted to know.

"We saw a need for more how-to classes for kids attending the Institute's school. Various therapies, field trips to help them adapt to various modes of travel, what to expect if fire or police department intervention is required, and even more simple things like going to the movies or eating in a restaurant."

"Sounds to me like somebody has already

written up the brochure," Frank said, grinning. "Any famous people this time?"

"I'm working on finalizing a few commitments." She'd done well with past events, but the gala's enormous success was due mostly to Ian's involvement. In his present condition, she didn't know if he'd participate. Or if she wanted him to, for that matter.

But depriving the kids of bigger donations simply because she couldn't bear to spend more time with the man she'd loved, lost, found again…but could never call her own seemed beyond wrong. The height of selfishness.

"A little bird told me your convict friend arranged for some big names," Frank said.

Who but Eliot could have passed on information like that? "That little bird chirps entirely too much."

"Maleah has things well in hand," Ann said. "She knows better than to get involved with him on anything but a professional level. Isn't that right, sweetie?"

Not one of the lines she'd practiced in the event Ian's name came up would help with this turn of the conversation. So it made no sense when she heard herself say, "You wouldn't believe how much he's changed over the years, mostly for the better."

All four adults sharing the table fell silent.

"I only say mostly because on the outside, he looks the part of an ex-con."

"Oh?" Ann dipped buttered bread into her stew. "He was a good-looking boy, as I recall…"

If she described him now, the shock of seeing him—if they ever saw him again—would be lessened. By a long shot.

"Ponytail, tattoos, an earring…"

Pat snorted. "Your brother said he aged a ton at Lincoln."

"So have I. Spied my first gray hair last week!"

That inspired a smattering of quiet chuckles.

"Don't give it another thought," Ann said. "Eliot started going gray years ago, and if you ask me, he looks even more handsome—and distinguished!—with white streaks at his temples."

"Better for the job, too," Pat pointed out. "New recruits pay more attention when an older cop doles out advice."

"Precisely why I wanted to talk with the young'uns the other day!"

"Dad, you know as well as I do that the rules have changed. Nobody gets to run roll call unless they're certified and approved."

"So thirty years on the job isn't good enough?

That stinks, if you ask me. Those greenhorns could learn a lot from us old geezers."

"You'll get no argument from me. But the rules are in place for a reason."

"Yeah, to protect the politically correct jerks who are more interested in appeasing the media than protecting the public." Frank leaned forward to add, "Which is the basis of the oath every cop takes before he or she pins on the badge." He sat back again and groaned. "Good grief. Did you hear that? I just said he or she. They've even got me doing it!"

Maleah almost pointed out that since female officers put their lives on the line exactly as their male counterparts did, it was only right to include them. But the change of subject had saved her from discussing Ian, so she kept her opinion to herself.

"More stew anyone?" Ann asked. "And there's cherry cobbler…"

Frank shoved his stew bowl away and scrubbed his palms together. "Make mine double-double."

"Coffee? It's decaf…"

"Sure. But keep that phony sugar away from me!"

"Frank, no need to shout," Teresa said. Her grandmother had been uncharacter-

istically quiet all through the meal, raising
Maleah's curiosity about the doctor's visit.
It seemed just as strange that neither of her
parents had asked any questions about the
appointment. What did they know that she
didn't? Maleah stood, and while her mom
dished up the dessert, she cleared the table.
"Okay," she said, depositing plates and silverware into the sink, "what's up?"

Her mother shot her a "not now" look, which
turned curiosity into fear.

"We're about to enjoy a Turner family clas-
sic," Ann said, delivering a huge portion of
cobbler to Frank. "And by the way, I happen
to agree with *some* of what you so often call
PC nonsense. You can't disregard the dangers
faced by female officers. They're just as likely
to die in the line of duty as the men. And don't
give me that 'more men die on the job than
women' craziness, because that's only because
the ratio of male to female officers isn't equal.
Yet."

Maleah admired her mom, the only Turner
brave enough to stand up to Frank. And since
it took the attention even farther from Ian, she
appreciated her, too.

The conversation veered away from Ian yet
again as they ate dessert, from Eliot's boys to

the Thanksgiving menu and the day's snowfall. Frank emptied his bowl and got up.

"I need to stretch my legs," he said, heading for the hallway.

Maleah followed him.

"I could use some fresh air. How about we take a walk around the block, like we did when I was a kid?"

He slung an arm over her shoulder and led her into the foyer. "Sounds like the perfect ending to a perfect evening."

They put on their coats.

"We're going for a walk," Frank hollered, and pulled the door shut behind them. They'd barely hit the walk when he said, "Curiosity got the cat, did it?"

"Only because I adore you." She linked her arm through his. "I want to know what's going on, so I can help if I can."

"Not much you can do, sweetie. At least not until we know what we're dealing with."

Now, he was just scaring her.

"Which doctor did you see?"

"Valenti."

His cardiologist. "Why, specifically?"

"Had a routine exam couple weeks ago, and he suggested a couple of tests. Run of the mill stuff."

"Such as?"

They'd reached the corner.

"Can you believe anyone could let their property go this way?" he said, pointing at the Stewarts' weedy, unkempt yard. "It's where they *live*, for the luvva Pete. Have they no pride of ownership?"

"It's a shame they let the place go," Maleah agreed. "But maybe it's because Mr. Stewart has a heart condition or something."

"Well, aren't *you* the subtle one?" He laughed. "Valenti brought me back for an ECG, MRI…" He patted his chest. "And sent me home wearing this Holter monitor."

To track his heartbeats during a twenty-four hour period. "How long before you'll have all the test results?"

"A week, give or take."

She pulled him closer to say, "You'll be fine, I'm sure."

What she really meant was *You have to be fine, because I don't know how to live without you.*

She glanced up, into the golden glow of the street lamp.

"Looks like those li'l snowflakes are sliding down the light beam, doesn't it?" Frank observed.

He'd always been the poetic one in the

family. But why did she get the feeling he was about to ask about Ian, again?

"At the risk of being labeled a nosy old man, can I ask you a question?"

"You can ask…"

He chuckled. "You still love the guy, don't you."

It wasn't a question.

"What makes you say that?"

"A lifetime of interrogating people. And picking up your cues over the years."

Dare she admit the truth? "I hate upsetting the family. Their behavior is rooted in love. I've always known that. But what they *think* they know doesn't exactly jibe with the truth."

"Few things in life do. But I didn't ask what you'd do if the clan approved. And you still haven't answered my question." He slowed his pace. "You have my word. Whatever you say is between you and me."

She had good reason to believe him. It had been Grampa who'd helped her care for the kitten she'd found at the playground up the street, getting it cleaned up before she asked permission to bring it home. It had been her job to grab the mail on her way into the house after school, and on the day she'd found the letter, detailing why she was in danger of failing chemistry, it had been Grampa who'd signed the form…after soliciting her oath that she'd study hard and bring up that grade before report cards came out. And it had been Grampa who'd held her, without saying a word, when they took Ian away.

"Sometimes," she began, "I think maybe I do still love him. Other times—hate is way too strong a word—but the memories bubble up and overshadow any good feelings. It's enough to make me wish I'd never run into him again."

"You two were pretty much inseparable in the beginning, despite your dad's reservations."

She couldn't even try to deny that.

"You enjoyed working with Ian on the Kids First events…"

"He's good at what he does. And works tirelessly. *And* everyone on the team loved him, because when he puts his mind to it, he's so easy to be around."

"Always was a charmer, that boy."

A charmer. She visualized his gorgeous smile and the way it lit up his dark eyes…and just about everything around him. "Let me ask *you* a question."

Frank met her eyes.

"What did you think of him, before, you know…"

"I was ambivalent. He seemed okay. Too

quiet for my taste, but then, he didn't exactly give off bad vibes, either. It just seemed there was something a little sinister—for lack of a better word—brewing in that head of his. I blamed his so-called mother, leaving him at a time when kids most need a stable home. And that sorry excuse for a father." Frank shook his head. "Not to excuse what he did, mind you, but considering who raised him, I wasn't surprised when he started running around with that pack of two-legged wolves. What he did with them, though? Now that puzzles me to this day."

Maleah sighed. "Same here."

"Ah well, live and learn, I guess. If you say he's a changed man, that's good enough for me."

He fell silent as they passed the old playground, where the swings, merry-go-round, and spring-loaded horses wore a thin coat of snow that glittered under the lights.

"So what will you do, cupcake?"

"What will I do about my, um, my friendship with him?"

"Friendship, you say?" Frank huffed. "Potato, potahto."

"If I knew, I'd tell you, Grampa. Honest I would."

He patted the hand that held onto his elbow.

"I know, I know. Thing is, I want you to be happy. Same goes for Grams, your mom and dad, Joe. Heck, put his feet to the fire, and I'll bet Eliot wants that, too…even if it means you found it with Ian."

For a moment, hope pulsed in her heart. And just as quickly, it faded, thanks to too many doubts.

"You're a young, beautiful woman, Maleah, with a heart that's bigger than your head. You deserve the whole white-picket-fence scene, and there's no reason you shouldn't have it just because the guy made a stupid, stupid, *stupid* mistake when he was a lonely, confused, bitter kid."

In other words, if she and Ian miraculously managed to get beyond the wall separating them, he'd back her up? Maleah shook her head. It was just too much to hope for. "Guess we'd better get to the house."

"Or your grandmother will send out a search party."

Turning, they headed back toward the Turners'.

"Any idea what color you'll paint your kitchen this time?"

She looked at the pristine blanket of snow that swathed each blade of grass, every tree limb, and the rooftops. "I'm kinda leaning to-ward white."

"Great minds think alike."

They walked the rest of the way in compan-ionable silence, and as he led her up the walk, she stepped in front of him, wrapped him in an enormous hug and said, "Love you to pieces, Grampa…"

He kissed the top of her head. "Ditto, kiddo."

"…so take real good care of yourself, okay?"

Laying a fingertip atop her nose, he winked. "All right, I'll give up the cigars, just for you."

"Cigars! I thought you quit, years ago!"

"Hey, you've got your secrets, I've got mine." This time, he kissed her forehead. "But we've always had each other's backs. Still do, right?"

"Right."

"If this Ian guy makes you happy, go for it."

"Much as I appreciate your support, if that means you're not really giving up the smokes, no way. I'll go to my grave a lonely old spin-ster before I make a deal like that."

Frank laughed. "Man, you drive a hard bar-gain. All right. Soon as I get home tonight, I'll hunt up every cigar stashed around the house and trash the lot of 'em." He held up his hand, as if taking an oath. "Word of honor."

The hand then wrapped around hers.

"Now let's get inside."

She had her grandfather's approval to fix the broken connection between her and Ian.

The big question now echoed what he'd asked moments ago:

What will you do?

Maleah had no idea, but she knew this: it was high time to make a final, firm decision, one way or the other.

CHAPTER FIFTEEN

THANKSGIVING AND CHRISTMAS passed with the usual Turner fanfare: too much food, an overabundance of decorations and more gaily-wrapped packages than in years past. Maleah believed her grandmother and mother went overboard because of her grandfather's diagnosis: Dilated cardiomyopathy, the cause of his shortness of breath, swollen ankles and vague complaints of fatigue. Test results showed that unbeknownst to him, Frank had survived a mild heart attack, prompting a prescription for an anticoagulant. If exercise, changes in diet, and the now-official no-smoking orders didn't improve the condition, he might need a pacemaker.

But since another more serious heart attack was possible, the family agreed during no-Frank-allowed meetings to coddle him…until he noticed and fought it. And so far, so good. She might have enjoyed the festivities more if her brain hadn't fixated on Ian. How had he celebrated?

As the new year approached and the subject of resolutions flooded social networking sites, the media and even the Institute, Maleah could think of just one major change that needed to take place in her life: Ian.

It shouldn't be so difficult, choosing a time and place for the face-off that would provide them both with a conclusion that would open the door to healing…or heartache. The timing needed to be right. Had he recovered enough to return to the bistro?

As she parked in her assigned space at Washburne, Maleah's cell phone rang.

"Is this my sweet Leah?"

Kent O'Malley. Who else would dare call her that? The only person she'd ever let get away with it had been Ian…

"You've reached Maleah Turner," she replied in her most businesslike voice.

"Oops, my mistake. I forgot you're not crazy about the nickname."

"That's true." And to assure he realized how disinterested she was in moving forward with him, Maleah added, "Who's calling, please?"

He punctuated the brief pause with a grating snicker. "Well you've sufficiently deflated my bloated ego, *Mah-lee-ah*. This is Kent. Kent O'Malley?"

"Oh, of course. Hi. Sorry…"

"No problem. But hey, the reason I'm calling… I know it's last-minute, but I'm hoping you're free on New Year's Eve. All day, and beyond the witching hour."

Day after tomorrow? Nothing like waiting until the last minute. Especially for one of the most important date nights of the year. She considered playing the "Let me check my calendar and get back to you" game, but few things annoyed her more than pretense.

"As it happens, I've made other plans."

Kent laughed. Not the deep, robust sound that made her heart pound, like Ian's, but not exactly annoying, either.

"My own fault, I guess, for waiting until the last minute. Looks like I'll have to ring in the new year alone again."

Again? A self-made millionaire who'd been photographed at red-carpet events with fashion models, TV personalities and corporate types? Maleah had a hard time believing it.

"Well, Happy New Year," she said, ending the conversation.

The back doorbell rang, and when she saw Vern on the porch, Maleah threw open the door.

"Looks like you got more of that stuff on you than on the walls," he observed, stepping inside.

"I know. I'm a very sloppy painter."

"But your cut-ins look professional."

Hands pocketed, he walked around the room. "Much better than that green. I approve."

"I was just about to put on a pot of tea. Want some? I have chocolate chip cookies…"

"Homemade or store-bought?"

"What do you think?"

"Then I'll stay." He laughed. "It isn't like I have back-to-back appointments."

She plunked the brush into the bucket that held her collection of paint tools, washed her hands and filled the kettle.

"So what're your plans for New Year's?" Vern wanted to know.

"I have a date, but he's got some surprise lined up."

"With the ex-con?"

Maleah hid a frown.

"No, he's a business associate. Sort of."

"Sort of, eh?" He smirked. She gave his shoulder a playful smack. He got real serious, real quick. "Just pullin' your leg. Didn't mean anything by it."

She slapped his shoulder again. "I know, I know."

"What are you doing for New Year's?"

"Same ol', same ol'. I'll park myself in front of the boob tube with a bowl of buttered popcorn and a can of Bud and watch the fireworks over the Inner Harbor. Gotta find a good movie to watch, though, 'cause those bands and singers drive me nuts."

"I tend to channel surf while that stuff is on, too."

"Young'un like you? You're kidding."

"It just so happens I love big band music. And that's never part of the entertainment, not on any of the stations."

"Big band, huh?" He bit into a cookie. "So… can you jitterbug?"

"People have called me Ginger Rogers, I'll have you know."

"You're one of a kind, Maleah Turner," he said as she slid a mug in front of him. "One of a kind."

She held out a box of brightly packaged tea bags. "Choose your poison, Vernon."

He decided on Earl Grey chai, unwrapped it, and dropped it into the mug.

"That's my favorite, too," she said, following suit.

"If I'm not getting too personal, how are things going with the, ah, the ex-boyfriend? Is he back to normal after the big accident?"

"I'm ashamed to admit it, but I have no idea. I stopped by to see him soon after his release from Hopkins, but haven't made the time to look in on him since."

"That's too bad."

"Because…?"

"Keeping your distance that way sends a message, loud and clear."

"Such as?"

"If you're avoiding him when he's all messed up like that, well, what message would *you* take from that?"

"That I don't care," she said, mostly to herself.

"Do you?" He spooned sugar into his mug. "Care about him, I mean?"

"Of course I care. He asked me to marry him, once upon a time, and I said yes."

"Maybe so, but a lot of water has sloshed under that bridge since then."

Not so much that she didn't still wonder what life might be like with Ian at her side… "Piece of advice? When you finally get around to checking on him, don't mention this date you're going on."

"Why not?"

"'Cause if he's still burnin' a candle for you, it'll send the wrong message, that's why."

He slurped the tea. "Then again, maybe that's the idea…to let him know you're not interested…"

"That's my dilemma. I need to figure out what I want, and get some idea what he wants."

"I take it you like livin' in limbo, then."

"I don't follow…"

"You ask me, you're playing it safe. Or so you think. No decision postpones the inevitable."

"Which is?"

"Finding out he beat you to the punch…and decided he doesn't care about you that way anymore."

And that, as the cliché said, hit the nail square on its head. Without realizing it, that's precisely what she'd been afraid might happen.

"I only have one New Year's resolution…to figure things out about him, once and for all."

"I'll believe it when I see it." Vern drained the mug and got up. "Thanks for the conversation and the snack." In the open doorway, he said, "When you clean yourself up, be sure to get that blotch of paint out of your hair."

Maleah locked up and, yawning, put the mugs into the dishwasher. And after returning the tea container to its shelf in the pantry, she decided to skip the shower and go straight to bed. Maybe, just maybe, an idea would come to her as she slept, and by morning, she'd know how to arrange a meeting with Ian.

CHAPTER SIXTEEN

SHOULDN'T HAVE TURNED off your cell, Ian thought, reading the phone's caller ID screen. Maleah had called shortly before midnight. "Sorry I haven't checked in with you sooner," the short message began. "I hope you're healing up well. Happy New Year, Ian. See you soon, I hope."

The way she'd rushed from the apartment that day, he'd thought it best to leave her alone.

"Wrong again," he growled. When it came to Maleah, he couldn't seem to do anything right.

"You're up and at 'em early."

His dad, seated in Gladys's usual morning spot, turned a page in the paper.

Ian limped over to the island and poured himself a cup of coffee. "I could say the same." For the past week, he'd been walking with just one crutch, but hadn't yet figured out how to carry liquids without spilling them. Much as it bugged him to ask for help, he said, "Hey

Dad, would you mind setting this on the counter for me?"

Brady relieved his son of the mug. "Are you joining me here, or should I put it by your chair?"

"Right here's fine," he said.

"Your hard work is paying off," Brady said with an approving nod. "Gotta hand it to you, son. You came through this like a real trouper."

Weeks of hobbling around the apartment helped build his strength enough to endure the fifteen-minute drive up Broadway to Hopkins, where time on the treadmill, climbing up and down a short set of mobile stairs, and stretching workouts rounded out his on-site physical therapy. Most frustrating were exercises designed to regain control over his fine motor skills. According to the staff, he'd progressed at twice the usual pace…not nearly fast enough for Ian.

"Gladys had some errands to run," Brady said. "That's why I'm here." He folded the newspaper. "What time is your session this morning?"

Ian would have bet his remaining crutch that Gladys spelled things out: Today's therapy had been postponed because of the after-New Year's holiday. What important activity, he wondered, had so preoccupied Brady that he hadn't heard her?

"Think I'll fix myself some cereal," he said, shuffling to the pantry. "Have you eaten yet?"

"Yeah, dunked some cookies in coffee."

Ian's go-to breakfast…before the accident. He made his way around the kitchen, filling his bowl, grabbing a spoon, then pouring milk over the puffed flakes. Impatience, he'd discovered, was his worst enemy. In his rush to complete simple tasks as he had before, he only succeeded in creating a mess that he couldn't clean up by himself, doubling his frustration.

"What's bothering you, son?"

"Nothing really. Just annoyed at how long it takes to get things done."

"Looks like more than that to me."

"Is that so."

"You're still hung up on Maleah, aren't you?"

Hung up didn't even begin to cover it.

"Gladys tells me she stopped by."

Ian slid onto a stool, wincing when he bumped his arm on the counter.

"Phone works both ways, y'know…"

"Gets a little tiresome," Ian began, "reaching out only to have your hand smacked all the time."

"How many times has that happened?"

It hadn't, technically. But knowing that it

might was reason enough to sidestep the possibility of rejection.

"Your aunt seems to think the girl still has feelings for you."

"Gladys is a dreamy-eyed romantic."

Brady smirked. "So you disagree."

"If Maleah has feelings for me, she sure has a funny way of showing it."

Brady pointed at the cactus garden that sat in the center of the island, the mostly empty box of chocolates, and deflating balloons that bobbed in the breeze whooshing from the ceiling vent.

"I read the card…"

"Hey, don't read between the lines. Besides, all this stuff is just…stuff. Thoughtful enough, I guess, but way easier to give than *self*."

"Whoa, that's deep. Real deep. Been reading the old philosophers again, have you?"

"Ha ha."

"Guess that means you haven't thanked her for all this, ah, stuff?"

"No, but I will."

He'd considered calling, texting, asking Gladys to invite her over again.

"The longer you wait, the tougher it'll get."

"Maybe I won't bother. She'll add 'ungrateful pig' to the list of reasons she dislikes me, and we'll both be off the hook."

"Hmpf. Sounds like self-pity to me. And if anybody oughta know about that, it's me." Ancient history had never been his best subject, so Ian hoped his dad wasn't planning to dredge up the past. He'd spent years saying things like *It's all right; you did the best you could under the circumstances.* It seemed to Ian that his dad had grown far too comfortable, living with his defeatist mind-set.

Brady glanced at the clock. "Gladys should be back in an hour or so. Will you be all right on your own until then?"

Time to head for the office, Ian realized. Another way his father hid from reality.

"Sure. I'll be fine."

"Leave the dishes. I'll get to them after work, if Gladys doesn't beat me to it." He grabbed his coat. "Tell her I'll pick up a pizza on the way home, save her having to cook supper."

"Sounds good." Ian grinned. "But no black olives."

"Speaking of food…have you been down to the bistro yet?"

"No," he said again, "but I'll go soon."

"Why not go now? I know your regulars are eager to see you."

One at a time, his staff had come upstairs to ask for advice about private parties, ask his approval on menu changes, to get him to sign paychecks. Without exception, they'd stressed how much they'd missed him and his leadership. Could he make it down the stairs and up again, unassisted? *Only one way to find out...* If he succeeded, could he return not only to *Sur Les Quais*, but to his SAR activities?

Cash ambled over, used his nose to nudge Ian's hand. "Guess you're ready to get back to work, too, aren't you, buddy?"

The dog dashed into the foyer and, after some huffing and tugging, loosed his leash from the hook beside the door.

"Okay, I get the hint," he said. "Give me a minute and I'll grab my jacket." Cash would provide an excuse to avoid the bistro, at least for now; how would it look if he violated his own set-in-stone rule about animals—except service dogs—on the premises?

It felt good to get outside longer than the amount of time it took to stagger into Gladys's ancient black Caddy. Not a horrible day, for this time of year. A frosty wind rippled harbor waters and blew a briny scent across the sidewalk. Ian took his time, passing the Oyster House, the Waterfront Kitchen and The Horse You Rode in On Saloon.

A water taxi putted by, filled with tourists that huddled deep into down parkas and faux fur coats. He didn't realize just how far he'd walked.

"Sorry buddy," he said, "but the leg is giving me a fit. Time to get back."

Cash slowed his pace.

"We'll do it again tomorrow." He glanced at the sooty, cloud-streaked sky. "Weather permitting, that is."

Back home, he hung up his jacket and Cash's leash, and shuffled into the kitchen. After refilling the dog's water bowl, he placed a cup of water into the microwave. Hot chocolate sure would hit the spot right about now. And when he finished it, he'd make his way downstairs just in time for the lunch rush. Ian popped the last chocolate into his mouth, a chewy caramel-vanilla cream combo, and tossed the empty box into the trash can. If he survived the visit, ego intact, he'd call Maleah and thank her for stopping by the other day.

Who was he kidding? He'd call even if his self-esteem took a slight hit.

He missed hearing her sweet-yet-sultry voice. Missed those big glittery blue eyes, too. Once, that cheery smile had the power to light every dark corner of his life and make him forget that his mother had chosen another man over him and his dad.

His mother had left a message a few weeks

ago to give him her new phone number. He looked at the kitchen clock. Nearly eleven o'clock London time. If he called now, he might wake her new baby boy...

That wasn't fair, and he knew it. The kid wasn't to blame for what his parents had done, and Ian had understood that, right from the start. It's why he'd made a point to send birthday and Christmas cards every year. He'd decided to start the new year with a clean slate, and that included touching base with his mother. He envied people who had families, and considering the fact that the estrangement had been his doing... When he finally worked up the nerve to make the call, Ian would ask her about his half brother's likes and dislikes, and send something more personal than a gift card for a change.

Cash flopped down on his thick corduroy bed, staring at Ian as if to say, *Well? Aren't you going to keep me company?*

Admittedly, it had been a while since they'd walked that far, and the walk had taken its toll on his sore muscles and healing bones.

Ian decided to pay a visit to the bistro after physical therapy tomorrow.

The cactus garden caught his eye and he decided Brady was right: the longer he waited to thank Maleah for the gifts, the harder it would be.

He got settled in the recliner, hands shaking as he picked up the closest phone within reach—his dad's—and dialed.

"No WAY TO know yet whether or not it's serious," said Pat Turner. "We're following the ambulance to Howard County General, right now."

A familiar *ping* sounded in her ear, and she ignored the incoming call.

"Want me to call Joe and Eliot?"

"Thanks, honey. That'd be great."

"I'll leave just as soon as I get hold of them. You guys drive safely, and if they'll let you see Grampa, give him a hug for me."

It was almost a relief that he hung up before saying more; hearing the tremor in her dad's voice had been almost as upsetting as the word *ambulance.* Her grandfather would be all right.

He had to be!

"…and we're expecting a relatively minor storm," the radio announcer said. No surprise there. Historically, Baltimore's biggest snowfalls happened at the end of the month, and into February.

"But be careful out there," the reporter continued. "This one snuck up on us, and the roadways haven't been treated…"

Great, she thought, turning off the radio, *just what we need during a family emergency.*

Maleah left a message for Eliot, then dialed Joe's cell number and left one there, too. Her brothers were on duty. If the weather forecast was accurate, the department might assign officers extra hours, to rescue stranded drivers, direct motorists onto safer roadways, even escort accident victims to the ER. She'd try them again, just as soon as she checked on Grampa.

She found her parents in the waiting room outside the cath lab, talking with a doctor. She sat beside her dad and took his hand in hers.

"Is Grams in with Grampa?"

"Yes," her dad said. He turned to the doctor. "This is our daughter, Maleah. Maleah, Dr. Peters."

"Where's Dr. Valenti?"

Her mother said, "In Europe."

"Don't worry," Dr. Peters said, "I promise to take good care of your grandfather."

Maleah's cell phone buzzed…a number she didn't recognize, and once again, she ignored it.

"We're prepping Mr. Turner for surgery now," Dr. Peters continued. "His type of cardiomyopathy makes him a good candidate for a pacemaker. It's a routine procedure that only takes a couple of hours and doesn't even require anesthesia."

Pat exhaled a relieved sigh. "And afterward?"

"We'll monitor him here for a day or two, and as long as things look good—and I expect they will—we'll send him home." The doctor explained how easy it would be to monitor the function of Frank's pacemaker, thanks to wireless technology.

"Will he need special medications?" Ann asked.

"If tests determine he needs a blood thinner, we'll prescribe one. But from what I've seen, he probably won't need anything. Once he's home, though, if he experiences discomfort at the implant site, an over-the-counter pain reliever like acetaminophen is fine."

Eliot joined them, and Ann said, "This is our eldest son."

Dr. Peters nodded. "They'll fill you in soon, I'm sure."

He seemed to take the hint and sat beside Maleah. "I've heard that cell phones interfere with pacemakers," she said.

"Only if they're carried in a pocket directly over the device."

"And security systems, like those at the airport?"

"It *could* sound the alarm, but if it does, he'll have a wallet card to explain things to agents. Might not be a bad idea to get him one of those medic-alert bracelets."

Her cell phone buzzed. "They're ready for me," she said after reading the text message. "I'll send your mom out to wait with you." Standing, she shook each relative's hand.

"Thanks, doc," Pat said.

"I'll find you when it's over."

Joe approached, pink-cheeked and breathless. "What's going on?" He'd clearly rushed from the parking lot to the waiting room.

Pat repeated what Dr. Peters had told them, and just as he finished, Teresa walked into the waiting area.

"Did the doctor explain things to all of you?"

"She did," Ann said, guiding her to the three-seater couch. "And did a thorough job, too."

"Snowing like a son of a gun out there," Joe said. "An inch deep and counting."

Pat frowned. "Thought they said it wouldn't accumulate?"

"Shouldn't last long," Eliot said, "with these warm temperatures."

"Warm!" Ann rolled her eyes. "Last I heard, it wasn't even thirty degrees!" Typical Turner nervous small talk, Maleah thought. She wouldn't put it past her brothers to start reciting every knock-knock joke they knew.

"So as long as we're all together," Joe said, "I have something to tell you guys."

Everyone turned toward him.

"I, ah, I met this girl, see, and I think maybe, *maybe* this is the one."

Teresa giggled. "Let us be the judge of that."

"You're gonna love her, Grams. She's amazing. A kindergarten teacher. Never married, no kids, owns a town house in Columbia, loves to cook, and drives—get this—a pickup truck."

Eliot elbowed him. "Sounds too good to be true. Can she go out in public without a bag over her face?"

Joe held out his cell phone, showed his brother a picture.

"Man. Some guys have all the luck," Eliot said, passing the phone to his mom.

"She's lovely." Ann handed it to Pat, who gave an approving nod before giving it to Maleah.

Joe's dark-haired, dark-eyed girlfriend could have been related to Ian. "She's gorgeous, Joe. What's her name?"

He smiled at the picture before sliding the phone back into his uniform shirt pocket.

"Molly. Molly Mucchino."

"When are we going to meet Miss Perfect?" Eliot asked.

"I was hoping this weekend, but with Grampa out of commission, that isn't a good idea."

"He should be home by Saturday," Teresa

said, "and the doctor told us he can get back to his usual activities...within reason."

"Yeah, but Molly teaches five-year-olds, and he'll be tired. Wouldn't want to take the chance she might carry some germ home from school."

"Good point, son," Pat said.

Eliot elbowed him. "Nice to see you use that noggin for somethin' more than a hat rack."

Maleah checked her watch. It had only been ten minutes since the doctor left them. Could the Turners keep up with the one-liners for another hour...perhaps two?

Shortly after midnight, the doctor appeared in the waiting room, a surgical mask hanging around her neck.

"He's doing great," she announced. "Give the nurses half an hour or so to get him settled in his room, and you can see him."

"All of us?" Eliot asked.

"As long as you're quiet."

"Soon as we've seen him," Maleah said, "I'll go to your house and bring you some toiletries and a change of clothes." She turned to Dr. Peters. "It's all right if she stays, right?"

"Of course it is. There are lounge chairs in the rooms. Tell the duty nurse you'd like a pillow and a blanket."

"Wonderful," Teresa said. "But I'd stay even if I had to sleep standing up, like a horse!"

Maleah laughed and squeezed her forearm as Joe said, "Eliot and I will drive you, Maleah."

Joe said. "The roads are pretty dicey."

Teresa's eyes filled with tears. "You kids are wonderful." She hugged them both. "I don't know what I'd do without you."

"You'll never have to find out," Eliot said. He faced the doctor. "So, no complications at all? Everything went exactly as planned?"

"If you don't have any more questions," the doctor said, "I'll be on my way. I make rounds any time after nine, so if you think of anything between now and then…"

The Turners looked at one another but no one spoke.

"I hope you won't all feel the need to stay," Dr. Peters said, backpedaling toward the OR.

"Sheesh, sis, what's up with your cell phone?" Eliot frowned. "It's been buzzing all night."

"Only three times," she corrected. "Caller ID says 'unknown.' At this hour, it has to be a wrong number. I'll take care of it later, once we've seen for ourselves that Grampa is all right."

Twenty minutes passed before a nurse appeared. "Are you the Turner family?"

Everyone stood at once.

Grinning, she said, "I'll take that as a yes. If you'll follow me…"

Frank was sitting up in bed, pink-cheeked and smiling when they entered his room.

"Relax, you guys. I'm not dead yet."

"Frank!" his wife scolded. "That isn't even remotely funny!"

"Just trying to turn those frowns into smiles, that's all," he said as she hugged him.

"You're amazing," Maleah said, patting his hand. Bending to press a kiss to his forehead, she added, "You look great."

Situations like this were precisely why she'd avoided the topic of Ian. The family had enough to contend with, and didn't need anything more upsetting them.

"All right. You've all had your eyeful, now skedaddle. This old goat is pooped."

Teresa rolled her eyes. "He *must* be fine."

Pat and Ann said their goodbyes to Teresa and promised to return first thing in the morning. And after they left, Maleah drew her brothers into the hall.

"I'll be fine going to Grams's alone. You two need your rest, so I'll drive myself. Think you'll be back to talk to the doc, or wait until he's released tomorrow?"

"Listen to Little Miss Sure of Herself," Eliot said to Joe.

"We'll call you," Joe said.

"Take it slow and easy," Eliot said. "We don't need two Turners in the hospital."

The siblings exchanged a three-way hug, and as the brothers headed for the elevators, Maleah stepped up to the nurses' station to ask for a pillow and blankets. Back in her grandfather's room, she adjusted the grayish-pink chair until it lay flat, then made it up like a bed.

"I'll bring your toothbrush," she told Frank. "Anything else?"

He rubbed his stubbled chin. "My razor. It's charging on the bathroom vanity."

"And something for him to wear home," Teresa said.

Maleah turned out the lights and palmed her keys. "I won't be long. You two try and get some sleep while I'm gone, okay?"

On the way to the parking lot, she checked her phone again. She'd been right: Three calls from the same unknown number, and no messages. Coworkers never called after ten, and even in the thick of a fund-raising campaign, neither did volunteers.

Tomorrow she'd dial the number.

Right now, Maleah concentrated on the roads. Joe had been right. The streets between

Howard County General and her grandparents' house were slick. She took it slow and steady… exactly as Ian had taught her.

He'd been soft-spoken and patient, even when she nudged trash cans and scraped fences, learning to parallel park. Astonishingly, after just two weeks, he announced, "You have insurance. You know the manual inside and out. And you can maneuver this old boat like a pro. Let's go to the DMV and get your license." The Turners hadn't been pleased when they learned who her driving instructor had been. But after a year's worth of flimsy excuses and broken promises, of course she'd taken Ian up on his offer to teach her.

Maleah pulled into the elder Turners' driveway and did her best to let go of the bittersweet memory. It took all of fifteen minutes to pack the items her grandparents might need, and twice that long to find the shovel and clear the front walk and drive. *Worth every minute*, she thought, returning the tool to the shed, because it almost got her mind off Ian.

Back at the hospital, she found Frank and Teresa fast asleep. And no wonder. It was nearly 2:00 a.m., and the long harrowing day had taken its toll. Maleah quietly stored the small suitcase in the closet and tiptoed to the straight-backed chair to the right of Grampa's bed. Boots propped on the radiator and using her coat as a blanket, she promptly dozed off.

The squeak of crepe-soled shoes crossing the polished linoleum floor roused her. "Didn't mean to wake you," a nurse whispered. "I should take Mr. Turner's vitals, but I hate to disturb him when he's resting so comfortably."

Unless her watch had stopped, she'd only been asleep a few minutes.

"I'll just use the monitor's readings and give him a few more hours." The nurse scribbled numbers on a small tablet, and slid it back into her pocket. "Can I get you anything?"

"I'm fine, thanks," Maleah whispered back. "And thanks for letting him sleep."

The door hadn't fully closed before Frank whispered, too. "Have you called him yet?"

"Hasn't been time."

"Make time. Life is unpredictable."

"I'll call."

"Promise?"

"Promise."

"Good. I want you to be happy."

"I'll be tickled pink if you go back to sleep."

Eyes closed, he said, "Love you, cupcake."

She finished their decades-old game with "Love you more."

His soft snores were proof that Frank hadn't

heard her. *Life is unpredictable*, he'd said, and Maleah understood, perfectly.

Yes, she'd call Ian. The sooner the better. That way, if her grandfather raised the question again, *yes* would be an honest answer. It wasn't likely she'd fall asleep again, which gave her plenty of time to practice her opening line …and a closer that guaranteed to get off the phone as fast as possible.

Because all right, she'd admit it: She cared about him. A lot. And probably more than was good for either of them.

CHAPTER SEVENTEEN

A FIRST-THING VISIT to the bistro, Ian decided, was probably better than dropping by during the dinner rush. He didn't expect any of the staff to take shortcuts or get things done the easy way, *But there's a first time for everything.*

Dan had already been to the farmer's market, and now stood at the stove, stirring the soup du jour.

"Smells great," Ian said.

"Hey boss, you're a sight for sore eyes!"

"You just saw me on Tuesday."

"Yeah, but it can't be repeated enough times— we can't wait until your doctor gives you the green light."

"I'm okay to put in a couple of hours, starting today."

The chef looked dubious. "You sure?" He sprinkled chopped parsley on top of the soup.

That wasn't what he'd hoped to hear.

"Where's Lee?"

"Sent him to The Restaurant Store for some

paper cups and lids. Lot of diners have been ordering coffee to go at lunchtime."

"Great idea. Compostable?"

"Of course." Dan cranked the pepper grinder above the kettle. "No sense riling the tree huggers."

Ian picked up the *Sur les Quais* specials menu choices: Shrimp sautéed with sun-dried tomatoes, chicken breast tenderloin, or herbed smoked salmon, and the assorted dessert crepes the bistro was known for.

"Perfection," Ian said.

"Easy when all I have to do is copy what you've already done."

His phone pinged with a text.

"Love note? Bet you get a lot of those…"

"Hardly. My doctor's secretary, asking to reschedule tomorrow's appointment."

"My mistake. I thought you and that little blonde were an item." He smirked. "You two looked mighty cozy on the night of the gala."

He'd almost forgotten Dan and his fiancée had attended.

"Maleah was in charge of the shindig. And she's a, ah, a friend. I've known her for years."

For a lifetime.

He should try to reach her again It wasn't like her not to return calls. "How's the mutt?"

"Great. He took me hiking yesterday and wore me out."

"Leave it to Cash to make sure you meet your exercise quota. I sure wouldn't want to explain to Mad Max the physical therapist that I'd skipped a day."

"Aw, Maxine isn't so bad, once you get to know her. I'll be back in a couple hours, after I take Cash for a walk."

"I won't tell the rest of the crew." Dan started chopping onions for the lunch dishes. "Wouldn't want to disappoint them. You know, in case you change your mind."

Only one thing could stop him: Maleah. And since connecting with her was about as likely as another house falling on him, Ian could say with confidence, "I'll be back in a couple of hours."

With Cash safe at the end of his leash, Ian headed out for another walk around the marina. The sky had turned steely gray, and he guessed the gusts had reached 20 mph or more. The weather report warned of an impending snowstorm that could produce several feet of the white stuff. But at least this time, road crews were prepared.

"Looks like we're in for it, buddy."

Cash didn't react, save to slow his pace.

Dog and master spent an hour in the cold

wind before returning to the apartment. Ian filled Cash's water bowl and handed him a biscuit, then flopped into his recliner and turned on the TV.

Just in time for the local news. The screen filled with a colorful map, and as Marty Bass explained what the lines and squiggles meant, Ian wished he'd thought to grab something to drink sitting; getting into and out of the chair posed a bigger challenge than walking. Now, with a mug of coffee and a bottle of water on the side table, he settled in, hopefully for the last time.

His phone rang.

Dan, probably wondering when he planned to go back to the bistro.

"Sylvestry's Bar and Grill," he said, grinning.

"Oh, you're a riot. Hey. Turn on the news. We're about to get bombarded with a full-fledged blizzard."

"Yeah, I'm watching now."

"I'm going to cancel tonight's bachelor party. No sense having a bunch of drunk groomsmen driving home in that stuff."

"I'll do it. Offer them something down the road that'll salve their disappointment." Dan provided the best man's name and contact information.

"No point in you coming down now. We'll be lucky if a dozen people show up."

"People who live within walking distance."

"Skeleton crew, then?"

"Anyone who doesn't need to hit I-95 to get home."

When Ian disconnected, he scrolled through his contacts list. Should he give Maleah another try?

"Why not?" he mumbled, hitting Call.

But instead of her familiar, musical voice, an impersonal, methodical recording:

"You've reached Maleah Turner. Leave your name and number and a brief message, and I'll return your call as soon as possible. Thanks."

For a moment, he considered hanging up. But having used his own phone this time, Ian didn't want to take the chance of riling her.

"It's me, Ian," he said. "Tried calling you a couple times… I picked up my dad's phone, so you probably didn't recognize the number. I've got his settings figured out now, though," he said, chuckling. He cleared his throat to add, "I'm mostly calling to say thanks for the gifts. You won't be surprised to hear the chocolates are gone…"

Now what? Say goodbye? Have a good day? See you soon?

"Stay safe in all the snow that's headed our way. Hope to hear from you soon."

He hit End.

"Well," he said, patting Cash's head, "at least I tried to behave like a gentleman, right?"

"OH GREAT," MALEAH SAID.

"What's wrong, cupcake?"

"Nothing, really." She glanced at the TV, where dire warnings of a blizzard scrolled across the bottom of the screen. "I forgot to pack my phone's charger, and this thing is as dead as King Tut."

"See if mine fits," her grandmother offered.

It did not.

"Here, try Grampa's."

No luck there, either. And to complicate matters further, their phone batteries were dead, too.

"I'm going to see if maybe there's one in lost and found that I can borrow. Or ask a nurse. Surely someone on the staff has a similar model!"

"Here's a novel idea," Frank said, pointing at the handset near the nurse Call button. "Use the hard-wired phone. I paid extra for the room because there's a land line in it."

"If only I could. All my contact numbers are

stored in my phone. And unless I can charge it…" Maleah shrugged helplessly.

"What's so important that it can't wait a day or two?" Frank asked.

She'd planned to call Ian, to find out how his therapy was going…

"Nothing really. I suppose."

"See, that's why I think it's crazy to rely so heavily on electronic devices," Frank said. "If you had one of those date books like I used in the old days, you'd have everything at your fingertips, and you *could* use this old-fashioned, *normal* piece of equipment."

He'd made a good point, and Maleah admitted it. "First chance I get, I'm going to the office supply store. I had one of those calendars, years ago. It took up a lot of space in my briefcase, but it sure would be worth it right about now."

"Relax," her grandmother said. "How often does an opportunity present itself when you can just forget about all the demands of work?"

"Not often." But she wasn't worried about bosses and coworkers. *Ian must be thinking I'm a self-centered idiot, waiting so long to check on his progress…*

"Buzz the nurse, Teresa."

She leaped up. "What's wrong? Are you in pain? Feeling woozy?"

"I feel right as rain. But I want to get home before that storm hits."

Teresa followed his gaze to the TV. "I suppose it would be better to sit it out at home than here in the hospital. Let me check at the nurses' station."

"I'll do it," Maleah offered. "Need to see about a phone charger, anyway."

She stood at the desk for less than five minutes. "Sorry," the floor nurse said, dialing Dr. Peters's number, "no chargers, but maybe we can get your grandfather out of here a little ahead of schedule."

Translation: If the storm caused accidents—and knowing Baltimore drivers as she did, it would—the hospital would need every available bed.

"Dr. Peters is on her way up."

Maleah thanked her and returned to her grandfather's room. Outside, fat flakes floated to the ground. So many that she could hardly see the buildings across the way. But she pretended not to notice. Pretended, too, that it didn't concern her.

"The doctor will be here soon. I'm sure once she reads your chart and gives you a once-over, you'll be good to go."

"But...we got here in an ambulance," Teresa said, gnawing on a knuckle.

"I didn't, and I'm happy to drive you home."
With any luck, she could get them settled, whip
up a quick lunch, and get home before the
snow started falling in earnest. Cozy as their
house was, and much as she'd enjoy a few quiet
hours in their company, curiosity about calls
and messages got the better of her.

Dr. Peters breezed into the room, white coat
flapping behind her. "So you want to escape
this place, do you?"

"The sooner the better," Frank said.

"I'll try not to take that personally." She
scrolled through his file's notations on the in-
room computer screen. A glance at the moni-
tors told her his heart rate, blood pressure and
pulse were fine, and tugging at his hospital
gown, Dr. Peters peeled back the bandage that
covered his incision. "A-plus," she said, gently
pressing it back into place.

"So I can leave?"

She draped the stethoscope around her neck.
"Sure. Why not. But remember…no straining,
and take it easy. That means *no shoveling.*"

"Yeah, yeah, yeah."

Maleah recognized that tone. It meant that
first chance he got, he'd insist he felt well
enough to go outside and clear the driveway and
walks. *Not if I have anything to say about it.*

Dr. Peters smiled. "I'll put in the discharge

order right now. One of the nurses will come in for your signature in just a few minutes."

"But hospital time is like football time," Teresa said, frowning. "We could still be here an hour from now."

The doctor typed something into his file. "I'll put a big red *rush* on it. But if you haven't signed those papers in a half an hour, you have my cell number."

"Thanks, doc," Frank said. "Yer a peach."

Half an hour later, true to Peters's word, Maleah was helping her grandparents into the car.

"I can stop at a fast food drive-through on the way home," she offered.

"No thanks," Teresa said. "There's already two inches of snow on the ground. And we have plenty of food in the fridge."

Maleah breathed a sigh of relief and, as before, took her time getting to their house. "Would you look at that!" she said, pulling into the driveway. "I shoveled all this just last night."

"That's Mother Nature for ya," Frank said, unbuckling his seat belt. "Unsympathetic old shrew…"

Once inside, Maleah insisted that they both relax in their matching recliners while she prepared lunch. Soft snores greeted her when

she returned with a fully loaded tray of sandwiches, sliced apples, chips and ice water.

They needed rest more than food right now,
she decided, and retreated to the kitchen to
cover the tray with plastic wrap.

Everything outside the kitchen window was
white. Tree limbs, shrubs, the walkways Frank
had installed to make it easier for Teresa to tend
her roses, even the big colorful urns that held
her artful arrangements of annuals. Ordinarily,
Maleah could see the neighbors' houses from
here…the pool where she and her brothers had
splashed as kids, the tree house where kids held
important meetings about homework and their
least favorite teachers. Today, the only things
visible were rough-hewn split-rail fences that
separated one yard from another.

If Maleah wanted to get home before the
roads became completely impassable, she'd
need to leave soon. Very soon.

She peeked around the corner, saw her
grandmother had picked up a magazine.

"He can sleep later," Teresa said. "Let's have
lunch."

Maleah set up the TV trays and brought the
food back out. They wasted no time, diving in.

"It's a little chilly in here. I think you need
a fire."

Maleah grabbed her coat and the straw

broom that stood in the back hall for as long as she could remember. After opening a thick braided rug on the laundry room floor to absorb melting snow, she headed for the wood pile and carried two armloads inside. Balled-up newspapers, kindling and the smallest logs went into the belly of the stove before she struck a match.

"Good job," Teresa said.

"Just like I taught her." Frank gave the thumbs-up sign.

"Now eat, before the bread gets all stale and crusty."

Smiling, Maleah sat down and bit the corner off her sandwich.

"So tell me, cupcake, have you called him yet?"

"Called who?" Teresa asked.

"Never you mind, *dear*. It's a private joke." He winked at Maleah. "Well? Did you?"

"Not yet."

Groaning, he said, "What. *Are*. You. Waiting for!"

"Courage, mostly."

"Oh my gracious." Teresa clucked her tongue. "You don't mean to say you're actually encouraging her to get in touch with that…that *boy*, are you?"

Neither Frank nor Maleah spoke, prompting Teresa to say, "If your son and grandsons get wind of this, you'll never hear the end of it." She clucked her tongue again. "Don't do it, Maleah. He isn't worth alienating your family."

Her grandmother had just put her greatest fear into words.

"Think about that, honey. Really *think* about that." She took a sip of iced tea. "Do you have any idea how scary it is, knowing you're considering a reunion with that...that criminal!"

He'd committed a crime. Yes, a serious one. But it had been nearly fifteen years ago, and he'd paid heavily for it. Maleah only shook her head and sighed. Maybe it had been wishful thinking that Grams had defended her when Eliot launched into yet another anti-Ian lecture. She wished her grandmother had the heart and soul of a romantic, like Grampa. But, as he was so fond of saying, "If wishes were fishes, you'd stink up the house."

"I'm going to clear some of this snow from the front walk and driveway. From the looks of things, the weather will only get worse. No sense letting it pile up."

"You don't have to do that, cupcake."

"I know. I want to do it. Need anything before I head for the tundra?"

"We're fine," Teresa said. "If we need anything, I can get it." She got up and wrapped Maleah in a big hug. "You're a sweetheart."

After donning her coat, she stepped into the swirling storm and said a silent thanks to her grandmother, whose furry boots fit perfectly. When she turned to head back into the house, Maleah couldn't see any evidence that she'd just spent an hour in this finger- and toe-numbing weather. Groaning, she plowed her way back to the porch. Leaning on the shovel handle, she stared into the white-gray sky. *Looks like you're stuck here for the duration.*

Inside, she added a few logs to the woodstove and slumped onto the couch. "What's the latest forecast?"

Teresa huffed. "They're calling for record-breaking low temps."

"And up to three feet of snow here in Howard County."

She remembered a similar storm. Then, it had taken days to clear the highways, rescue stranded motorists and dig out.

Frank shook his head. "What do you bet we'll break a snowfall record, too?"

"I just hope the power doesn't go out. In this neighborhood, if a mosquito sneezes, we lose electricity."

"Guess we're lucky the pesky skeeters have frozen to death, aren't we?"

The bulletin that scrolled across the bottom of the TV screen said the governor had called in the National Guard to assist the state highway administration.

"Multi-car accidents have already claimed the lives of fourteen," the broadcaster said, heaping bad news atop bad news, "so stay inside and off the roads."

Maleah closed her eyes, but it didn't help get her mind off the weather map, or being stuck at her grandparents' house, or the fact that a week or so ago, she'd loaned Joe her phone's car charger.

The house phone rang. For a full thirty seconds, Frank and Teresa bickered about who'd answer it.

"It's probably Mom or Dad," Maleah said, picking up the handset.

"Everything okay over there?" Pat asked. "Your mother called the hospital to check on Dad, and the nurse said you brought him home this morning."

"Dr. Peters checked him out and signed the release. Everything here is fine. And speaking of which, have you heard from the boys?"

"Both safe and sound at the station house."

Why did she hear *for now* at the end of that sentence?

Her mom picked up the extension. "Do you have everything you need, honey?"

It had become a joke around town that even before the first flake hit the pavement, Baltimoreans flocked to the stores to pick the shelves clean of bread, milk and eggs, and the all-important toilet paper.

"Oh, you know Grams. This place is as well-stocked as a warehouse."

"Well, if you need anything…"

Pat laughed. "How do you propose to get it there if she does? Dogsled?"

At the mention of the word, Maleah's mind went immediately to Cash. And then to Ian, sitting alone in his apartment. Was Gladys there with him? Or Brady? *Why do you care? He's a grown man, perfectly capable of—*

"No sense trying to shovel," her dad said. "The way this wind is blowing, it'll drift over everything before you can say Frosty the Snowman."

"Hmpf," his wife cut in, "ask how he figured *that* out."

Maleah could hear the smile in her mother's voice. "Like father, like daughter." She pictured her car, nearly hidden under one of those drifts. "Don't worry. I have no intention of going back out there until this mess has ended."

Frank wiggled his fingers, and Maleah handed him the phone.

"Got the old woodstove crankin'?"

"Not yet. I need to muster the gumption to find the wood pile first."

"Maleah found ours and we're basking in the fire's glow right now."

"You didn't lift logs, I hope!"

"Never got the chance, Ann. This kid of yours is kinda bossy." He winked at Maleah.

"Somebody's beeping in," he continued. "Can't see the caller ID without my glasses. Let me get back to you."

He hit the Talk button. "Yellow…"

Teresa groaned. "I don't know why he can't just say hello, like a normal person."

"Sure, sure," Frank said. "She's right here. Let me put her on."

He handed the phone back to Maleah. "You might want to take this in the kitchen. Better still, upstairs in the guest room."

"Why?"

"You'll see…"

"Hello?" she over-enunciated.

"Man, it's a relief to hear your voice."

Instantly, she understood the reason for her grandfather's suggestion and started up the stairs. "You didn't answer your cell or your work phone. Thanks for being safe. And for being *there*. I would have called your folks' house if I had to, but…"

Maleah could hardly blame him for feeling skittish about making *that* call.

"Call me crazy, but I pictured you alone and freezing on some deserted side road. Say the word if you think I'm prying, but where were you?"

"You aren't prying." By now, she'd reached the landing to the second floor. "My grandfather was rushed to the hospital night before last. Well, technically, very early yesterday morning."

"Maleah, that's awful. I'm sorry to hear that. I hope he's all right."

"He's fine now. They implanted a pacemaker."

"And he did well?"

"Well enough that his doctor sent him home. We barely beat the storm."

"Glad he's all right. How's your grandmother? Is she holding up all right?"

"She's fine. Thanks for asking."

"Hey, I always liked Frank and Teresa."

And why wouldn't he, when—before they fell into step with the rest of the Turners— they'd been welcoming and polite.

"He's like the Turner family rock," Ian continued. "What's the prognosis? He is gonna be okay, right?"

"His doctor is very pleased with his progress."

"Good. Good. Glad to hear it."

"How are *you* feeling these days?"

"Me?"

He seemed surprised that she'd asked, and Maleah felt bad about that.

"I'm fine. Getting around a little better every day, something Cash is grateful for. Poor pup was getting cabin fever, I think."

"Good, I'm glad to hear it," she echoed.

"One of the reasons I tried so hard to track you down was to thank you for the cactus garden. And those balloons really brightened the place up until the helium leaked out. Hey... how weird is this—that dog of mine doesn't think twice about racing into a burning building, or digging through mud or ashes to find a lost kid, but let a couple of half-deflated balloons bob around the apartment and he's totally freaked out."

Maleah laughed. "Aw, poor Cash."

"But anyway, I'm glad to hear you and your grandfather are all right."

"Thanks. I would have called you, too, if I'd had a working phone. I rushed out of the house so fast that I forgot my phone's charger.

No one had a charger to fit it, and since all my numbers are stored in there, I couldn't use another phone."

She was rambling and knew it, but couldn't seem to stop herself.

"I had no idea who called. Couldn't listen to messages…it was so frustrating."

"Now I know what to get you for your birthday this spring."

Please don't get me a gift, Ian. She couldn't help but remember all the thoughtful little presents he'd given her. A pocket folder specifically for her English Lit projects. Gloves with the fingertips snipped off so she could write reports and term papers in her favorite place, her parents' unheated sunporch. Sherbet ice cream and butterscotch candies…

"No, thank you, but this has never happened before, and I doubt it'll happen again."

"You know what they say…"

"There's a first time for everything?"

"Bingo."

"How are things in Fells Point? Are you buried in snow yet?"

"It's pretty bad. About a foot and a half out there so far."

"Guess you'll have to close the bistro until you can dig out."

"Lee said he'll stay. Gladys and I will go

down later, take care of the few stragglers who'll come in. Fells Point is populated by a whole bunch of people who like nothing better than to brave the elements. It's not so bad really, since they do it on foot."

"Ah, the adventure seekers."

"Good name for them. So yeah, we're open." He paused again. "Too bad you live so far away."

Because...?

"Because I think it'd be a lot of fun, being snowed in with you."

Now really, how was she supposed to respond to that?

"It's good you don't have to go outside to reach the bistro. The last thing you need is to slip and fall, and reinjure yourself."

"True. I guess."

It sounded to Maleah as though he'd run out of things to say. And since she had nothing more to ask, either, Maleah said, "I'd better get back to the grandparents."

"You're staying put there, right?"

"My car is buried. Literally. I'm here for the duration."

"Any idea when the plows will reach you?"

"The man across the street is on the county council, and while I was shoveling earlier, he said tomorrow by midnight at the earliest."

"Bummer...but if I know you, you'll make it fun for them. Popcorn, hot chocolate—better still, cooked-on-the-stovetop chocolate pudding. Couple of old movies on TV..." It was so similar to her plan that Maleah wondered if Ian had developed mind-reading talents at Lincoln.

"I'll enjoy it, too," she said. "I haven't spent an over-nighter here since I was in junior high."

"High school, you mean, when your folks went to New York for some sort of police convention. I remembered how furious you were with them when they insisted you couldn't stay home alone."

Because they were convinced a certain someone would worm their way into the house and not leave until ten minutes before Mom and Dad got home.

"I'm going to enjoy every minute. Who knows when an opportunity like this will present itself again. Before we know it, the road crews will get things cleaned up, and that, as they say, will be that."

The silence was so long that Maleah wondered if the weather had caused interference and ended the call.

"I, ah, I think I hear Gladys in the hall. Probably wondering what's taking me so long to get down to the bistro. I'm, I, ah, I'm glad your grandfather is okay. And it's a relief knowing you're safe."

Had she said something to change his mood from jovial and talkative to standoffish and uncomfortable?

"It's good to hear you're on the mend, too. Keep up the good work and—"

"Well, ah, later then."

He hung up, and Maleah stared at the handset. Why hadn't she thanked him for calling?

Or wished him a nice weekend? Or told him to be careful, and not overdo it at the bistro?

"Because you're an airhead."

The worst kind of airhead…who doesn't know her own mind, and who's probably in love with an ex-con.

CHAPTER EIGHTEEN

"YOU SURE ABOUT THIS, dude?"

Ian handed up his shovel, then climbed into the plow's cab.

"I appreciate this, Andy. I know it's out of the way for you."

"You're footin' the bill—enough for that down payment on Helen's new used car—so I'm happy to go a little out of the way."

"Times like these it's good having a pal who's president of his own construction firm."

"Just so you know… I promised Helen's sister, her folks, couple of her teacher friends that I'd plow them out. So this might take a while."

Ian snickered. "You're talking to a guy who stared through steel bars for ten years. I'm a patient man, Andy. Real patient."

But it was a lie. He'd waited nearly fifteen years for a chance like this, and *patient* didn't begin to describe his current state.

The ride was noisy, rough, and when the big machine teetered atop five- and six-foot snowdrifts, borderline terrifying. It took nearly four hours to make the forty-minute trip, and when Andy idled the rig several houses down from the Turners', he said, "You're serious. Every driveway on the street…"

It wasn't nearly as easy, getting off the rig as it had been climbing on, thanks to sore muscles and achy bones. He handed Andy a generous check. "Yeah, the whole shebang."

Pocketing the payment, Andy shrugged. "It's your money."

"And it's our secret."

"I think you're nuts, but okay."

He'd shared his opinion earlier: "Best way to win a woman's heart is to do a good deed for somebody she cares about. A grandpa recently released from the hospital? Can't get much better than that."

If things worked out tonight as he hoped they would, she'd come to him willingly and happily, not because she felt beholden to him.

"How you gonna get home again?"

Ian stood stock-still in the thigh-deep snow, unable to believe he hadn't considered that.

"I, ah, I don't know."

Andy's laughter echoed in the enclosed cab. "No worries, pal. Getting this whole neighborhood plowed out will take until morning.

If you haven't been arrested before then, you can ride back with me. No charge."

Arrested. The word sent a cold chill through him.

"Thanks. You're all heart."

"I'll call you when I finish," he shouted over the plow's diesel engine.

It had been a mistake, asking Andy to drop him this far from her grandparents' drive. Walking on flat ground had been a challenge with crutches, and then the cane. He took his time, but tromping through deep snow made him wince with every step. *If you put yourself in the hospital, you'll only have yourself to—*

"Ian?"

Maleah...

He'd hoped for a few minutes to catch his breath, to pull his thoughts together, and find a way to mask his pain. It lessened some when he took stock of the woman who stood before him, snow-dampened blond curls clinging to her cheeks and forehead, cheeks as rosy as those on the painted cherubic faces of Gladys's Hummel figurines. If she'd ever looked more beautiful, he couldn't remember when.

"What're you doing out in this mess?" he asked.

"Trying to stay half a step ahead of this beastly storm." She followed the narrow path she'd shoveled and met him at the mailbox. "What are *you* doing here? No…" She held up an ice-encrusted mitten. "The better question is, *how* did you get here?"

Ian pointed to the plow just up the street. "Hitched a ride with a friend."

"From Fells Point to Ellicott City. In a snow-plow."

He shrugged. "Uh, yeah."

"Why?"

"So I could see for myself that you're all right."

"And put your own life on the line in the process?"

Ian hadn't realized until that moment that he'd been massaging his aching thigh. He grinned, trying to make light of it. "I'd hardly call the ride over here life-threatening…"

She snorted. "I wonder if your surgeon would agree."

"Good question."

"You look awful," she said. "Pale, dark circles under your eyes… You arranged for that plow, didn't you?"

"I might've influenced the driver. A little."

"You're shivering." She jammed the shovel into the slip-sliding mound of crumpled snow she'd tossed beside the driveway. "Come inside."

She punctuated the order with a smile, and

linked her arm through his. His heart beat hard. *That oughta warm you up.* "But…your grandparents…"

"They're fast asleep. Have been for hours."

"So," he said as she led him to the back steps, "they have no idea you're out here, alone in the dark, in the middle of a major blizzard."

"No."

"And if you slipped, clunked your head on something—"

"It's snow, Ian. *Snow.*"

"With a half inch of frozen stuff on top of it."

She paused at the bottom of the stairs. "Says the man who traveled miles, on a snowplow, to earn a few brownie points by having my grandparents' driveway cleared."

Ian hung his head. "I'm that obvious?"

She blinked up at him through snowflake-dusted lashes, blue eyes glittering in the golden glow of the porch light. Once upon a time, a look like that might precede a passionate kiss. At the very least, a loving hug.

Maleah took a step closer. Licked her lips. Exhaled a sweet sigh. Those minutes on the dance floor, holding her close enough to feel her heart thrumming against his chest, had been wondrous and memorable…and woke a yearning in him as nothing before it had. Would she actually take another step forward, and bridge the gap that had separated them for so long?

Rattled, hopeful and more than a little scared, Ian decided to take that step, instead…and lost his balance.

He landed on his back in a deep drift, taking her with him, a warm and petite, parka'd blanket that covered him from chin to shins. Instinct made him wrap his arms around her.

Instinct…and an aching desire to hold on to the moment for as long as he could.

He'd heard people say "Time froze," but until now, hadn't experienced it. What seemed a full minute passed as those incredible eyes bored into his, searched his face, then squeezed shut.

When she opened them again, Maleah whispered, "Are you all right?"

"No. I'm not."

Both eyebrows disappeared under wet bangs. "I'll get your snowplow friend to help get you up."

She started to get up, but Ian tightened his arms around her. "The only thing wrong with me," he managed to say, "is…is…"

Where to start? By telling her about the self-loathing he'd experienced every hour since that night at the convenience store? With regrets he'd recited like a litany when sleep eluded him? Or the list of "if onlys" he'd tried so hard to bury in his mind?

"Maybe you shouldn't have braved the elements so soon."

Her lyrical voice, soft as the falling snow, touched a long-forgotten place in his heart. Ian didn't trust himself to speak. Last time she'd brought tears to his eyes had been the day the letter arrived, unopened like the others, demanding that he leave her alone, forever. Eyes burning, he struggled for self-control, and the courage to tell her what he'd come here to say.

"Guess I am a little crazy. Crazy about you," he ground out. "Still. Always." Hands pressed into the snow on either side of his head, she raised up, repeated the mesmerizing study of his face. The pale yellow glow of the porch light haloed her head, making it impossible to tell if her lashes were still damp from the snow...or if she had been moved to tears, too.

"I know."

She knew? He held his breath, waiting for her to follow up with "Me, too." Or "That's how I feel." When she didn't, another old saying came to mind: *No one ever died of a broken heart.*

Right here, in this moment, he wasn't so sure about that.

Her lips touched his, softly, gently, slowly at first.

But only at first. Where he ended and she began, Ian couldn't say. Did she realize that as her kisses slid from his mouth to his cheeks, from his forehead to his chin, she'd awakened every hope and dream he'd secreted away? It seemed she was reaching into his soul. How would she respond after reading years of unanswered love he'd written there?

Had he thumped his head hard when he flopped onto his back? *Open your eyes; it's the only way to know for sure.* He hesitated, because if this was some sort of weird dream, Ian didn't want to wake up. Ever.

"What day is it?"

She'd just turned his world upside down, made him question his sanity, and that's what she wanted to know?

"Saturday. January twenty-third."

"That's what I thought."

She rolled to the left, and lay beside him.

"Let me help you up before you freeze to death." She pressed a light kiss to his cheek. "Besides, what will the neighbors say?" He looked over at her, into eyes that once blazed bright and blue with unabashed love for him. What were the chances he'd see them shine that way again?

She scrambled to her feet, dusted snow from her backside, from the knees of her snow pants.

Then, hands on hips, she said, "Would you look at that?"

Already, the narrow path she'd shoveled from the mailbox to the porch had drifted over.

Snow filled their boot prints, too.

"All that work and what do I have to show for it?"

She might not see any positive results from her hard work, but Ian did: If she hadn't been outside, shoveling at two in the morning, he never would have lost his balance, starting a chain reaction that ended with kisses and sweet smiles…things that would comfort him when this dream ended and he had to face the ugly reality of life without her.

Maleah held out a hand, and he grabbed it, let her help him to his feet.

"I'd forgotten that you're a lot stronger than you look."

"Aren't we all?" she said, brushing snow from his back. "This jacket isn't the least bit waterproof. You know that, right?"

"I, ah—"

"Let's go inside." She mimicked the bunny-hating cartoon hunter: "If you're vewwy, vewwy quiet, I'll make us some hot chocolate and let you dry out beside the fire."

Lord but he'd missed this, missed *her*.

"Well, what are you waiting for, siwwy wabbit?"

"Are you sure about this? With your grandparents asleep upstairs?"

She opened the door and, forefinger to her lips said, "Don't worry. You won't wake them. They sleep more deeply than my folks."

Guiding him onto the bench in the laundry room, Maleah tugged off his snow-caked boots and stood them beside the door, then helped him take off his jacket, gloves and cap, and clipped them onto the clothesline Teresa had strung between the cabinets above the laundry tub before removing her own wet gear and hanging it up.

They made their way into the kitchen as he limped along behind her. "I have a feeling my dreams will be mighty sweet tonight, thanks to you," Ian said.

Her back was to him as she filled the teakettle, so he couldn't see her reaction. "Y'know, on second thought, I should go. Don't want to miss my ride, get you in trouble with your family."

In less than the time it took to utter the words, everything—from the caring light in her eyes to her relaxed posture and affectionate smile—changed. She left him alone in the kitchen, returned with his still-dripping coat.

272   THE MAN SHE KNEW

"You really need something that repels water." Then, as if she regretted doling out that helpful piece of advice, she said, "It probably wouldn't be easy, explaining why I invited the notorious Ian Sylvestry into my elderly grandparents' house, in the middle of a blizzard."

First, capable of robbing a children's charity; now, notorious.

"Sorry I couldn't help you shovel," he said, pulling the stocking cap onto his head.

"Don't give it another thought. I'm sure once Andy makes his way to this end of the block, he'll make quick work of the job."

Had he dreamed that perfect, unforgettable scene outside? If so, maybe he *was* crazy. Yeah, that had to be it. How else could he explain that, for those exquisite moments, he'd talked himself into believing Maleah saw hope for their future, too?

He zipped up and walked toward the back door, wondering what a good parting line might be. He didn't think "It was great, kissing you. Hope we can do it again, real soon" would fly.

"Be sure to thank your friend for us. Who knows how long we'd have to wait for the county to send a plow?"

"Yeah, can't put much stock in what politicians say."

As she reached for the doorknob, Ian reached into his pocket.

"Found this in a little shop on Thames Street the other day." Taking her hand in his, he deposited a silver chain and white enamel daisy pendant into her upturned palm. "The minute I saw it, I thought of you."

She held it up to the light. "It's lovely. But why did it make you think of me?"

"Because I remembered how many decisions you made with your invisible daisy... Pink sweater or white at the blue-light-special sale. Fries or potato salad with your burgers. An old movie on TV or something new in the DVD player..."

She bit her trembling lower lip. "It's a very sweet gift."

"Surprising, coming from a notorious outlaw, huh."

Eyes and lips narrowed, Maleah opened the door. "Thank you, Ian, for arranging for the plow—I know you did it to ease the family's mind, in case Grampa needed to go back to the hospital—and for this, too." She closed her fist around the daisy, let the chain dangle between her fingers. "I'm sorry if I seem ungrateful. It's just..."

He sandwiched her fist between his hands.

"You don't owe me anything, not even an explanation."

Ian opened the door and stepped outside. What more could he say except "Sleep well, Maleah. Keep me posted on Frank's progress."

With that, he ducked into the collar of his coat and, hands pocketed, walked away, praying with every difficult step that Andy wouldn't ask how things went.

CHAPTER NINETEEN

MALEAH LEANED INTO the mirror above the guest room dresser and, satisfied the daisy pendant was hidden in her turtleneck, headed downstairs to start breakfast.

She'd slept all of two hours, most of it tossing and turning, and remembering her bold and brazen attack on Ian. She felt the heat of a blush creep into her cheeks. *You should be ashamed of yourself*, she thought, and nothing—not sleepless nights or moving hundreds of pounds of snow from the driveway—excused or explained her behavior.

Maleah stood at the window, waiting as water filled the coffeepot's carafe. From this vantage point, one might think her grandparents had grown so tired of lawn care that they'd paved the entire yard with white concrete. Sunlight flooded the fenced-in space, painting pale blue shadows behind every glittering wind-blown ripple. Gently sloping drifts inched up tree trunks, making it easy to guess at the snow's depth…

Thirty inches, she calculated, minimum. She and Ian had fallen into a snow heap at least that big. Thankfully, Andy had cleared the driveway and sidewalks, covering up any indentation they might have left behind.

When her lips first touched his, Maleah knew Ian had been stunned. And why wouldn't he be, when the only warmth she'd shown him to that point had been when she leaned into his arms on the dance floor. Learning that he'd arranged to clear her grandparents' drive and every street leading to the main highway had moved her— Water sloshed over the pot's rim, rousing her from her daydream. Grabbing a dish towel, she dried it, then filled the pot's reservoir.

"Add an extra scoop of grounds," Frank whispered, padding into the room in corduroy slippers. "Your grandmother's coffee is as weak as tea."

Maleah stuffed a filter into the basket. "I thought your doctor said no more caffeine."

"I get one cup a day, and by golly, I'm gonna enjoy it."

"Makes sense to me," she said. But instead of the rounded extra scoop of grounds he'd asked for, Maleah only added half that much.

"Is Grams up yet?"

"Yup. She's in the shower." He parted the

curtains behind the corner booth. "Man. It'll take days to dig out of this mess."

She'd let him find out for himself that here on Waterford Street, at least, cleanup wasn't necessary.

"Pancakes for breakfast?" she asked.

He parked himself at the table as Teresa appeared in the doorway. "Sounds good," he said.

"But no eggs," Teresa said, cuffing her plaid shirtsleeves. "Remember what Dr. Peters said."

"Yeah, yeah, yeah...two eggs a week." He scowled.

"I'm impressed with our councilman neighbor," Teresa said. "He said midnight tonight, and beat that time by a whole day."

"No way." Frank stood, said over his shoulder to his wife and Maleah, "That guy makes promises all the time, and I can't think of one he's kept."

Standing at the windows, he surveyed his driveway, walkways and porch. "That politician didn't do this. No way those county guys would have plowed all this. Wouldn't have shoveled the walks, either."

He looked at Maleah. "What's the scoop, kid?"

"How would I know?" Maleah returned to the kitchen.

"You're the one with a hundred big shots in your phone book…"

"If only I had that kind of pull, my job would be a whole lot easier."

Frank and Teresa exchanged a look, something between surprise and suspicion.

Maleah poured their coffee and juice, then started the batter.

"I heard that snowplow last night," Teresa said. "Thought it was wishful thinking, though, so I didn't get up to check it out."

From the corner of her eye, Maleah saw Frank focus on her. She oiled the griddle.

"And I thought I heard a man's voice down here," he said.

"If you ask me, dreams that realistic are proof that you two need to quit snacking before bedtime. You need at least six hours of uninterrupted sleep a whole lot more than ice cream or pudding."

"Or popcorn and hot chocolate?" Teresa asked.

"Okay." Maleah hoped she'd diverted their attention away from male voices. "Good point. But that was special. A once in a lifetime thing. The likelihood we'll get another blizzard like this one in our lifetimes is slim to none."

"Aw, we get hit every ten-twelve years," Frank said.

"But not like this…nearly three feet in twenty-four hours?"

"Okay, I'll give you that."

She poured two circles of batter onto the griddle and, while waiting for the edges to form bubbles, sipped her coffee.

"You gonna keep us in suspense, or tell us who it was?"

Maleah flipped the pancakes, happy to have something to look at besides her grandmother's face. "His name is Andy." Not the whole truth, but not a lie, either. "We went to high school together. Sort of."

She slapped pancakes onto a paper plate and poured two more circles of batter.

"Sort of?" Teresa grabbed three rooster-decorated stoneware plates, distributed them around the table.

"I was a freshman when he was a senior… for the second or third time. But at least he hung in there long enough to get his diploma."

Frank rearranged the silverware, earning a cross look from his wife. "So now he drives a plow for the county?"

Without thinking, Maleah said, "It's his plow. He owns a major construction firm."

"Wait…are we talking about Andy Palmer, that big gawky kid who hung around with Ian?"

Too late to take it all back now, Maleah thought. "One and the same, Grampa."

"Well, I'll be," Teresa said, putting butter and syrup on the table. "I've seen his trucks all over the county."

Frank nodded. "Read an article in *Baltimore Magazine* couple months back. I have to admit, he did pretty good for a kid who didn't go to college."

"Well," Teresa corrected. "He did well."

Maleah brought six pancakes to the table, and went back to the stove to make more for the freezer. Standing here gave her a valid excuse to avoid eye contact. "Makes one wonder," Teresa said, "what your ex is doing these days, doesn't it?" She squirted her stack with syrup. "He didn't attend college, either, did he?"

Maleah saw nothing to gain from telling them he'd earned the equivalent of a degree... at Lincoln.

"Not everyone needs to attend a university, Grams."

"Exactly," Frank said. "Where would all those sheepskin-flaunting folks be without people to do the real work?"

"*I* have a teacher's degree. Are you calling me uppity?"

"'Course not, sweetie. Just highlighting

our granddaughter's very astute point." He leaned over and kissed her cheek. "Besides, I know plenty of cops and firefighters, EMTs, too, who don't have degrees." He took a gulp of coffee. "And we all sleep better knowing they're on the job."

"Ian is sole owner of a very successful bistro in Fells Point." Maleah didn't know what possessed her to say that. Or what prompted her to add, "And lets his dad and aunt live in the apartments above the restaurant, rent free."

"And you know all this because..."

She should have known that providing details like that would awaken her grandfather's interrogation skills.

"We had to talk about *something* other than the Kids First campaign."

"She's right, Frank. It's better to let the boy boast about his accomplishments than encourage a reunion."

Maleah carried more pancakes to the table. She could only imagine how much it would distress her grandmother that, not only had she heard a man's voice last night, but it had been Ian's. And if she found out that Maleah had nearly suffocated him with that long, delicious, heart-pounding kiss? She didn't even want to think about that!

"Have you been to this bistro of his?"

Frank shot his wife a look.

"It's called *Sur les Quais*. French for 'on the water.' And yes, I've been there." She wouldn't tell them how many times… "A few weeks before Thanksgiving, I attended a holiday party in his banquet room, and saw him on the far side of the dance floor. It wasn't until quite some time later that I realized he owned the place."

"Oh yes, I remember now. You went with Kent O'Malley." Teresa wiggled her eyebrows. "Now, *that's* the sort of man you deserve. Rich, powerful, intelligent, and oh so handsome, too. Didn't he play professional football, too?"

"He's a blowhard. Every time I've seen him interviewed, he's bragging about how much he donated to this charity or that. What happened to the old-fashioned principle of doing good deeds just because they need to be done, not because of the glory or free publicity—and tax deductions—they'll buy you?" Frank polished off his coffee. "For all we know, O'Malley served jail time, too," he said, banging the mug down on the table. "Because who knows how he came by his rich and powerful status?" He banged the mug down on the table. "He can keep his money. And, no, he never played pro ball."

Maleah loved him for trying to defend her,

and in a roundabout way, Ian, too. But the subject had agitated him, not a good thing so soon after surgery. And it might cause an argument between him and her grandmother. She decided not to tell them that Kent had asked her to spend New Year's Eve with him.

She turned on the TV. "I wonder if the weather reports will say Mother Nature has finished with us, or that this is just the calm before the next storm."

"I think we're out of the woods," Teresa said. She pointed at the window. "The sun's trying to burn through the clouds."

The anchorman described the aftermath of what the media called Snowzilla: two hundred thousand people without power in the mid-Atlantic region alone, nearly two dozen storm-related deaths, stranded motorists and canceled flights, and hundreds of traffic accidents, all resulting in millions of dollars in damages and lost wages.

"I feel so guilty," Teresa said. "Here we sit, comfy-cozy, while others have no heat, no lights, no food."

Frank slid an arm around her. "When we can get out and about safely, we'll call the county executive's office, find out how we can help."

"Certainly not with manual labor, because you're in no condition to—"

He silenced her with a kiss. Nothing like the kiss Maleah had foisted on Ian, but sweet and loving nonetheless. It made her smile, seeing how much in love they were, even after all their years together.

"New necklace?" Teresa asked.

Maleah's hand automatically went to her chest, surprised it that the necklace now dangled over the collar of her shirt. She sipped her orange juice, buying time.

"Brand new," she admitted.

"Very cute. A little juvenile for a woman of your age, but different strokes for different folks, I suppose."

How odd that Ian remembered her fondness for daisies when her own grandmother hadn't...

If her grandfather had Grams's talent for mind reading, he'd no doubt spout one of his family-famous, paraphrased witticisms: "Don't read more than what's on the page." When the page told the story of how he'd come out in one of the worst blizzards in history while still in recovery from a near-fatal accident to make sure she was all right...

She loved her grandparents, but oh how Maleah wished it was safe to climb into her car and drive home, where she could think clearly and make some hard decisions.

CHAPTER TWENTY

"I THOUGHT YOU had better sense than that,"
Gladys scolded. "What were you thinking,
going out in the middle of the worst storm on
record when you're not fully recovered from
the accident?" She held up one hand. "No,
don't tell me. You weren't thinking."

Ian sat quietly while she delivered acetaminophen and a tall glass of water. His own fault.
If he'd thought to call her, or at least leave
a note...

"I was in a snowplow," he said. A flimsy
defense, but unfortunately, that's all he had.
"When's the last time you saw one of those
stuck in the snow?"

"Oh, and you had a letter from God, I suppose, guaranteeing the motor wouldn't conk
out." She threw both hands into the air. "Did
you even check to see if your friend had some
means to communicate with the outside world
if you *had* been stranded?" He had not.

"Andy said he'd call when he finished the

work, so I assumed he had his cell phone, at least."

"You assumed." She stomped into the kitchen and stirred the pot of chicken soup simmering on the stove. "You know what they say about that word."

Yes, he knew, and it only added to the misery he was in. Every muscle and joint ached, far more, even than during those first days following surgery. That, too, had been his own fault. Gladys dished up a bowl of the steaming brew, then set up a TV tray near his chair. He thought surely she'd crack the thin wooden legs. He'd only seen her this angry on one other occasion: the night he was arrested.

"You're right," he said, "I should have called, or left a note. What can I say? I'm an idiot."

"So was it worth it?"

Gladys might have been referring to any number of things, and rather than rile her further, he sat, quietly sipping soup and waiting for her to tell him.

"Did she even say thank you?"

"Yes."

"Did she mean it?"

"Yeah, I guess."

She sat on the end of the couch nearest his chair.

"Soup's delicious," he said.

"You must think *I'm* an idiot, too, trying to placate me with compliments."

"You're the least idiotic person I know."

"How many idiots do you know?"

"I dunno." He shrugged, and he laughed to hide his pained grimace. "Never took a head count."

"The fact there's more than one only proves the old 'birds of a feather' adage. If you spent less time with empty-headed numbskulls…"

Gladys's voice trailed off, and for her sake more than his own, Ian hoped her vexation had reached his peak.

"I'm genuinely sorry for worrying you, Gladys, and the soup really is good."

Tears shone in her eyes when she said, "If you ever, *ever* do anything like this again, so help me, I'll… I'll give you that butt-whoopin' I've been threatening all these years!"

That would sting a lot less than seeing the hurt and disappointment on her face…the same expression his mother had worn when he'd stubbornly refused to attend her wedding…and Maleah, too, as they led him from the courthouse. If he didn't shape up soon, his tombstone would read:

HERE LIES IAN SYLVESTRY
HURTER AND DISAPPOINTER
OF THE WOMEN WHO LOVED HIM

Gladys's phone rang, a jarring punctuation mark on his epitaph. "Ruthie," she said, "so glad you called." She dragged a kitchen stool into the hall and, began an animated conversation with her sorority sister.

Her friend's name—the same as his mother's—reminded Ian that he still hadn't made that call to England...

Satisfied that he could take care of himself, Gladys had been spending less time at his apartment and more in her own. As soon as she left, he'd dial his mother's number. Provided he could convince Gladys he could take care of himself tonight. Unless he could demonstrate that he didn't ache from scalp to heels, she'd insist on bunking down in the guest room, forcing him to choose: put off the call yet again, or endure another dressing-down—this one *un*deserved—for wanting to reconnect with Gladys's nemesis, Ruth Sylvestry Allen.

Ian took a deep breath and held it as he slid the tray aside and hoisted himself from the chair. On the exhale, he picked up the empty soup bowl and carried it to the kitchen island. *Slow and steady.*

He could almost feel her gaze watching for the slightest hitch in his step. As he helped himself to a second bowl of soup Gladys ended her call and came back inside.

The plan had been simple: fake hunger—everyone knew that pain diminished the appetite—and get to and from his recliner without staggering or scowling with pain. So far, so good. Now if he could get Gladys's mind off the reason he'd ridden a snowplow to Ellicott City in the first place—

"You never answered my question."

Ian was tired, physically and emotionally. He ached from head to toe and wanted nothing more than to get that phone call out of the way and crawl into bed until Cash roused him for their morning walk. But there sat Gladys. Her steadfast tough love had quite literally saved his life. The least he could do was show her the respect and patience she'd earned.

He gentled his voice to ask, "Which question?"

"You took an incredible risk with your life when you did that, Ian…"

Memory of Maleah's kiss resurfaced, along with the memory of her quick mood shift, from loving to withholding. The feelings that had warmed him earlier now chilled him to the marrow of his aching bones. He felt awful that his time at Lincoln made her so wary of him; if he could find a way he'd make it up to her. But he was *done* being toyed with. Gladys would say he deserved better than that. *Gladys* deserved better than that.

"Was she worth it?"

"Maybe, maybe not, but it sure feels good, knowing her grandfather will have a safe route to the hospital if, God forbid, he needs one."

She nodded. Smiled. Patted his hand. "I always liked Frank. He's good people."

"That he is."

"So, is that bottomless pit you call a stomach finally full?"

He hadn't even touched the second bowl of soup.

"Because if you are, I'm going home."

"Sorry," he said again, "that worrying about me kept you up all night."

Bending at the waist, she kissed his forehead. "Get to bed…idiot." She winked. "I love you, too."

Cash followed her to the door, waited for the usual pat-pat-you're-a-good-boy farewell, then trotted back to Ian's side. The dog would need another trip outside before settling in for the night, so Ian worked his way out of the chair, grabbed his coat and Cash's leash, and went out by way of the back door.

"No sense saddling her with a guilt trip, right buddy?"

Cash huffed his quiet agreement, front paws

clicking on the hardwood in anticipation of his walk.

It wasn't easy, finding a clear spot in all the snow where the dog could relieve himself.

Back inside, Ian changed into sweats and scrolled to his mother's number. Ruth lived with her husband and teenage son, so why hadn't he prepared himself for the possibility that a deep-voiced man might pick up? A man with a crisp British accent…

"Hi, uh, this is Ian. Ian Sylvestry."

"Hello. Yes, I know who you are. Mum will be so pleased."

So this was Frederick, his half brother. "I hope I'm not calling too late."

"No, not at all. It's just past ten here." The boy laughed. "I'm always up past midnight, trying to keep up with my studies."

"Ah, well, I'm sorry for interrupting."

"You didn't. It's quite a pleasant diversion, actually." Following a pause, Frederick said, "Would you like me to fetch Mum? I'm sure she hasn't nodded off just yet."

"Oh. She's in bed already, then." He should have known that. "Don't bother her. Just let her know I called, and that she can—"

"We were talking about you just yesterday. Your snowstorm made the news over here, you know. I think it's hilarious the way they're calling it Snowzilla."

"Yeah, hilarious. The American media cracks me up all the time."

"Mum's up," Frederick said. "Every floorboard in her room squeaks. Probably coming out to find out who I'm talking to at this hour." He lowered his voice to add, "She doesn't know it, but I often talk with my girlfriend, long into the night."

"I remember those days." If Ian had a dollar for every time Maleah's dad stomped into her room and unplugged the phone at midnight or beyond...

"Well, here she is. Pleasure chatting with you, brother."

"Same here. Good night, Frederick."

"Ack. Please, call me Fred."

As the boy handed over the phone, Ian heard him say, "He sounds quite nice, Mum. Funny, too. I wish you'd let me talk to him before."

He couldn't hear her whispered response, but it was clear from Ruth's tone that she'd told Fred the same lies she'd told Ian: "He's afraid to talk with you." He'd never asked why, and evidently, neither had Fred. What possible reason could Ruth have for keeping her sons apart?

"Hello, Ian. I'm so glad you called."

"Sorry to call so late, though."

"We're five hours ahead of you. You never were very good at math."

"I'm doing better with it now," he said. "Had to learn. Keeping the books myself is cheaper than hiring a pro."

"How are things going at the bistro?"

"Closed today, thanks to the blizzard. But fine, otherwise."

"You're all right? I mean, you have power and all?"

"We're doing fine here. Some of the suburbs weren't as lucky, though."

"We, meaning Brady and Gladys. How *is* she?"

"She's great. Busy. Active. Ornery as ever."

He'd called to see how *she* was doing, not talk about his aunt.

"Still no husband?"

What difference did that make! "By choice."

"Of course. I didn't mean anything by that."

The conversation was hard work, and Ian didn't much feel like putting more time and energy into it. He'd say a gracious goodbye and promise to call again soon. Maybe once he got the green light from his surgeon, his patience level would rise.

"Did your Christmas gifts arrive?"

But…it was nearly Valentine's Day. "Uh, not yet."

"I thought it best to send them to the post office box."

There were two things wrong with her line of thought: first, that's where his business mail went, and she knew it. She also knew that packages, no matter how small, had to pass through customs before being delivered. He'd mailed their gifts early in November. Amazing, he thought, how not even living with an Oxford professor and having a second son had changed her. Ruth, he'd learned long ago, thought first of Ruth.

"How long ago did you mail them?"

"A week? Two, maybe? I sent it by standard post."

If time allowed, she might give a thought to others. It made him feel sorry for Fred.

"Fred sounds like a great kid. Not the least bit like a—how was it you described him? Oh yeah. 'Fraidy cat.'"

"Thankfully, he has outgrown that."

Yeah, same here, Ian thought.

"He reminds me a lot of you."

"Good grief. For his sake, I hope not."

"You made one mistake, and paid dearly for it. But there's nothing to be gained from living in the past."

The past, where people hoped secrets and sins would die before they had a chance to contaminate the future. Ruth had buried her share of bad memories. He supposed he ought to feel grateful that he hadn't been one of them.

"Are you seeing anyone?"

Tried to... "Nah. No time for dating."

Her soft sigh filtered into his ear. "Ian, sweetheart, you deserve a good woman at your side. Someone to celebrate your successes with, who'll comfort you when things go wrong, keep you warm on cold winter nights."

The way Maleah had kept him warm in the snowdrift before kicking him to the curb? No thanks.

"If such a woman exists, I sure haven't met her."

"What about Maleah?"

Punch to the gut. Giving her up once had been hard enough.

Doing it again...

"Maleah has issues," he said.

"That dreadful, judgmental family of hers, I'll bet."

Judgmental, he'd give her. But dreadful? No way. "They're good people. If I had a daughter, I'd want to protect her from a guy like me, too."

"A guy like you?"

"I committed a crime. Spent time in prison. I have long hair. A beard. Tattoos and an earring. Drive a Harley. You get my drift… Your son isn't exactly what a family of cops wants for their little girl."

"But she isn't a little girl. Maleah is a grown woman with a mind of her own. If they're such good people, why is she afraid to tell them how she feels about you?"

"I don't think she knows how she feels about me."

"In all this time, you haven't asked her?"

Ian hoped Gladys's mind-reading antennae were up, because he sure could use an interruption from her right about now. "Ah, because you're afraid of the answer."

He'd never considered it from that angle.

"Mum," Fred said from the background. "Look at this…"

"I'm still on with your brother, son. Can't it wait?"

"You'll want to see it, I promise. I Googled Ian just now—and Ian, I know you can hear me. And I found this article from the *Baltimore Sun*." Ian groaned. If he hadn't been half-lit on pain meds in the hospital, he never would have agreed to the interview.

"I can save you the bother of reading the whole boring thing," he said. "A few weeks ago, there was an accident. A water main burst and took a house off its foundation. We went in to get the couple who lived there and the roof collapsed."

"It *isn't* boring!" Fred shouted. And at the same time, Ruth said, "Ian! Sweetheart! Why didn't you let me know? Frederick and I would have come immediately." He'd considered it, but Ruth and he hadn't been all that close, even before she ran off. So why worry her with something completely out of her hands?

Ian heard the click that told him the kid had picked up an extension.

"Oh, Ian. It just breaks my heart to know you went through all that alone."

"I wasn't alone."

"Brady and Gladys again…"

"She moved into my apartment."

"But Gladys was a teacher. *I* was a nurse."

"Why can't we go see him now, Mum?"

"You have exams coming up. That school costs a fortune, and your father will flip his lid if you miss any more days."

Ian thought he could almost hear the long distance call dollars whooshing from his bank account as they bickered.

He'd just spent a small fortune to impress a woman who couldn't *be* impressed…

"Well, guys, it's late. It was good hearing

your voices. I'll watch for that package, and when it arrives, I'll shoot you a text."

"Ian, sweetheart, I know international calls are expensive. Hang up, and I'll call you right back."

"But Mum… Dad hasn't sent the check yet this month."

Ian heard whispering, and Ruth, trying to muffle the phone with her palm. He caught some words: "Ian isn't well…" and "…this is our problem…" then "…but Dad left you, not the other way 'round…"

"Guys, guys," he interrupted, "I can hear you. Don't worry about what this is costing, and don't worry about me. What's going on over there?"

"Dad's got himself a *girl*friend."

"Frederick! Didn't I just ask you not to bother Ian with this? Besides, your father and I are working things out."

Almost word for word what Ruth had told him before her dramatic exit on his sixteenth birthday. His aunt, in typical Gladys fashion, had predicted the new marriage would end this way: "Once a cheater, always a cheater. Only question is, which cheater will cheat first, and how long will it take 'em to find someone to cheat *with*!"

"Look, you're both welcome here, anytime. No questions asked, no explanations required."

"See there, Mum? Ian's not resentful *and* he's kind."

Kind of crazy, because where would he put them if they took him up on the offer?

Head pounding and bones aching, Ian stifled a yawn.

"Fred, text me after you two have figured things out."

He rattled off his cell number, wished them well, said he loved them, and hung up. "Good thing you already took your walk," he said to Cash, "'cause the way I feel right now, you'd have to wait until morning."

Ian bolted the door and turned out the lights. In his room, he kicked off his shoes and dropped heavily onto the bed without even pulling back the covers. All things considered, life was as close to perfect as it gets. The business was thriving, family was close by and in good health...

Cash leaped onto the bed and flopped down beside him.

...he had a four-legged pal who thought he'd hung the moon, money in the bank, and his battered body was on the mend.

Eyes closed, Ian began to drift off, thinking, what more could a man ask for?

Ian, sweetheart, Ruth had said, *you deserve a good woman at your side.*

Deserve…

"Cash, ol' buddy, I think I just figured something out."

The dog rested his chin on Ian's uninjured thigh.

"I'm getting what I deserve."

CHAPTER TWENTY-ONE

SHE'D CALLED HALF a dozen times without leaving messages, thinking Ian would recognize her number and return the calls. When he didn't, Maleah dialed him another half-dozen times, and left voice mails... She loved the daisy necklace. How's the cactus garden holding up? Is Cash enjoying walks more now that most of the snow had melted?

And still nothing.

If he really *had* injured himself on the night of the blizzard, she'd have two reasons to feel guilty. One, he'd put his recovery at risk for her, and two, she'd sent him away with little more than a half-baked thank-you. After throwing herself at him.

It was only after she considered calling his aunt that Maleah realized what should have been obvious from the start.

She'd finally pushed him far enough away that he wasn't coming back.

The knowledge should have come as a relief. Instead, every day that passed, she found it more difficult to concentrate at work. The only time she could truly focus was when a special needs child and parents were in her office.

On Valentine's Day, since she and Eliot were, as he put it, unattached, he suggested they share a pizza at Leonardo's and catch a movie. It stung, but Maleah laughed right along with him, pretended the pizza tasted terrific, and cringed when he did as giant metal dinosaurs consumed unsuspecting townsfolk.

The 5K was slated for the first weekend in April, just weeks from now. Mere weeks after that, Washburne's annual Trek to the Mountains. Thankfully, she'd booked campground space near Rocky Gap months ago, but she hadn't reserved buses to drive teachers, kids and parent chaperones to the Alleghenies, hadn't lined up a single interview with staffers or volunteers for the marathon, either.

All facts that hadn't escaped Stan's observant eye.

He marched into her office one afternoon and, arms crossed over his chest said, "What in the name of all that's holy is going on with you, girl?"

This, she thought as he stood, cowboy boots shoulder width apart, is what Mr. Clean might look like in a suit and tie.

"I, um, going on? With, ah, with me?"

He puffed up his cheeks and let the breath out slowly. "Stuff like that, right there!" he bellowed, pointing at her. "Stammering and stuttering, looking like Little Girl Lost…that isn't you. At least, it didn't used to be."

Stan plopped into the chair beside her desk. "Now, hon, I realize things have been a little hairy in your world these past couple months, what with your grandpa's heart thing, and playing catch-up after the blizzard, but good golly, kid, I would've bet my new Caddy that you'd bounce through it like one of those superballs my grandkids toss around the house."

Grandkids? He didn't seem like a "sit on my lap and I'll tell you a story" guy. "Out with it, girl. I promised the little woman dinner at The Charleston."

"I'm fine. Really. Just a lot to do." She patted her in-box. "And not enough hours in the day."

"See, now you're *really* scaring me. The Maleah I know and love could juggle six oranges while spinning a dozen plates on bendy poles."

"Wow," she said, laughing, "even I admire *that* Maleah!"

"It's Ian, isn't it?"

"Ian? Ian Sylvestry?"

He got up so fast that, for an instant, the chair came with him.

"Kids today, my own included, drive me

plumb crazy. You want something, go after it! Don't like something, put a stop to it! If you're waiting for somebody to hand you a script, you'll be waiting until you're pushin' up daisies."

What any of that had to do with Ian, Maleah didn't know. But by the look on Stan's face, she had a feeling she was about to find out.

"Somebody's gotta make the first move, and men his age," he tapped his temple, "they're *thickheaded.* Pick up that phone and arrange a face-to-face. Tell him what he needs to hear, or demand he say what *you're* waiting for. Then kiss and make up and get back to being reliable Maleah. There are a lot of people, me included, counting on you, y'know."

He started for the door. "Well? What're you waiting for?"

"A little privacy?"

Stan smiled. "I feel better already."

After ten minutes of pretending to read the file on her desk, she picked up her desk phone's handset. Stan had a point.

By now, she knew all three of his numbers by heart. Maleah dialed the apartment first.

"Leaving a message to say I'm thinking about you and hope you're better. Call me." Next, she punched in his cell phone's digits.

"Called your apartment, left a message.

Maybe instead of calling me back, you should call the cops, because not hearing from you makes me feel like a stalker."

Last on the list, the bistro. Someone had to answer that phone.

"*Sur les Quais*, how may I help you?"

"Hi Terri, it's Maleah."

"This is Linda, Terri's mom. She's home with Avery."

"Uh-oh. Picked up a cold at school, huh?"

"Yes, and it's a doozy. I'm just standing in until he's back in school."

"I hope he's better soon. Is Ian in his office by any chance?"

"I think so."

"Do me a favor? Don't tell him it's me. I want to surprise him."

"O-o-kay, whatever you sa-a-y…"

What does she know that I don't?

"Hey."

"Hey, yourself. It's me."

"I know."

"But… Linda said she wouldn't tell you it was me."

"She knows how much I hate surprises." He cleared his throat. "So what can I do for you?"

She recognized his "want to make a reservation or book the banquet room" voice. "Couple of things, actually. Let me buy you dinner. It's kind of a lot to go into over the phone. Wait. Scratch that. You own a restaurant. Why would you want to go out to eat? I can make something at my place. Lasagna. Meatballs. Garlic bread. Tiramisu."

"You planning to murder me, 'cause that sounds like a last meal."

It very well could be his last meal...with *her*.

"The bistro is closed on Mondays, right?"

"Not since New Year's."

"Then...you choose a night."

"What's wrong with tonight?"

"Nothing, except...you're working."

"The crew can get along without me for a couple hours."

"But it's nearly four o'clock."

"So?"

With every second that ticked painfully by, it became clearer that Ian had no intention of making this easy for her.

"So it takes hours to make sauce from scratch. And I'd need to stop by the store for ground beef. All the cheeses. Noodles. Do you have any idea how long it takes to make homemade lasagna and tiramisu from scratch?"

"Matter of fact, I do."

Of course he did. "It'll be midnight before dinner's ready."

"Good point. Order a pizza then."

"I wanted to cook for you, though, as a goodwill gesture."

"You started off asking me to dinner at some random restaurant…"

Maleah heard one quick click, and would have bet her lighthouse collection that he'd just snapped his fingers and whispered "Gotcha!"

"All right. Pizza. Is six o'clock too early?"

"Nope. See you then."

I hope you appreciate this, Stan. She grabbed her coat from the hall tree. *Something tells me I'm about to begin the longest, hardest night of my life.*

THE WEATHER HAD warmed enough that Ian could have ridden the bike to her house. But the doctor had said that although his body hadn't rejected the steel pin in his left leg, one good twist or bump could damage the tibia.

So he'd driven the pickup, but made sure to look every bit the Harley-driving ex-con she believed him to be. He'd spent the entire time between her call and leaving the apartment doing what Gladys called *gussying*. His plan wouldn't work unless he dressed the part: faded jeans with a frayed hole in one knee, plaid shirt with a half-torn pocket, scuffed biker boots, and a baseball cap worn backward.

She valued punctuality, so he showed up ten minutes late.

She hated it when people rang the bell repeatedly, so he leaned on it for all he was worth.

As if on cue, the deep-green-painted door swung inward, and he stepped inside before she had a chance to ask him to.

"How was traffic?"

"It's Baltimore. What more can I say?"

Maleah went from gnawing her lower lip to plucking at her cuticles, sure signs he'd made her nervous. Ian didn't like seeing her this way— didn't like being the cause of her distress, either.

But, as someone once said, "It's a tough job, but somebody's gotta do it."

"Nice place." He walked into the living room. Would have swaggered, except it hurt to do that. "Been here long?"

"Couple of years."

She started for the kitchen, and he followed before she could ask him to.

"I made iced tea and lemonade…"

Such a sweet, innocent face, but he couldn't let it shake his resolve.

"How about half and half."

He noticed the pizza box in the middle of the table. "How long has it been here?"

"You probably ran into the delivery boy on your way up the walk."

So he couldn't complain about hating cold pizza… Maybe the tea or lemonade would be too sweet. Or not sweet enough.

Their fingers touched when she handed him the glass, and Maleah pulled back as if stuck by a pin. He hated doing this to her.

It has to be done…

But did he have the stomach for it?

If you want to end this, you'll have to develop one.

She poured her own drink. "Wish I looked half as well-rested."

"Amazing what a clear conscience will do for a body."

He'd never heard napkins and paper plates hit the table with more force. And that face… Ian didn't think he'd ever seen her this angry before. With any luck, it would all be over before the first slice of pizza left the box.

"I know what you're doing, Ian."

Impossible, he thought; he'd only figured it out a few hours ago, himself.

"But it won't work. It takes two to argue."

The lid of the pizza box creaked quietly when she opened it to help herself.

He sat across from her and took a piece. If she meant it, he'd have a fight of a different kind on his hands.

"How's Cash?"

"Good. Almost brought him tonight."

"You should have. He's a great dog."

Not only didn't he have the stomach for this, as it turned out, Ian didn't have the backbone, either. She was hurting, and he'd been the cause. *Just get it out there, and get yourself out of* here.

"So why am I here?"

Placing the pizza on her plate, she dabbed the corners of her mouth with a napkin. "I need to apologize. First, because I was out of line the night of the snowstorm. Way out of line, not just with that ridiculous kiss—"

"Ridiculous?" He blew a two-note whistle. "Maybe I'm the one who should apologize. As I remember it, I gave as good as I got."

A bright pink flush colored her cheeks. "I'm not talking about the kiss itself. I'm talking about the way I… Let's just say it wasn't my most ladylike moment."

"Another way men and women are different. In my opinion, you were never more *woman*."

The blush deepened as she said, "Well, still. It never should have happened."

"Why?"

She opened her mouth only to clamp it shut again. "I didn't thank you properly for everything you did that night."

"There she goes again, seesawing like a

campaigning politician." He grinned to show he was teasing, but Maleah plowed onward.

"I can only imagine what it cost to hire Andy."

"Maybe he did it out of the goodness of his heart. Ever think of that?"

"Oh, please. I never got to know him well, but he's a businessman. It makes no fiscal sense that he'd fuel up a piece of equipment that size, expose it to wear and tear, without getting something in return."

Ian shrugged, took a bite of his pizza. "Free lunch at the bistro?"

She continued as if he hadn't interrupted. "So, thank you for what you did. It eased all of our minds knowing we could get out in an emergency."

And sliding her thumb under the silver chain around her neck, Maleah freed the little white daisy he'd given her that night.

"Thanks for this, too. It was a sweet, thoughtful gift."

"Was…"

"My attitude took the shine off it. And I'm sorry about that, too."

"It's real silver. So it shouldn't lose its shine…"

"Ian, come on. Meet me halfway, at least."

"Okay. I'll accept your apologies...if you'll accept mine."

Genuine surprise widened her eyes. "But you didn't do anything."

"Oh, yeah, I did. I robbed a store."

"That wasn't you. It was the other guys."

"I knew what was going down, and did nothing to stop it. That's caused trouble between you and your family since day one. I robbed you, too, that night, of your ability to trust in anyone, least of all your choices in men."

"That isn't true."

"Then why is a woman as wonderful as you still single?"

Whether Maleah hung her head because she agreed that he was largely responsible for her marital status, or because, like him, she'd held tight to a hope that could never be fulfilled.

"If I hadn't been such a fool, we'd be married now. We'd have a couple kids. Maybe Cash would, too."

That, at least, produced the hint of a smile on her face, and eased his guilt.

But he hadn't come here to make either of them feel good. The sole reason he'd accepted her invitation had been to say goodbye. Not in the literal sense, because some of their charity work would still overlap. But the love that had bonded them one to the other...

"You trimmed your beard."

Ian stroked his chin. *So much for trying to look like a rough-around-the-edges criminal.*

"Just a little."

"What's the real reason you wear it?"

"Thought I told you…to hide a scar."

"Lots of people have scars."

So far, he'd taken two bites of the pizza, yet despite having just two coffee-dunked cookies and a handful of oyster crackers to eat that day, Ian didn't feel the least bit hungry. Breaking hearts, it seemed, was a great appetite suppressant.

"I think I get it," she said. "If it wasn't hidden, every glance in the mirror would remind you of Lincoln."

Ian started to deny it, but she already knew that in his opinion, it made no sense to hide his past, neither on a personal nor a professional level.

"The scar is…" She lifted both shoulders and, palms up, said, "It isn't about some inmate meting out his insane brand of prison justice. It's a reminder of who you used to be. You don't like that person very much, so…"

He leaned back, stretched out his legs—far easier to do now that the cast was gone.

"Boy. You don't even need a hammer to hit the nail on the head, do you?"

"I'm sorry if I overstepped my bounds."

"You didn't. We're friends."

"Friends…"

Disappointment rang in her voice. There'd be plenty of time to cope with the guilt and self-recrimination of causing that. Right now, Ian needed her to hear him out. "You know I have a one-track mind," he began, "so do me a favor and just listen for a minute, okay, because I need to say this before I chicken out. Again."

Hands folded on the table, Maleah sat up straight. "Let me have it, *friend.*"

"You already know that I fell for you in the school library when you stood in front of a guy twice your size and blasted him and his friends for stuffing a kid into a locker. The robbery, Lincoln, time, nothing—*nothing*—changed that."

She'd obliged his request, and sat ramrod straight and silent, blinking those long-lashed eyes and squeezing her hands together. He couldn't tell what she was thinking. Not that it mattered. He'd made a promise to himself, hand on his grandfather's Bible and everything: This ended today.

"I love you. Probably always will. One of the reasons is, you're too nice to tell me flat out that it'll never work. So I'll say it: *It. Will. Never. Work.* Not with fourteen—no, it's fifteen now—not with fifteen years, four cops and two angry women between us." He frowned, drove a hand through his untethered hair, groaned with frustration. "Wait. That came out wrong. It sounds like I'm asking you to choose me over your family. I'm not. *Definitely* not. You have to believe that. Say you believe that."

"I believe you, Ian."

"Whew. Anyway, let me start again, and shoot for nonthreatening and nonaccusatory this time.

"We were great together...as naive kids. But we're older and wiser now. We both know there were better ways for me to grow from a smart-mouthed kid with a chip on his shoulder to the man I am today."

"I like the man you are today."

Ian couldn't afford to believe it. Not even for a split second.

"I'm done, Maleah. Just...done. Tired of hanging on to something that never had a chance to develop into anything more than it was at its inception...an innocent teenage infatuation."

There. He'd said his piece. And she hadn't flipped the rest of the pizza onto his lap. Her calm demeanor told him she agreed...just because they couldn't be a couple shouldn't stop them from being friends.

If he had anything to say about it, Maleah would never hear how he really felt: Her family *was* the reason she'd cut him off then, why she couldn't make up her mind about him, now. For him, it had always been full-out, no holds barred, one-hundred-percent love. He'd never stand between her and them, but if what they'd shared—what they could share—wasn't worth telling the hard truth to her family, then she wasn't worth fighting for. It had taken time, but he'd adjusted to life at Lincoln…and he'd adjust to life as only her friend, too. "I hear Washburne is sponsoring a camping trip to the mountains," he continued. She blinked. Maybe Maleah had expected him to give her a chance to speak her mind, too. Well, it may seem harsh, but she'd had a hundred opportunities to do that, and let each pass at his expense.

"Did Stan tell you that?"

"No, Terri. She signed Avery up for the trip. But her mom's surgery is scheduled for the same week. So she asked if I'd stand for her."

"Nothing serious, I hope."

"Double knee replacement. She'll need help that first week."

"You said yes?"

"Sure. Terri's a friend. And I think the world of that kid of hers. I'd hate to see him miss out again this year."

She nodded slowly.

"I've been camping plenty of times. Got all kinds of gear in the storeroom behind the bistro. My tent sleeps six, so if there are other kids without chaperones..."

"I'll look into it. Thank you."

"I've already filled out the paperwork, and Terri signed it. So if you need help in the planning phases, what to pack, what to expect, stuff like that, let me know."

"That's very thoughtful of you, but this isn't Washburne's first camping outing."

"So I've heard."

"You know because Avery couldn't go last year."

"Or the year before. He's pretty psyched." Ian forced a grin. "Wants to pitch a tent in his basement this weekend. I told him we couldn't build a fire down there, so he agreed we'll conduct the test in his backyard, instead."

"Sounds like fun." She paused. Ian tried not to let it bother him when their conversation went back to being stiff and formal. Maleah would come around to the friendship idea, or she wouldn't. Either way, he'd made up his mind, and made himself clear: after tonight, there'd be one fewer rubber ball in her toy box.

MALEAH HADN'T ASKED for a camping gear list, but Ian provided one, anyway. And because it was far more complete than the old one, she made copies to include with the information folders. She opened the get-acquainted meeting by handing out the packets, and gave everyone time to peruse the contents.

Without exception, moms and dads, teachers and counselors agreed it was the most efficient compilation of its kind they'd seen.

"Your friend is remarkable," the administrator said. "He thought of everything from flashlight batteries to zipper bags for collecting rocks and bugs."

Her friend.

"I'm just glad he'll be with us in the woods." The counselor shivered. "I don't know the first thing about the woodland creatures that live on Ragged Mountain!"

"Don't worry," Maleah assured. "Most of us have made the trip before. We'll gather everyone together and talk about all that once we arrive."

"I hope it'll include a lesson on building and maintaining a fire," one of the dads said. "Left to my own devices, I'd burn down the forest."

"We'll do our best to teach you everything you need to know. We want you to stay safe, but we hope you'll have fun, too."

Stan, who'd assumed the role of camp director, stepped up front.

"As Maleah said," he told the worried mom,
"we've all been there before, and learned a lot
with each trip. The campground makes their staff
available to answer any questions we can't...
and as I said, we've done this before, so there
won't be many." He gave a brief speech about
the route, recommended supplies, meals in the
campground's mess hall, and transportation, then
drew their attention to the camp's map, high-
lighted on an old-fashioned roll-up screen.

"We'll go over this again, of course, but I
hope you'll each take a few minutes to study
the map included in your folder. Once we've
assigned campsites and everyone is settled in,
we'll meet up again for a walking tour, so you'll
know which areas are off-limits."

"Is it dangerous? I mean, should we be worried about bears or wildcat attacks?" asked a
guy in the front row.

"There has never been a cat sighting in the
Town Creek Campground, but just to be on the
safe side, you might want to pack some tuna
treats to distract the cat while you're making
your getaway."

Laughter filled the room.

"Seriously, folks, the place is perfectly safe.
You'll find the staff friendly and helpful, and

those of you who've been there with us before know how hard we try to keep your kids—and you—safe as babes in their mamas' arms. That lovely young lady over here," he said, pointing to Maleah, "pulled this event together."

Smiling, Maleah gave a little wave.

"If you don't already have a tent, sleeping bag, backpack or first-aid kit, come see me," Stan continued, pointing to a stack of supplies in the corner.

"They're included in our registration fee?" a woman in the back row asked.

"No, ma'am, they are not. They were purchased and delivered by Ian Sylvestry, who asked that we distribute them to folks who need them. They will be yours to keep."

Quiet murmurs now circled the room.

"Where is he?"

"You'll get a chance to meet him on Monday in the high school parking lot where we board the buses."

The meeting ended, and while attendants gathered around the refreshments table, Stan pulled Maleah aside.

"You make me proud, girl. I tell ya, it's hard to believe that just a few weeks ago, you seemed unprepared for this meeting."

"I had a little help."

"Sylvestry?"

"Yes, and my secretary. My next door neighbor pitched in, stuffing information into the folders."

"Well, you assembled a good team, as always." He gave her shoulder a fatherly squeeze. "Now admit it, aren't you glad I persuaded you to call Ian?"

"Of course. As it turns out, he's becoming a good friend."

"Friend? You wouldn't kid an old man, would you?"

From across the room, a woman hollered, "Maleah, can you come here for a moment?"

It was Mrs. Bealle, who'd honed her talent for finding problems to a keen edge. It was just as well. Maleah would rather help look for a solution than talk with Stan about Ian.

Saved by the Bealle, she thought.

"Sorry, Stan, but duty calls."

"You can run," he called after her, "but you can't hide."

Wanna bet?

TWO DAYS LATER, Maleah was the first to arrive at the high school parking lot. The sun burned bright in the cloudless sky, and a calm breeze rustled the trees' newly-unfurled leaves. Weather analysts predicted lower temperatures and the possibility of storms later in the week, and she hoped they were wrong. No one enjoyed huddling in a damp-floored, leaky tent, even during a gentle rain. But with Washburne's sensitive-to-noise kids, wind, thunder and lightning had the power to take the campground from calm to chaotic in seconds.

She unlocked the trunk and reached for her wheeled backpack.

"Let us get that for you."

"Ian, Avery, good morning. I didn't even hear you pull up."

"I'm so excited!" the boy said, flapping his hands as Cash cozied up for a pat. Maleah obliged them both, stroking the dog's nose, then drawing Avery into a sideways hug.

"We're gonna have a blast."

"You bet we are, pal."

"Hey, can I climb on that wall over there?"

Ian followed the line of his pointer finger. "Yeah, I guess. But no jumping down from it. We don't want to go to the emergency room instead of the campground, do we?"

"Okay. I'll be good."

Hands flapping excitedly, he ran off, leaving Maleah with Cash and Ian.

"I'm glad you brought him along," she said, bending to kiss the top of his furry head.

"It'll be good for the kids to learn about search and rescue dogs."

She glanced around the lot. "Did someone drop you off?"

"Gladys needed my truck. So I'm driving her car." He pointed to a sporty red coupe. "Took a while to unfold myself from behind the steering wheel, but listening to that motor purr made it worth it."

He grabbed the backpack's handle and tugged. "Holy smokes! There are plenty of rocks around this place. Why would you bring more?"

"Ha-ha. I loaded the bag into the car myself, so I know it isn't that heavy. But thanks for saving me a bonk on the head." She narrowly missed clipping her forehead as she slammed the trunk closed. "See what I mean?"

"We need to find you a stretching machine, short stuff," he said, patting her head, "so things like that won't happen anymore."

They both leaned back against her trunk to watch Avery. On the other side of the parking lot, he pretended to walk a tightrope atop the three-foot-wide brick wall.

"If the powers that be ever see fit to give me a son, I'd want him to be just like him."

"He's a good kid, all right." Maleah nodded. Shading her eyes, she looked toward down the road. "The buses ought to start arriving soon. The kids, too."

"And the counselors."

"And the teachers."

"And Stan."

Maleah groaned. "He means well. I think."

The first of six yellow school buses lumbered toward the center of the lot. Close behind it, an SUV and a modest sedan.

"Are you ready for this?"

She shrugged. "Ready as I'll ever be."

"Let's make a deal, before the rest of 'em roll in." Ian held out his hand. "If I get into any hairy situations, I'll find you."

"Ditto."

They shook on it and grinned. This friendship thing might just work after all.

The woman in the SUV climbed out of the passenger seat. Young, curvy, with long glistening auburn hair. Ian noticed her, too. This might work as long as she didn't have to watch him admire other women.

But she had no right to feel jealous. Friendly distance was exactly what her surly behavior told him she wanted. "They're calling for storms. What's the plan if they're right?"

"Panic."

Eyebrows high on his forehead, he looked into her face.

"Kidding. Just kidding." Maleah gave his shoulder a playful slap. "We'll start by making sure everyone knows to head straight for the clubhouse at the first sight of lightning. I've made clipboards for teachers and chaperones, names and ages of each child in their charge, and individual things to watch for."

"Things they're scared of, or haven't done before, you mean."

"Right. Plus, who can't swim, who tends to disappear, who gets stuck in the tree branches…"

"Looks like folks intend to show up on time."

"Parents of kids on the spectrum keep things calm and organized, starting out with a strict schedule. It helps with just about everything." Bus drivers paced near the open doors of their vehicles, while parents offloaded their children's packs. Counselors and teachers headed for Maleah.

"You know what I feel like?"

"Queen bee in the hive?"

"I was going to say Mother Goose, but I like yours better. Guess I'd better buzz on over there, make sure this trek starts off on a sweet note."

Since Avery left them to teeter atop the wall, Ian had only taken his eyes off the boy long enough to admire the lady from the SUV.

"You keep this up, you'll be bleary-eyed and jittery when we leave that campground."

"Keep what up?"

She could have said "Ogling pretty women," but chose to say, "It's impossible to watch him every minute. That's why we assembled so many volunteers. And why we'll hang name tags round their necks." He nodded, and she added, "Want me to hold off on the 'let's do this' pep talk until you round up Avery?"

"Can you do that?"

"'Course I can. I'm the queen bee. Meet me in front of bus number seven." Had Ian heard her? Maleah couldn't tell. But he was a big boy—a big, handsome boy—and no doubt he'd figure it out.

Keep thinking that way and this friendship thing will fall before it takes off.

She'd never been a woman who settled. But she'd do it in this case, because having spent so many years without him, Maleah would take friendship over absence, any day.

CHAPTER TWENTY-TWO

AFTER SUPPER ON the third day at Town Creek Campground, the aftereffects of two all-nighters presented themselves. Yawning, Ian walked beside Avery, pointing out the types of twigs that made good kindling, and the stems in the ground that, in just a few weeks, would develop three reddish-gold leaves each.

"You know what it's called?"

Avery kept his distance. "Poison ivy. When it gets big enough, it'll climb up the trees and if anyone touches it, they'll be sorry."

Ian ruffled his hair. "Did your mom teach you that?"

"Yes. She likes to walk. Walking is good for the soul."

"She's right. And a good teacher, too. You're lucky to know how to recognize things like this in the woods."

The boy yawned and knuckled his eyes.

"Sleepy?"

"Yes." He looked up at Ian.

He sat on a folding camp stool, gestured toward a second. "Have a seat, Avery, so we can talk a bit before you turn in."

"Can I ask a question?"

"Sure you can. What's up?"

"How come the kids have to be quiet and get to bed by nine o'clock, but some of the grown-ups get to make so much noise that nobody can sleep?"

"That's a very good question. In fact, I was wondering the same thing. And you know what?" He reached out, gave the boy's forearm a gentle squeeze. "I'm going to talk to the boss about the problem, just as soon as we get you zipped into your sleeping bag."

"Awesome. Thanks, Ian!"

"Did you brush your teeth?"

"Not yet, but I'm gonna. Will you go to the community center with me?" The restrooms, attached to each end of the building, could be intimidating to autistic kids. Even when empty, the constant flicker of bright fluorescent lights, reflected by a dozen mirrors and stainless steel stall doors, set off an optical commotion in the kids' heads. Add three or four more excitable kids to a room where even the sound of a penny hitting the tile floor echoed from every surface, and you had the makings of a full-blown anxiety attack.

"You bet. And as long as I'm in there, I might

as well brush my teeth, too. But first, let's find some wood, so we can feed the fire during the night. I hate to wake up cold, don't you?"

"Yeah."

He high-fived Ian, who stacked logs in the crook of his arm, carried them to the tree nearest their tent, and placed them one atop the other.

"Looks like a pyramid," Avery observed, hands together to form a triangle.

"Let's make another one on the other side of the tree."

"We can make three, and then the pyramids will be pyramids!"

Ian didn't get it, but somewhere inside that brilliant mind, it made perfect sense.

It took half an hour to complete their chores and stow their toothbrushes in airtight plastic containers. Garbed in fleecy sweats and thick socks, the boy slid into his sleeping bag and waited for Ian to zip up the sides.

"Why do bears have better noses than people do?"

Obviously, Avery had been paying full attention when Maleah explained the importance of storing away anything that might attract bears, coyotes or even raccoons.

"Here's how I see it… We can go into any fast-food store and say, 'One burger, please!'"

"And an ice-cream cone!"

The sleeping bag's plaid lining muffled Avery's giggle.

"Can you imagine what the people who work there would say if a big ol' bear lumbered up and said the same thing?"

"They'd scream. And run. Or throw pots and pans at it."

"They don't *like* scaring people, but that's just how things are. And can you imagine eating nuts and berries, every day, all day, for the rest of your life?"

"Bo-o-o-ring."

"You said it. But do bears complain?"

"I would if I was one… 'Waa-waa-waa, the mean restaurant people won't sell me fo-o-od, and I'm tired of woodsy stuff.'"

"Yup. So they sniff the air and smell the ground to find things that *don't* smell like nuts and berries."

"Stuff like toothpaste."

"And trail bars."

"And candy."

"Especially candy."

"But bears are a little selfish. And scare easily. So if they rousted out some cookies or brownies, and there was a person near it? They'd think 'uh-oh, he's going to take my treat.'"

"So *that's* why they attack people?"

"That's one of the reasons."

"How many reasons are there?"

Kids like Avery were very literal. So Ian said, "Nineteen."

"When will you tell me about the other eighteen?"

As soon as we have Wi-Fi and I can look it up.

"After we get home, and make sure your grandmother is all right."

"Okay," he said around a sleepy yawn.

"I'm going to see if I can find Maleah, tell her how we feel about all the noise." He tucked the cover around the boy's chin. "Stay tucked in there, okay? Weatherman said it's only going to be thirty degrees tonight."

He dimmed the lantern and ducked out the tent's flap as Avery said, "…love you, Ian."

After hearing that, it took a second or two to gather his composure. "Some kid," he whispered.

"Yes, he is."

"Holy smokes, girl. Sneak around much?"

Smiling, Maleah said, "I was just checking in to see how you boys are doing."

"Funny thing, that…" He led her farther away from the tent. "What's with all the racket at the other end of the campground?"

"The banjos and guitars, you mean?"

"And accordions."

"I'll have a word with them."

"Good. Saves me the trouble of doing it at tomorrow's meeting." He held up his fist again.

She wrapped warm fingers around his. "Put that thing away. Somebody's liable to see it who doesn't know you're all bark, no bite."

Ian didn't mind that she no longer thought him incapable of violence. Liked it so much that he had to resist the urge to pull her to him in a big hug. The only thing stopping him was wondering whether or not she meant it.

And then that kiss came to mind...

"Well, I'd better get back to my side of Tent Town," she said, looking gorgeous standing there in the firelight.

"Yeah, it's been a long day."

He waited until she disappeared into her tent to add logs to the fire. Thunder rolled in the distance, and he hoped it would stay to the west.

Maleah exited her tent and looked at the sky. She'd heard the incoming weather, too. He had an idea that might prevent pandemonium, and hurried over to ask if she agreed.

"Not a sliver of moon nor the spark of a star," she said when he approached. "How about if we pass the word to the counselors...tell the old 'the angels are bowling' story to the kids before the storm reaches us. Even if they've heard it before, it might ease some anxiety."

"Let's do it."

Ian walked north, Maleah moved south to deliver the message. Word spread fairly quickly among the campers, and before long, the area was abuzz with a cacophony of voices, each sharing the bowling angels tale.

And then, the blessed peace of Cash's quiet snores and Avery's steady breaths. Tree frogs, peeping from every branch, harmonized with the few crickets that decided to brave the sometimes-cold spring nights. Times like these, it was easy to forget that just a few miles away, traffic whooshed by on Maryland's Interstate 68. Now and then, the far-off wail of the train's horn floated down from the tracks that paralleled the Potomac, and lulled Ian to sleep.

He didn't know how much time had passed when the sound of thunder woke him, but from the sound of things, it was raining on Warrior Mountain. If anyone else heard it, they weren't stirring yet. Easing from the sleeping bag, he made his way to the tent Maleah was sharing with her secretary and an autism counselor, thinking to offer his help in guiding kids to the community house before the storm reached its full peak. Standing at the back of the shelter, he whispered her name, twice. In one moment, he heard the soft snarl of her sleeping bag's zipper; in the next, she joined him outside, the bag draped over her shoulders.

"You heard it, too?"

"How soon do you want to round 'em up?"

"Before the rain starts. No sense letting the kids get wet. They'll be miserable enough, crowded into the hall until it passes."

The wind picked up and changed direction, and she tugged her thick, zippered cape tighter around her.

"It could blow over. Or go around us."

Nodding, she gathered up the bag and, taking care not to let it touch the ground, bent to step through the flap.

"Let's tell them tent by tent, same as before."

She nodded in agreement and took a last glance at the sky. "I really hate waking the children if it's going to fizzle out before it hits."

"They've had three great days walking the trails, learning to identify critter tracks, collecting bugs. Even if they went home right now, they'd say a good time was had by all."

Taking a knee, he picked up the long stick she'd been using to stoke her campfire. It wasn't out, but it soon would be.

"Go ahead and do what you need to," he said,

stirring the coals. "Soon as I get this going again, I'll wake Avery, have him get—"

A young woman ran up to them. "He's gone," she cried. "Billy isn't in the tent!"

Ian straightened. "Let's not panic, Jen." *Yet*... "What time did you turn in?"

"Ten-thirty, quarter of eleven, maybe?"

"And Billy was sound asleep?"

"Yes. I remember worrying I'd wake him, zipping up the tent flap."

"What woke you just now?"

"I'm not sure."

His watch said one-thirteen. No telling how long ago Billy slipped out of his tent, or which way he'd gone.

"He probably just crawled into a friend's tent."

"Steven, most likely."

"There y'go. You check on that, and we'll look around here."

Once she was out of earshot, Ian asked Maleah to recommend her most qualified counselor.

"Betty."

"Will you see if she can stay with Avery? I'll go explain things to him."

"Definitely." She took off.

Billy's mom showed up, carrying the T-shirt

Billy had worn before changing into a sweat-suit, and handed it to Ian.

"Thanks, Jen. Now, I know how impossible this sounds, but you need to relax. We're going to find him, and when we do, he'll need his mom."

Ian followed as the dog sniffed every corner of every tent.

Still no Billy. So much for the theory that he was sleeping peacefully someplace within Washburne's area of the campground. Ian quickly called SAR.

Maleah raced up, breathless. "The camp director is sending two of his employees to look around. He said kids get lost in the woods all the time, and these guys always find them, happy and healthy...until their parents get hold of them."

"That'll help once the local SAR team gets here."

"What? Already?"

"Walk with me and I'll explain." She fell into step beside him as Ian said, "I put in a call to the operations leader on a lot of my missions. He has a SAR pal up here, says they'll issue a call-out within a few minutes. I told them to meet us right here, so they can set up a base camp and start conducting interviews."

"With Billy's mom?"

"With everybody. Sometimes the weirdest detail points us in the right direction." When they reached the camp director's office, Ian pounded on the door. An elderly woman across the way yelled, "He ain't in there, mister. He's in bed, fast asleep, like the rest of us would be if not for you."

"Sorry, a kid is missing, and we'd like to find him before this storm hits."

"His cabin is up there—" she pointed west "—last one on the left."

"Thanks."

"Good. There's a light on," Maleah said as they approached.

The door flew open and a balding, paunchy man stepped aside. "You the guy who's organizing the call-out?"

"Ian Sylvestry." He stuck out his hand.

"Duke Olinski. Operations leader. You want to take charge of the perimeter search?"

"Nah, your guys already know the terrain. It'll save time if I start knocking on doors and unzipping tent flaps."

"Give me five minutes to get dressed, and I'll meet you in the community center."

"Our group is on their way there," Maleah said.

"We won't take up much space."

"But these are special needs kids, as I explained to the woman who booked our reservation. Noise, activity, flashing lights…not good for them."

"Yeah, I remember that now. Okay, then we'll move into one of the empties." He handed Ian a key ring. "Tall Pines, just two cabins down."

On the way over, Ian said, "You might want to consider canceling the rest of the week. With all the lights and people running around yelling for Billy—and the thunder moving closer—the kids will go bonkers."

"You're probably right."

"Hey." He turned her to face him and, hands on her shoulders, said, "Billy going missing, that's not on you. It's not on his mother, either. He has a penchant for wandering, and from what I've heard, these kids are escape artists."

"Nice of you to reassure me, but I'm the psychologist. I should have assigned a pro to keep an eye on him."

"And insult his mom? That doesn't sound like you."

Stan joined them, huffing and puffing and mopping his brow. "Somebody bring me up to speed. Maybe I can pull a few strings back home to get things moving up here."

Ian said, "You know how you can help, right

here, right now? Start asking questions. Everybody should be under one roof soon, and that'll make things easier for you."

"What sort of questions?"

Ian slipped the pen from Stan's shirt pocket, then picked up a campground brochure to write on.

He scribbled in the margins while he talked:

"First, see if Billy's mom—her name is Jen—can give you his approximate height, weight, shoe size, what he was wearing, if he'd brought any electronic gadgets or stuffed animals on the trip that aren't in their tent now. Then find out from his classmates if they know about Billy's tendency to go off on his own. Chances are good their answers will shed some light on what lures him away. The rest of the adults...when did they see him last, and what was he wearing?"

He handed the list to Stan. "Think of this as a conversation, not a police interrogation. Don't push too hard, or people will clam up."

Stan said, "You continue to amaze me, Sylvestry. Is there anything you *don't* do well?"

"Receiving compliments."

"Still, I don't know whether to salute you or hug you."

"Save it for the 'we found him' celebration."

The operations leader cut loose with a shrill

whistle as four men, geared-up and ready to join the search, entered the room.

"There's a topographical map over here," Duke said, pointing to the cabin's kitchen table.

"Have a good long look at it before you head out. If you have any questions, let me know. Otherwise, see me to find out who your team leader is."

Stan, Ian and Maleah headed outside. The crisscrossing beams of flashlights that bounced from tree trunks and scrub brush told them that at least one team had already gone into the woods.

"Be careful out there, you two," Stan said, and headed for the Washburne camp area. As Ian and Maleah headed for their tents, a misty fog swirled around their ankles, beading up on their clothes.

"Where should I meet you once I've changed into rain gear?" she asked.

"Meet me? I figured you'd be on the bus with Avery, explaining why I couldn't take him home."

"A boy went missing on my watch. My place is here." In her shoes, he would have said the same thing.

"I'll call Terri, give her a heads-up."

"Good idea. She'll need time to find another sitter for him in time for her mother's surgery."

"God willing, we'll be back by then, and he can hang with me."

She pulled her jacket tighter around her and stared at her boots, probably thinking about that kid, alone in the dark woods, without a coat or any real protection from the cold, soggy air. He slid an arm across her shoulders. "We'll find him, so quit worrying."

She looked up at him through long, mist-dampened lashes, just long enough to double his heartbeat. "Any last-minute tips for what I should put into my backpack?"

"Just that it'll feel three times heavier in this uphill terrain, so leave those rocks in your tent."

"Yes, boss," she said, snapping off a smart salute.

He'd probably fail miserably at this friendship thing, because all he wanted to do was gather her close and kiss those full lips.

CHAPTER TWENTY-THREE

NOSE TO THE GROUND, Cash led them into the woods.

"But all the others are going in the opposite direction," Maleah said.

"I'll trust his instincts over theirs any day."

For the better part of two hours, they'd been zigzagging over rocks and fallen trees, taking turns yelling Billy's name. If her own legs were aching, how must Ian's feel, just two months after his doctor gave him permission to return to normal activities?

"How are you holding up?" she asked.

He'd just pulled himself onto a flat-topped boulder and, reaching down to give her a hand up, Ian said, "I'm fine. How're you?"

"I don't have steel pins in my leg."

"There's a cop-out answer if ever I heard one." He pointed to the left. "According to the map, that's Town Creek down there. Watch your step. These rocks are slick."

Every few minutes, Cash stopped and looked

back to make sure they were still following before darting back into the underbrush.

"I can't believe Billy would have come this far," Maleah said.

"You'd be surprised how far a scared kid can travel. Don't know why, but in a lot of cases, they head toward the sound of moving water."

"Makes sense, though I don't know why."

"Basic survival instincts. We're all born with them. Kids listen to them better than adults, because they haven't survived decades of second-guess mistakes."

"Like second-guessing a trained rescue dog?"

"Yeah. Like that."

They snaked their way back downhill, ducking low-hanging branches and stepping around teetering rocks. When they reached the flat ground that ran alongside the creek, Maleah leaned against a tree.

"I can't believe you do this on a regular basis."

"Somebody's gotta do it."

Cash woofed, and Ian said, "It's okay, buddy. She's just catching her breath."

The challenge was just enough to get her moving again, and he noticed that she steered clear of the steep drop from the path to the water below.

"How far would you say it is," he asked, "from where we are to the creek?"

"You should know that math wasn't my best subject, professor."

"Ha-ha," he said over his shoulder. "Go ahead. Make a guess."

"Twenty, thirty feet?"

"More like ten."

"Why?"

"No particular reason. Just a random question."

It wasn't anything of the kind. He'd kept a careful eye on her since they left the campground, teetering slightly when their hike put them anywhere near a ledge or overlook. Experience had taught him that volunteers who watched their feet were more likely to trip and fall than those who kept their eyes on the trail ahead.

"Never realized you had a fear of heights."

"I wouldn't call it a fear, exactly…"

Mostly pointless conversation, he hoped, would keep her calm…and her eyes off her boots.

It happened without warning: the jarring sound of shifting gravel. A quiet gasp, followed by a tiny scream. Ian turned in time to seize the strap of her backpack, and kept her from going over the edge. His own backpack prevented him from gaining the leverage he needed to pull her up. He wriggled out of one belt, then switched hands to shrug out of the other one. This was the arm he'd broken, and it hurt like blazes, but Ian managed to roll, and bring her with him onto the narrow creek bank.

She lay flat for a full thirty seconds, eyes squeezed shut and gasping, one hand on her chest.

"You're okay," he said.

"Easy for you to say. Ask me again how far it is from here to the water."

"Okay, so maybe I underestimated a bit."

Levering herself onto one elbow, she branded him with a stare. "A little bit? You need to make an appointment with an eye doctor when we get home."

She tried to stand, and in the process, kicked Ian's backpack. He reached for it and missed, and it went over the edge, and splashed into the creek. The pack bobbed, like a cork in a whirlpool, before racing south toward the Potomac.

"Great," he muttered. "Just great."

Maleah, on all fours beside him, watched the camouflage pack disappear around a bend in the creek.

"Everything we need to stay in contact with Duke is in there."

Not to mention gloves. A lightweight tarp.

Flashlight and extra batteries. The first-aid kit. Flares. The all-important radio. And when he'd noticed her unsteady steps, he'd added the heavier items from Maleah's pack. And two sweatshirts…

Half an hour or so after hitting the demanding trail, he'd removed his Ravens sweatshirt to forestall overheating. It hadn't been easy, squeezing it in with the one he'd brought to put on Billy, if they were lucky enough to find him.

Maleah sat back on her boot heels. Ian could tell that she was on the verge of tears, and he saw no point in adding to her misery.

"Hey." He gave her hand an affectionate squeeze. "Thing like that could've happened to anybody. I'm the dummy who put the pack so close to the edge."

"To keep me from falling." She hid behind her hands. "What are we going to do?"

"We're going to stay calm and follow Cash. Worst-case scenario," he said, walking toward the dog, "we'll head back to the campground and take our lumps for losing our gear."

A few minutes later, he looked over his shoulder, and saw that she'd fallen behind by at least thirty yards.

Ian backtracked, and when he reached her, said, "Why are you limping?"

Her lower lip trembled when she answered. "Did something to my ankle, trying to climb back up onto the path."

He helped her sit. "Let me have a look at it."

She gulped air when he wrapped a hand around the joint. Already, the swelling had started to bulge over the top of her boot. "My guess is, it's a bad sprain. We'll just sit here a minute, give you a chance to catch your breath."

"I don't want to sit. I can rest it after we find Billy." Maleah scrambled to her feet, and would have lost her balance if Ian hadn't steadied her. "I'm serious. Let's keep moving."

She took a tentative step and nearly collapsed again.

Ian picked her up and, backpack and all, threw her over his shoulder. He climbed the bank just ahead of them, stopping in the first clearing.

"We'll hunker down here for a couple hours. When the sun comes up, I'll head back to the camp, bring some help."

"I'll never live this down."

"Only if you tell them what happened."

Maleah met his eyes, and as realization dawned—that he'd keep her secret—hers filled with tears and she fell into his arms. It touched him, not only because it wasn't like her to cry when things didn't go her way, but because she trusted him.

He helped her sit at the base of an ancient oak that was wide enough that they could both use it as a backrest. Cash trotted up, assessed the situation, and lay down beside Ian.

"You're shivering," Maleah said.

"It'll pass." He hunched deeper into his lightweight sweatshirt.

She took off her quilted ski jacket and draped it over them. Petite as she was, it barely went from her right shoulder to his left.

"Put your hand into the pocket," she suggested.

And when he did, Ian found a pack of gum.

"Didn't you once tell me you hated this stuff, because it made you feel like a cow, chewing its cud?"

"It's for emergencies. For when I have spicy food for lunch followed by a meeting."

"Ah. *Those* kind of emergencies."

"You're still shivering." She pulled the jacket higher, tucked it under his chin, and snuggled closer. "Shared body heat," Maleah explained. "I'm surprised they didn't teach you about that in search and rescue school." Head resting on his shoulder, she said, "Warmer now?"

He was. "Wonder if the buses are loaded yet?" he wondered aloud.

"Probably not. With the weather and all, they'll probably wait until morning to hit the road."

"Who knows? We could be back by then."

She nestled closer. "Wishful thinking."

"How's the ankle?"

"It's throbbing. Small penance for stranding us out here."

"We're not really stranded. I know exactly where we are."

"Me, too. Cold, damp, achy and worried about Billy."

Ian added *tree branch digging into my behind* to her description, but wouldn't complain, because they'd put her here in his arms.

She wondered aloud where Billy might be hiding. He speculated about the reasons he'd left the safety of his tent in the first place. Did Ian think another team had found him by now? Hope so, he'd said.

And while they talked, Cash, settled happily between her right thigh and his left, looking from Ian to Maleah and back again as though he understood every word.

"Silly dog," he said, scratching between the pup's ears.

"What do you suppose he's thinking?"

Ian did his best Goofy impression. "If you

two weren't so busy jabbering, you might have noticed that the sun is coming up."

He pointed, and Cash took it as his cue to get back to work. He raced up the path and disappeared around the curve at the top of the hill.

"I wish I could do that," Maleah said.

Just then, the dog started yapping.

"That's his 'found something' bark," Ian said, getting to his feet. "Stay put and I'll see what's got him all worked up."

He'd only gone a few yards when Maleah said, "Ian! Wait up!"

She was still limping, but nowhere near as badly as she had been. "Told you the rest would do you good," he said, pointing at her ankle. "But I still think you should wait here, make sure you don't make it worse."

"Says the man who rode a plow through a blizzard, wearing a cast on his leg and his arm."

"Touché…"

"Anyway, if Cash found Billy, well, you don't know what shape he'll be in. You might not have time to come back for me."

"What makes you think I'd come back for you?"

"You'd have to, because you love me."

Definitely not something she'd intended to say, and her big round eyes and gasp proved it. In all probability, she never would have said it if the ankle hadn't kept her awake all night. Ian thanked the power of her subconscious for allowing him that glimpse of her true feelings.

"Okay, you can limp along beside me," he said, extending an arm, "but only if you lean on me." She didn't say a word as they made their way to the spot where they'd last seen Cash.

"He doesn't sound agitated," Ian observed. "Which could mean he cornered a rabbit or found a ball some kid dropped during a hike."

"I hope it means he found Billy."

"Me, too."

It was an uphill climb to reach the spot where Cash now ran back and forth to coax them nearer.

"You have two choices. Wait here for me to check things out, or let me carry you up there."

Shoulders slumped, she released a sigh.

Ian picked her up and, as he had earlier, draped her over his shoulder.

"Sorry if this makes you feel like a sack of potatoes."

"I yam what I yam," she said. "Let's just hope this is the last time."

He saw the boy long before she did. After gently putting her on her feet, Ian hugged Cash.

"Good boy," he said. "Good boy! You found Billy."

"Is he your dog?" the boy asked.

"He sure is. His name is Cash."

"Yes, I know. I met him at the campground. Plus, I read his tag."

Cash, sensing he was the subject of their discussion, lay across the boy's lap.

"He's very warm. I sure was real glad to see him."

Maleah watched as Ian gave the boy a quick once-over.

"He's cold, a little dirty," he said, looking up at her, "and those mosquito bites will give him a fit for a couple days, but otherwise, I think he's fine."

She limped closer and, getting onto her knees, held Billy's face in her hands.

"Do you know what a miracle is?"

"Yes, it's a good thing from heaven."

Touching a finger to his nose, she said, "And that's just what you are."

She removed her jacket, and as she tucked it around him, Maleah's ring clicked against the hard plastic rectangle he'd been sitting on.

"A cell phone?"

"It's my mom's."

"Aw, is the battery dead?"

"I don't think so." He shrugged. "I fell asleep and forgot it was there."

Ian remembered that kids on the spectrum

didn't like surprise moves. "Mind if I have a look?"

Another shrug. "It's my mom's."

"Battery is at 47%," he told Maleah, "and reception is three of five bars."

He punched a few keys, hoping he hadn't misdialed.

"Olinski," the gruff voice said.

"Duke, it's Ian Sylvestry. We've found the boy."

The operations leader held the phone away from his ear. "They found him!" he shouted, inviting a chorus of applause and cheers.

"Is he all right?"

"He could use a bath and some calamine for the bug bites."

"That's it?"

"That's it."

"Well, I'll be…"

Ian recited coordinates to the best of his abilities, given that he'd lost his map and compass, and while waiting for the team to arrive, Ian sat beside the boy.

"Were you scared?"

"Yeah, a little. The woods are creepy in the dark."

Maleah rubbed warmth into his hands.

"And there are a lot of weird noises out here,

too." He looked up at Ian. "I heard a…an owl, and saw a deer."

Maleah had guided the kids through a couple of crafts. Ian's favorite? The binder where they could store pressed leaves, drawings, and even small flat rocks they'd found in the campground.

"There's an adventure for your memory book."

"Why isn't my mom here?"

"I'm sure she'll be with the team. They'll be here soon."

"Is she mad?"

"No, but she was real worried."

Billy sighed.

"Can I ask you a question?"

"Yes…"

"Why did you leave your tent last night?"

"I heard a noise. Mr. Stan told a story about raccoons washing their hands in puddles. I wanted to take a picture."

"You saw one? Washing its hands?"

"There were *three* of 'em, eating out of the trash can. But no puddles. So when they ran off, I followed them."

"And what about all the other times you wandered off?"

"Grown-ups like to tell stories, and they know kids like me get bored easy. So they make the stories exciting. Like the time I went to the train tracks, to see if the wheels really were made of iron, and could flatten pennies on the track."

Ian looked over Billy's head and watched Maleah's expression change from shock to disbelief to exasperation. Had he overstepped his bounds, or was her annoyance rooted in the fact that no one, not even Maleah, herself, had drawn that much information from the boy.

You're a fine one to talk, he told himself. One minute he thought life would be perfect and complete if she was a part of it. The next, he was questioning her sanity, and his...for loving her, still.

"You're awfully quiet all of a sudden," she said. "Are you all right?"

Billy's eyes widened. "What's wrong, Mr. Sylvestry?"

He heard the unmistakable sound of truck motors and tires grating over gravel. Tempting as it was to go down to the road and meet them, Ian concentrated on Billy.

"I'm just glad you're all right." Winking, he plucked a dried leaf from the boy's hair. "Will you do me a favor?"

"Sure!"

"Next time you get an idea to investigate something, tell your mom first, okay?"

"Okay."

"She's gonna be *so* relieved to hear about this."

"Really? Why?"

"'Cause she loves you, that's why"

"Yeah...she says that a lot. I didn't know she meant it, though."

Kid, he thought, *I know exactly how you feel.*

CHAPTER TWENTY-FOUR

WHAT BEGAN AS a fluke had become an annual event for Teresa and Maleah.

She'd been too young to remember the earliest Mother's Day shopping trips, but from the age of five or so, Maleah saw the event as one of the year's most anticipated.

"Do you realize we've been doing this for what seems like forever?"

Teresa looked over pink-framed reading glasses. "You were only a few months old that first time." She closed the Double T menu. "I don't know why I even bother looking. I'm going to order what I've always ordered."

"Two eggs over easy, sausage links and hash browns," Maleah said, "with coffee and a small tomato juice."

"Another thing we have in common." She rooted around in her purse and removed a coupon-stuffed envelope. "Would you believe I couldn't find one special sale that stood out?" Teresa slid the envelope closer to Maleah. "Ann is your mom—see if something jumps out at you."

"I already know what I want to get her." She unsnapped her own purse and produced a department store circular.

"A mother's ring…she'll love it. You always come up with the sweetest, most thoughtful ideas."

"But it's getting more and more difficult to get something she doesn't already have."

"And it'll only get worse as the years go by."

"This," Maleah said, tapping the full-color ad, "is an example of a happy accident. Mom has no idea I overheard this conversation… When Grampa was in the hospital, Mom actually took a nurse's hand to get a better look at her ring."

"Like I always say, it pays to pay attention."

They ordered breakfast, and while they waited, Teresa said, "So what's the latest on the little boy who ran away from the campground?"

"I talked with his mom just yesterday, and he's doing great."

"What makes a kid run off that way, I wonder?"

"You'll hate hearing this, I'm sure, but thanks to Ian, I know exactly why Billy wandered off." She told the as-told-by-Billy story. "He made Billy promise to tell someone next time the urge to wander struck, and according to his mom, he's keeping that promise."

"Now, why would I hate hearing something so uplifting?"

"Because it involves *Ian*."

"What involves Ian?"

"Joey!" Teresa slid farther into the booth. "What a great surprise!"

"You're kidding, right?" He sat beside his grandmother. "You two have been doing this every year for what, a hundred years? I knew exactly where to find you."

"You've never tracked us down before. What's up, little brother?" Maleah said.

"I need some help thinking of something to get Mom for Mother's Day. Flowers...meh. Candy...meh. She has every kitchen gadget ever invented, and if I buy a gift card she'll give it to Eliot because," he drew quote marks in the air, "'he's struggling since the separation.'"

"It can't be easy, paying a mortgage and apartment rent on a cop's salary," Maleah said.

"I know, I know, and I'm glad to help him out in a roundabout way. But it's frustrating... if I find the right gift, something personal that she actually wants..."

"You've always been a sweet, thoughtful boy," Teresa said, elbowing his ribs.

"Yeah, well, I can't package sweet and thoughtful."

The waitress reappeared and took Joe's breakfast order, and once she was gone, he said again, "So what involves Ian?"

Teresa brought him up to date, adding, "She thinks I hate the man. Which couldn't be further from the truth."

"Could-a fooled me," Joe said. "You guys— Mom and Dad, Grampa and Eliot—have never made a secret of your feelings about him."

"We don't have anything against him, personally. It's just…" Teresa frowned. "We think Maleah deserves better."

"Better than a man who built a successful business, pretty much single-handedly? Who volunteers to help kids? Who has enough money in the bank that he can afford to let his alcoholic dad and old-maid aunt live rent free in his building?" He shook his head. "Remind me not to make any mistakes around *you* guys."

"His father is a recovering alcoholic," Maleah said, "and it isn't PC to use the term old maid anymore. And how do you know so much about him, anyway?"

"Hey. Whose side are you on?" He took a sip from Maleah's water glass. "I'm a cop, so I have my ways of finding out…stuff." Turning to Teresa, he said, "Being a cop is also why I get how the family felt about him years ago. But let's be honest. He isn't that guy anymore."

Teresa frowned again. "We don't know what he might do, presented with the right…shall we say…opportunity."

"Nope. Hate to say it, but you're dead wrong, Grams. Couple pals of mine—parole officers—say recidivism is most likely in the first year after a con is released from prison." He shook his head. "If it hasn't happened by now, it isn't going to. I'd stake my reputation on it."

"Says you," Teresa retorted, and elbowed him in the ribs again.

"Have you been working out?" He wrinkled his nose and rubbed his side.

"Just my usual yoga classes." She winked at Maleah.

"One more question. You want to see Maleah happy, right?"

Their grandmother hadn't expected that, as evidenced by her wide, blinking eyes. "Of course I do. It's what I want for all of my grandkids."

"You think she's happy, *really* happy, being an old maid?" Grinning, he looked at Maleah. "Sorry. I don't know the PC-approved term, or how old a woman has to be to fit it."

"There isn't a specific age. And what's wrong with *single*?"

Joe sat back while the waitress delivered all three meals.

"We're way off topic here," he teased when she left the table. "Let's go back to the beginning: Mother's Day gift ideas. Please?"

"Last time I was over there," Maleah said, "a commercial came on TV. *Phantom of the Opera* is coming to the Hippodrome in a couple weeks. She told Dad they should get tickets, and when he said, 'All that money to see a chick flick on a wooden stage? No, thanks,' she looked so disappointed."

"So you're suggesting I get them tickets. Great idea!"

"Not *them*. I'm suggesting *you* take her."

He rubbed his chin. "Yeah, yeah, that'd be different, all right."

"She'll remember it for the rest of her life."

"Yeah, but…Eliot isn't the only one trying to make ends meet on a cop's salary, y'know."

"I'll loan you the money for dinner. You can pay me back later. And it'll be our little secret."

Joe and Maleah looked at Teresa, who said, "It's a great idea, so mum's the word."

"What's in the bag?" Joe asked, nodding at Maleah's purse.

She'd planned to give her grandmother the

gift during lunch. But it might be more fun, presenting it with Joe there.

"Since this is the thirtieth anniversary of our Mother's Day shopping spree," she told her grandmother, "I got a little something to commemorate the occasion."

She slid the silver-wrapped box across the table.

"Honey," Teresa said, untying the green satin ribbon, "you shouldn't have." But she ripped into the tiny package like a kid on Christmas morning. She lifted the lid, and at first sight of the gift, sat back, shaking her head. "A 'thirty' pendant…"

"Oh no. Don't tell me Gramps got you one for your thirtieth wedding anniversary…"

"No, he didn't." She dug through the big purse again and produced a silver-wrapped package.

"This is for you, Maleah."

Inside, the identical necklace. "I don't believe it…"

"I know. Talk about a coincidence…right down to the green ribbon…"

"…because green is the color for thirtieth anniversaries," Maleah finished. "I love it," she said, and put it on.

"I love mine, too."

While Joe helped Teresa put her necklace

on, Maleah said, "Guess it's true. Great minds think alike."

"Hmpf," Joe said, finishing his coffee. "You know what *I* tack on any time someone quotes that old saying…"

"…and fools seldom differ," all three said together.

"Well, much as I hate to leave this party," he said when the laughter waned, "I'm due at the station. Eliot has an appointment with his lawyer, and I promised to fill in for him."

"I'd really hoped he and Amber would work things out," Maleah said. "Divorce is so sad, and so hard on the boys."

"Can't work things out when both parties refuse to give an inch. She's insisting he find a less-dangerous job."

"He was a cop when she met him," Teresa pointed out. "She knew what she was getting into."

"In her defense," Maleah began, "I'm sure Amber *thought* she could deal with the worries and fears that go with being a cop's wife, but you know better than most that it isn't easy. And you know why."

"I suppose…" Teresa sighed. "If only Eliot would find something within the department that didn't require walking the beat."

"They've been up and down that road," Joe

said. "He says sitting behind a desk all day would drive him crazy."

"He's already crazy," Maleah countered, "if he's willing to break up his family for a reason like that."

"Hey, don't shoot the messenger. But in all honesty, I understand his side, too. I can hardly stand being inside long enough to write up reports. Desk work all day, every day? No way." He emptied his coffee mug. "I'll never get married."

"Didn't you just tell us you met a woman, and she might be 'the one'?" Before he could answer, Teresa added, "Does your new girlfriend know that?"

"Yup." Standing, Joe reached for his wallet.

"Breakfast is on me, little brother."

"Thanks, sis. And I can afford to take Mom to dinner…if I hold off on buying a flat screen for my bedroom."

He kissed their cheeks and left them.

"What a shame," Maleah said, "He'd make a great husband, and you've seen him with Eliot's boys. He'd be a great dad, too."

"He'll change his mind when the right woman comes along."

The right woman… The words echoed in her head through the rest of their meal, at the jewelry store while she and Teresa ordered Ann's ring, as they browsed the mall bookstore, during their impromptu manicure-pedicure visit.

Why hadn't *Ian* found the right woman in all these years? Memories of his caring deeds flashed through her mind like someone thumbing through a deck of cards. By contrast, the only thoughtful thing she'd done for him had been the easy-to-order gifts, delivered by a florist soon after his release from the hospital. No wonder he'd come to the conclusion they could never be more than friends.

Teresa suggested a late lunch at The Trolley Stop, an easy drive up Main Street.

"If I order dinner for Frank and me, I won't have to cook or clean up."

"I'm still full from breakfast, so I think I'll have the soup and salad."

Her grandmother scrutinized Maleah's face. "You feeling okay, honey?"

Physically, she was fine. Emotionally...

"It's Ian, isn't it?"

"I'm a little distracted, that's all. There's a lot going on at work."

"You're thinking about what Joe said, aren't you?"

The waitress took their orders...two Trolley Stop #9s for Frank and Teresa's supper, and two house salads for now.

"I love this old place," Maleah said. "I'm so

glad they didn't cover these gorgeous stone walls."

"Yes, yes. I'm not senile *yet*, so you're not getting off that easily. Is the reason you've been so quiet because you're upset that we haven't forgiven him?"

Maleah didn't want to discuss this. With anyone.

"Can we just enjoy the rest of our day?" she asked.

Teresa opened her mouth to say something, and quickly changed her mind. "Think I'll ask our waitress about the dessert of the day. I'll poke a candle in…whatever it is and pretend it's my birthday."

"Your birthday isn't until late June." *The day after Ian's…*

"I know." She giggled. "It'll be fun."

Maleah clucked her tongue. "I never would have guessed you have such a mean streak," she teased.

"Everyone has a dark streak. If we're lucky, it's overshadowed by good things in the people we love."

Was she talking about herself, or Ian?

"WHAT TIME SHOULD I have him there?" Gladys asked.

"Between two and two fifteen."

Maleah had pulled out all the stops and called in every favor to organize the party, and with Gladys's help, invited people he'd enjoy spending his birthday with.

"You're sure it's all right for him to bring Cash into the Institute?"

"Yup, I cleared it with the director." She'd had to promise to finagle tickets to an Orioles game, and if she had to buy them herself, it would be worth it. "Besides, the whole premise of the party is that Cash is getting a medal for finding Billy."

She'd put the streamers-decorated gift-and-refreshments table in the back, so Ian wouldn't see it when he entered the big conference room. By one forty-five, everything was in place: his favorite chocolate cake and ice cream, soft drinks and platters of cheese and crackers. His chef let her know which bistro employees could be spared to attend, and helped her get in touch with Ian's SAR buddies. She invited volunteers from every Washburne event he'd participated in, and Gladys, Brady, and Terri and Avery rounded out the guest list.

Gladys, true to her word, delivered Ian at two o'clock sharp.

"Wow, buddy, look how many people showed

up for you!" He smiled at Maleah. "I wasn't expecting a turnout like this."

She bent to hug the dog. "Have you picked out a place to hang your medal?"

Cash nuzzled her neck, and then she led Ian inside.

A chorus of "Happy birthdays!" rang out, punctuated by the off-key notes of tin horns, kazoos and paper blowouts.

He looked from Maleah to Gladys and back again. "What? You guys... I can't believe you pulled this off without me finding out about it."

"Speech! Speech!" one of the SAR guys yelled.

Blushing, Ian said, "I, ah, I'm speechless."

"There's a first!" Dan said.

"Thanks, everybody. This is..." He met Maleah's eyes as the right side of his mouth lifted in a silly grin. "This is great."

"Open your presents!" Avery said.

Terri pulled up a chair and Dan moved the gift table beside it.

"Which one is from you?" he asked the boy. And once Avery delivered it, Ian removed the wrapper. "A monster hunter video game. Now we'll see who's the best player, won't we?"

Pulling Avery into a warm hug, he said, "Thanks, kiddo. I love it."

The bistro crew chipped in on a fancy

mahogany-and-brass nameplate for his desk. His SAR buddies presented a gift certificate to the local tattoo parlor. "We noticed a blank spot on your forearm," Sam said.

Gladys arranged for a professional photographer to capture the bistro's exterior, and Brady had bought polo shirts for the staff that bore the bistro's logo.

An anonymous giver had wrapped a package of fluffy black scrunchies with a card that read, "To keep those dark flowing locks out of your face when you're on the Harley." Laughing, he added them to the neckties, soda-can coolies and bandannas. Maleah couldn't help but notice he'd saved her gift for last.

He took his time unwrapping the wallet-size box, dark eyes widening when he saw what was inside: one-on-one classes taught by one of Baltimore's most sought-after painters. The guests' reactions made it clear he hadn't told many people that, in high school, his sketches and paintings won awards, so she explained. "He's a talented artist, but the demands of work and volunteering hasn't left time for his art."

"I...I don't know what to say."

His voice, gruff and quiet, told her that he meant it. "Gladys, will you do the honor of lighting the candles?"

The gang gathered around the table to sing

the birthday song as Ian stood behind the cake, waiting to blow out the candles.

"Make a wish, Sylvestry!" Joe bellowed.

Eyes closed, Ian complied. When he opened them, he wordlessly zeroed in on Maleah.

THE PARTY HAD surprised him, but not nearly as much as Maleah's gift.

Gladys must have told her about his admiration for the artist's work. She'd turned a pipe dream into a reality, and Ian would always be grateful.

Now more than ever, he wanted Maleah in his life, and not just as a friend. He'd given it a lot of thought. Talk, as they said, was cheap. He needed a grand gesture, something to prove he really *would* do anything to make her happy... to make her *his*.

Ian remembered that, rain or shine, the Turner family had never missed a July Fourth parade.

Their favorite route was in Old Dundalk, where thousands lined the streets to watch clowns and antique cars, Old Glory–draped floats, and high school bands marching by. Afterward, they'd gather at the elder Turners' for burgers and dogs. If he timed it right, he'd catch them in the right mood. If he didn't, the neighbors might see a fireworks display that had nothing to do with pyrotechnics.

Frank believed in three square meals a day, holidays included. That meant they'd fire up the grill at noon, and have the food on the table by one.

IT WAS ONE-FIFTEEN when Ian parked the pickup truck on the street. He'd brought Cash, mostly for moral support.

Mostly…

Side by side, they made their way up the driveway. Just before opening the back gate, he whispered, "Wish me luck, buddy."

They entered the yard just as Eliot took his first bite of a charred hot dog.

"What're *you* doing here?" he mumbled around it.

The only sound in the shady yard was the spit and sputter of cheese dripping from the burgers onto the coals. Even Eliot's boys sat perfectly still and quiet at the picnic table. "I'd like to talk to you," Ian said, pocketing his hands. "*All* of you. Is Maleah inside?"

"None of your business," her brother barked.

"Let's hear him out," Joe said.

Frank walked away from the grill, tongs in hand, and said, "Out with it, son."

"I know how you feel about me, and I can't say

I blame you. But the Ian Sylvestry you knew is gone. This guy," he said, hand to his chest, "loves Maleah enough to walk away, if that's what she wants. But you need to know that I'll work harder to make her happy than I have to change my life."

She descended the porch steps, a pitcher of iced tea in one hand, a bucket of ice in the other. After putting them on the picnic table, she crossed the yard and crouched to pet Cash.

"You shaved."

"Because today, I wanted everything out in the open."

"Get this fool out of here," Eliot said.

"Eliot, shh," Teresa said.

Maleah looked up at him. "Why are there daisies on Cash's collar?"

"Not just daisies. Daisies with seventeen petals."

"Because we met on the seventeenth of—"

"I'm hoping they'll help you make your decision."

Maleah stood, took a step closer. "You're out of your mind coming here." She laughed.

He took her in his arms, oblivious to the shocked expressions of her entire family.

"Out of my mind about you, even though you aren't very observant."

Answering her unasked question, he pointed at Cash, who sat obediently at her sneakered feet.

"He has a little something for you. It's tied to his collar."

Eliot threw his arms in the air. "Are you guys just gonna stand here and let that—"

"Stow it, son," Frank said. "This is starting to get interesting."

Maleah, on her knees now, drew Cash closer.

Ian heard her gasp when she found it, tied to the dog's ID tag and license. Hands trembling, she couldn't undo the knot. On his knees beside her, he gave the white ribbon a good tug, and it fell into his upturned palm.

"Do you think you can spend the rest of your life with a long-haired, tattooed, scarred ex-con?"

She glanced back at her family huddled together, smiling, shaking their heads in disbelief.

There were tears in her mother's eyes. In her grandmother's, too.

Frank gave the thumbs-up sign, and Joe mirrored it.

Her dad strode purposefully across the yard and held out his right hand. When Ian grasped it, Pat said, "You know what'll happen if you hurt her, right?"

"You have my word on this, sir… I'm never going to find out."

The Turners gathered around them, shaking Ian's hand, hugging Maleah, laughing and chattering, wishing them luck and a happy future.

Eliot's youngest son stuck both pinky fingers between his lips and cut loose with a high-pitched blast. And when they quieted down, he said, "You guys! You guys! She hasn't said yes yet!"

"Thanks, Joey," Ian said.

Taking Maleah's hand, he picked up where he'd left off.

"So what do you think?"

The pause was long.

She held out her arms, and when he stepped into them, Maleah traced the length of the once-hidden scar. "This, *this* is the man I knew."

Little Joe whispered, "Is that a yes?"

Maleah drew him into the hug. "You bet it is, kiddo." Then she looked up at Ian and whispered, "It's a yes."

"Is he *cryin'*, Dad?"

"I dunno, son."

"But why's he sad?"

Teresa sighed. "Those are happy tears, li'l Joey."

Cash wedged himself between Ian and Maleah.

"We did it, buddy," Ian said.

The dog, tail wagging, responded with a quiet *woof.*

And Ian kissed her.

* * * * *